"WE HAVE TO STOP," EILEEN PLEADED

"I didn't intend for this to go as far as it has. Please believe me." There was a note of panic in her voice as she adjusted her robe, folding one lapel primly over the other.

"I know you didn't," Dan said softly as he smoothed the hair back from her face. "When I make love to you, we'll be alone, with no fear of intrusion. And the lights will be on because I want to see you when I love you, to see the passion in your eyes. There are enough secrets hidden in a woman's body without compounding them with darkness. I want to discover your secrets, learn how to bring you pleasure, hold you when we find satisfaction in each other's arms."

"Oh, Dan," Eileen murmured, pressing her face against his chest, her thoughts and her body alive with the images his words evoked.

ABOUT THE AUTHOR

Since her first Superromance, *Until Forever*,
published in 1983, Sally Garrett has attracted a
wide following of loyal readers. *Visions* is the
second book in Sally's newest series, a trilogy
about three cousins from rural Kentucky. Like the
women she writes about, Sally loves living far
from the city. With her biggest fan, husband
Montie, Sally makes her home in beautiful
Montana.

Books by Sally Garrett

HARLEQUIN SUPERROMANCE

90–UNTIL FOREVER
139–MOUNTAIN SKIES
173–NORTHERN FIRES
201–TWIN BRIDGES
225–UNTIL NOW
243–WEAVER OF DREAMS

Don't miss any of our special offers. Write to us at the
following address for information on our newest releases.

Harlequin Reader Service
901 Fuhrmann Blvd., P.O. Box 1397, Buffalo, NY 14240
Canadian address: P.O. Box 603,
Fort Erie, Ont. L2A 5X3

Sally Garrett
RAINBOW HILLS SERIES

VISIONS

Harlequin Books

TORONTO • NEW YORK • LONDON
AMSTERDAM • PARIS • SYDNEY • HAMBURG
STOCKHOLM • ATHENS • TOKYO • MILAN

Published September 1987

First printing July 1987

ISBN 0-373-70275-2

Printed in Canada

ACKNOWLEDGEMENTS

The plight of the American farmer is very real. As Eileen Mills's story unfolded, I tried to deal with her financial problems in a believable manner, avoiding the temptation of a miracle solution.

Daniel Page is not a wealthy hero, but together they find a love strong enough to survive whatever the outside world may bring their way.

Before starting to research *Visions*, my knowledge of growing potatoes was limited to my own garden. Deana Jensen, a fellow writer, and her husband, Don, opened their home near Shelley to me and introduced me to their neighbors. Onita Stoll and her sons Richard, John and Robert Hoff; Merrill and Bethea Hanny; Reed and Marilyn Hansen; all accepted the challenge of educating me on the commercial growing of Idaho spuds. Bill and Dixie Cottom told me about the seed potato side of the operation. Phyllis Letellier chided me when I made a flip comment about farm foreclosure in 1984 and then helped me understand what losing a home place does to a family. A special thanks to Blaine Larson who first planted the seed of a potato story in my mind when we shared a table at Yesterday's Calf-A in Dell, Montana a few years ago.

DEDICATION

To my sister,
Layne O'Nora Garrett Bales,
who helped during those years
when life was rough for me,
who sat with my four sons at night
so I could return to college,
and who helped in other ways
that shall remain private.

To her husband George Bales
and their two special children,
Rachel Layne and Andrew Elbert.
May God continue to bless you all.

EILEEN'S PROLOGUE

THE THREE GIRLS made their way along the creek bank to their secret meeting place in the wooded area behind Callie Hardesty's parents' farm.

Eileen Hardesty, the oldest of the three cousins, was in the lead. Her red-haired, eleven-year-old cousin, Abbie, was next in line, followed by eight-year-old Callie. Callie's hair was black as coal like most members of the Hardesty clan.

Eileen's bare foot slipped on a wet rock near the water's edge and a rush of irritation swept through her. She wanted to excel in front of her family and her favorite cousins, to prove to everyone who knew her she had the mettle to succeed.

Her mouth tightened as she glanced at the sun creeping toward the western horizon. "Come on, Abbie, you're such a poke-along," she called. "I have to get back and help Jordan and Les with the milking by five." She patted one long brown braid and tried to look sophisticated. Eileen's foot slipped again and she teetered on the rock, her arms waving in the air before, at the last second, she took one quick step into the creek to maintain her balance.

She tugged the bottom of her yellow and green calico blouse, trying to ignore the frayed edges of the hem. As she watched her pretty red-haired cousin admire a fern near the creek bank, her thoughts moved on to other concerns. She and her mother had gone to Greenville, Kentucky a few

weeks earlier and chosen fabric to make two new outfits for
the coming school year.

Eileen had wanted ready-made knit tops and two mini-
skirts but her father had already given his opinion and laid
down a warning. "As long as your momma can sew, there
ain't no need to waste our money on store-bought clothes,
and young ladies always cover their knees."

She and her mother had compromised by settling on two
pieces of bonded plaid for skirts and soft pastel broadcloth
for blouses. Her mother had promised to hem the skirts a
few inches shorter than last year.

Balancing on the boulder in the creek, Eileen put her fists
on her slender waist and pushed her budding breasts against
the frayed blouse as she waited impatiently, wondering if she
would ever have a decent figure like the other girls in her
grade.

The other girls were already shaving their legs. She had
been saving her small allowance to buy a pretty blue razor
and a supply of blades she had priced in the variety store.
Her father would be too busy with the crops to notice her
legs anyway, she reasoned.

As the three cousins chatted, Eileen mentally counted her
four brothers. Shelby Junior, was the oldest and had recently married his high school sweetheart on his twenty-first
birthday. Taylor, named after their grandfather Hardesty,
was eighteen and had just gone to work in the Rainbow
Mine Number Two. Jordan and Leslie were identical twins,
tall and lean at fifteen with black hair and brown eyes. They
were already pressuring their parents to let them quit school
and go to work in one of the mines that abounded in the
county.

All her brothers had spent years warning Eileen about
boys in general and had made it perfectly clear that if she

ever had a problem to let them know and they would settle
the matter for her. Eileen had thanked them, but privately
vowed to keep her personal life to herself. With four strapping brothers ready to defend her honor, she was quite sure
any young man would think twice before asking Eileen
Hardesty for a date.

Abbie and Callie were squabbling again. At times, Eileen grew weary of being the referee in their disputes. They
were standing nose to nose, their faces flushed and their fists
clenched, trying to prove their opinions about future careers to each other.

As usual she interceded. "My momma says that everyone should plan for something else besides what she wants,
just in case things don't work out. Momma says you should
never put all your eggs in one basket."

Abbie was two years younger than Eileen, and as Eileen
watched the girl's animated explanation, she smiled. At
times she envied Abbie's colorful hair and sparkling green
eyes. Her own hair curled only when the humidity was high.
Her mother had insisted her eyes were amber, but Eileen
knew her mother had only been trying to console her. All
she had to do was look in the mirror to see that they were
just plain brown, as colorless as her dirt-brown hair.

Abbie giggled. "Aunt Mimmie says I'm just stubborn
enough to get what I want." Each and every night, after I've
said my prayers, I think about what I'll be when I grow up."

Eileen nodded. "Me, too. Jordan says I can make it if I
try. I'm going to win a scholarship to college and someday
I'll be an independent woman and the boss of a whole bunch
of men. Wouldn't that be a barrel of fun? Most of my
brothers say they would never work for a girl." She laughed
and added. "Especially not their own sister. I'll finish high

school first, then I'm going to go to college. Mrs. Gray says it's never too early to plan for it.''

She managed to keep the two younger cousins moving up the creek bank until they found their secret meeting place, a small glen hidden in the thick undergrowth in an outcropping of rocks not far from the creek.

After a snack, Eileen called the club meeting to order. Feeling quite grown up because she had been elected president of their secret club, Eileen reached for Abbie's hand as well as Callie's. "The last meeting, until next summer, of the Rainbow Hills Secret Society of Sisters and Friends will now come to order," she said, her pretty mouth unsmiling. She searched her mind for the proper rules of conduct for a club meeting that her mother had taught her.

Quickly, she moved through the agenda. When she called for new business, Abbie opened a paper sack she had been clutching.

"Aunt Minnie has been making us something special. Here's one for you." She handed a small package wrapped in white tissue paper to Eileen. "And one for you, pipsqueak," she said, handing Callie an identical package. "And one for me."

Filled with anticipation, they unwrapped their presents. When Eileen spotted the shiny gold locket and chain lying in the nest of tissue paper, she gasped. "Oh, it's fabulous."

Callie looked at her own locket. "It's . . . it's wonderful."

Abbie leaned toward Callie. "Are they all alike?"

"Almost," Eileen said, after studying the three lockets. "But each has our own initial on the front. See?" She pointed to the fancy script letter *E* on her own locket.

They opened the lockets. On the inside left was a tiny counted cross stitch image of a rainbow and three small trees on a hillside. On each side of the center frame and the inside back was a clipped photo of each girl. The outside back of the gold case had been inscribed with the words, "Sisters and Friends."

"Now let's make our promises," Abbie suggested. "We'll never never take these off...or if we do, we'll never lose them, and we'll always remember what we want to be when we grow up...and we'll stay in touch with each other, always."

Eileen nodded. "And we'll always be willing to help each other if we need help. We'll never be too proud to ask for help. Now, that's important," she said, shaking her index finger at the two younger cousins.

"What do you mean?" Callie asked, her dark eyes solemn.

"I'd be willing to help you if you needed me," Abbie said patiently.

"Oh, that," Callie replied. "I know that. It's like the Golden Rule we learned in Sunday School. Do unto others..."

"Yeah, yeah," Abbie interrupted. "We all know that verse."

"No," Eileen said, and the other girls turned their curious gazes to her again. "It's more than that. Momma calls it the other side of the coin in lending a hand to other people. What I mean is we'll never be too proud to *ask* for help."

"The members of the Rainbow Hills Secret Society of Sisters and Friends will never forget each other," Abbie said, "and we'll be best friends forever and ever, even when we're grown up and living far far away from here, and our matching lockets will prove it. Now let's promise out loud, or it doesn't mean a thing."

Eileen reached for Callie's hand and then Abbie's hand. "Right you are," she replied. Clasping hands tightly, they sat cross legged in a lopsided circle and closed their eyes, repeating their sacred vows to be sisters and friends always.

CHAPTER ONE

"YOU WANTED to see me?" Daniel Page asked, pausing at his editor's door, his hands deep in the pockets of his brown woolen trousers. A Shaker-style knitted pullover in a deep shade of forest green, worn over a white dress shirt, darkened his sage-green eyes.

"Yeah, grab a seat," Gil Hadley replied as he shuffled a stack of papers to an uncluttered corner of his desk. "Welcome back to Boise," he said.

"Good to be home," Dan said, sliding into the nearest chair. He was curious about why his boss and friend had summoned him.

Gil dropped an empty paper coffee cup into the waste basket and arched his thick gray eyebrows at Dan, motioning toward a donut.

Dan shook his head and shifted his chair to avoid the bright rays of the midmorning autumn sun.

"Just as well," Gil said. "It's been here since six this morning. Its twin was stale when I ate it." The donut made a resounding thud as it hit the waste basket.

Dan glanced out the window at the Boise city skyline then down at his digital watch, wishing Gil would get to the point. He had an interview scheduled across town in less than an hour.

Gil searched the piles on his desk and found a copy of *Western Living* magazine. "You creative people seldom pay any attention to the financial side of the business, but we've just completed a three-month campaign to increase our circulation," the editor said.

Dan exhaled. "I'm aware of that part of the operation, Gil. Don't underestimate me. I'm more than a good speller, typist, and arranger of words."

Gil chuckled. "I know, I know. Sometimes you're so complex you scare the heck out of me."

Dan's features softened. "So how did the promotion go?"

"Great, just great," Gil said, beaming. "We have subscribers in every state west of the Mississippi River now. Not bad for an upstart publication, eh?" He chuckled. "And the experts said it couldn't be done."

Dan recalled the newspaper in Texas that had been his own life for a short time. "Win some, loose some," he said.

Gil frowned. "Yeah...but you were set up." He tossed the dog-eared magazine to Dan, its glossy pages glistening in the sunlight.

Dan caught the magazine in midair and noticed that a scrap of paper was sticking out of it.

"Remember that series you did last year on your women?" Gil asked.

Dan opened the magazine to the marker and flipped through the long article. The series had been one of his best and had earned him special recognition at a national conference for regional magazines several months earlier.

"My women?" he asked, smiling as he scanned the photographs of the women he had interviewed for a three-part series on successful women in unusual occupations.

One of the women selected had been his own former wife, Vanessa Harcourt, who had chosen her assistant vice presidency in a potato-processing company in Boise over moving with Dan to Texas when he had bought a struggling daily newspaper.

Vanessa had been right when she'd warned him he was asking for trouble. After a year of successful growth, the innovative newspaper had gone down in financial ruin, along with the personal assets Dan had pledged against a bank loan. A powerful competitor had driven his advertising customers away by threatening to refuse their business in the much larger publication. Bankruptcy had become his only way out of the ensuing legal mess.

The failure had left a bitter taste in his mouth, but when Vanessa had sent him a bouquet of yellow roses and invited him to dinner upon his return to Boise, he had swallowed his pride and accepted.

"You're a survivor," Vanessa had said. "You'll find another challenge."

"And how is Stephen?" he had asked, changing the subject to the son who'd been the reason they'd married years earlier. "He hasn't written for a few months."

"The military academy staff keeps the children very busy," she had replied. They had discussed their only child for a while, then parted after Vanessa had insisted on paying for dinner.

Their relationship had settled into one of amiable respect. The spark of passion that had brought them together had long since evolved into a platonic friendship. Stephen and Dan spent a week together each summer with the usual promises to visit often.

Dan turned the pages, glancing at the pictures of other women in the magazine. His attention was caught by the photo of a woman who had intrigued him more than any of the fifteen women he had interviewed.

As he studied the photograph of Eileen and Duncan Mills, he felt an unusual stirring in his chest. The other women were strong, determined, intelligent women who had fought their way to success in their chosen fields. Eileen

Mills was different, and he had sensed the difference from the moment he'd first heard about her.

When she had welcomed him to the family-owned potato farm near Shelley, Idaho, his heart had gone out to her and her ailing husband. Duncan had been struck down by a rapidly debilitating case of multiple sclerosis in his early thirties.

Now, gazing at the picture of the couple, Dan was glad he'd been able to make the husband appear healthier than he actually had been. A very handsome man well over six feet in height, Duncan had been open about his illness and accepting the limitations it had brought to his farming skills. Privately the sick man had expressed his regrets over putting his wife into such a predicament. Dan had asked him to elaborate, but when Eileen had returned unexpectedly, the interview had taken a different direction.

Since that time, Duncan had died. When Dan had read the obituary in the Idaho Falls daily paper, one of several the magazine publisher provided for the staff, he had decided to attend the funeral. And after he had expressed his condolences to the young widow, she had invited him to her home for the customary visitation.

Dan glanced at the calendar on Gil's wall. Several months had passed since that visit. He had chatted with Eileen's three young children, met her cousin Abbie and the owner of the sheep ranch where she worked, but had managed to talk with Eileen Mills only briefly.

Her black mourning dress had hung from her shoulders. Once when she had twisted around to respond to a call from one of the children, her dress had been pulled against her body. Her hip bones had been as visible as her breasts. Dan had wanted to take her away to a quiet restaurant, feed her a nourishing meal, and shield her from the tragic turn of her life.

When he had looked into her sensitive amber eyes and seen their sadness, he had yearned to brush away the dark shadows beneath them and erase the tightness of her mouth. Instead, he had given her his business card and insisted that she phone him if he could help her and the children in any way.

Eileen had written him a brief note a few weeks after the funeral, thanking him for coming and for expressing his concerns, assuring him that all was going well for them, that the crops had been planted on schedule, and that with the coming summer they would all be very busy on the farm.

Dan had read between the lines, sensing her determination to pick up the pieces of her life. She would continue to farm almost three thousand acres of potatoes, barley and alfalfa hay by herself. He had respected her desire to go through her period of mourning alone.

"Dan?" Gil leaned forward over his desk.

Dan started.

"You were a million miles away," Gil said.

Dan ran his fingers through his wavy brown hair. "Sorry. I was thinking about this assignment." He glanced at Eileen's smiling face again before closing the magazine and dropping it back onto Gil's desk.

"That's what I want to discuss," Gil replied. "We received a lot of positive mail from that series. I'd like you to do a follow-up article and give us an update on as many of the women as you can track down. See if they're still successful, if they've moved on to bigger and better opportunities, or dropped out of the rat race." He waved his stubby fingers through the air. "Take whatever slant you choose but I want to know where you're going. Well, what do you think?" he asked, tilting his swivel chair back on its spring.

Dan's fingers massaged his forehead. He reached for the magazine again and flipped through the pages, his gaze settling once again on the haunting eyes of Eileen Mills. He shook his head, amazed at the direction of his thoughts. Involvement with a young farm widow and her three children was definitely not in his best interests, but there was no denying the woman touched him and had from the first.

"Well, do you want the assignment?" Gil asked again. "I can pass it on to someone else."

Dan straightened in his chair. "I'll work up an outline and run it by you." He closed the magazine again and met Gil's gaze. "I'd enjoy meeting all those dynamic ladies again. Do I have my customary expense account freedom? A man can get a lot of information from a woman over a glass of wine and a good meal."

Gil nodded. "Whatever it takes to get the job done . . . within reason."

Dan rose from his chair and turned to go.

"Oh, wait," Gil called, waving a cream-colored envelope. "This came while you were out of town," he said. "It's addressed to you in care of the magazine. Whoever sent it must not know you too well or they would have addressed it to your apartment."

Dan slid his finger around the edge of the flap and opened it, then withdrew another envelope. Someone had handwritten his name in script. His forehead wrinkled as he opened the second envelope and withdrew an engraved invitation.

"Who's it from?" Gil asked.

Dan smiled as he read aloud, "Dane Axel Grasten and Abigail Berniece Hardesty invite you to share in their wedding celebration." He read the date and time aloud to Gil. "The bride is a cousin to my spud lady," he explained.

"Your what?"

Dan grinned. "The woman who operates the commercial potato farm in the series. I'll be damned. I ran into them last month during the big sale at the sheep experiment station north of Dubois. They didn't say a word about getting married." His smile broadened.

"Are you going to go?" Gil asked.

Dan nodded. "You can pay for the gas. This invitation is a great excuse to start a follow-up on the potato farmer. I'll bet you a steak dinner she'll be part of the wedding."

Gil extended his hand. "You're on. What's so special about this spud lady? Is there something between the two of you?"

Dan shook his head. "No, but the other women had a certain toughness about them...this one was different. She's pretty, she's one of the most feminine women I've ever met, she's like..." He searched for the right words to describe Eileen Mills. "Like turning back the clock to a gentler time. She's strong-willed and filled with pride, maybe too much for her own good. It will be good to see her again. She's from Kentucky."

"A steel magnolia?" Gil asked, arching a heavy brow.

"No," Dan replied, as a vivid image of Eileen Mills materialized in his head. "She's more like a moss rose. When she gets knocked down or hurt, she always comes back stronger and more beautiful than ever."

Gil laughed. "Sounds like you're smitten."

Dan grinned. "She's just a very nice woman whom I happened to have met in the line of duty, Gil." But as he left the editor's office, he knew Eileen could easily become much more to him, even though he had not seen her since her husband's funeral.

The hours passed quickly as Dan scheduled interviews with several of the women from the series. Some telephone numbers on his original list had been disconnected. Of the women he found, most were receptive when he explained the purpose of the new article. His appointment book pages were soon filled with names, times and places. Only one name and number remained.

He dialed the number. When he heard Eileen's soft melodious voice answer, he exhaled in relief. "Hello, this is Daniel Page from Western Living Publications. Is this my spud lady?"

"Dan? Dan, is this really you?" Eileen Mills asked, and Dan could imagine how she looked. "I'm...I'm so surprised. I...how are you? It's been months..."

"How have you been?" he asked.

"Fine," she replied.

"And the children?" He listened to progress reports on her son and twin daughters. "Good. I'm glad to hear it. Tell them all hello." He explained the reason for the phone call.

"I don't know," she said, mulling over his request for another interview. "What could we talk about that we haven't already covered?"

"Couldn't you at least think about it?" he asked. "I can call back in a few days. I'd hate for you to be the only woman missing from the update."

"I'll think about it," she replied, "but you'll have to give me more time. I'm taking a trip...out of state to a wedding, actually. Do you remember my cousin Abbie Hardesty?"

"Of course. I saw her at a ram sale at the sheep experiment station in September."

"You did? Abbie never said anything."

He chuckled. "She was with her sheep rancher. They had eyes only for each other and the two rams they bought."

"That's what love does to people," she replied. "They're getting married next weekend and I'm going to be matron of honor. It will be the first trip the children and I have made since . . . since Duncan's death.''

Dan heard her sigh. "I've taken a subscription to *Western Living*,'' she said. "You're a very good writer. I loved the interview of the couple who ran the bulb farm.''

"Glad you liked it.''

"And your job?'' she asked. "I suppose it's a career or profession to you. It must be exciting to travel around and meet all those interesting people.''

"It keeps the creditors away from my door,'' he teased.

"I know how that can be.'' She hesitated, then asked, "How is your son?''

He didn't remember mentioning Stephen. "The job's fine, I'm fine, Stephen's fine. He just had his twelfth birthday. And Jordan? Is he eleven yet?''

"Last month,'' she said. "The twins were eight in June and growing like weeds.''

"I know what you mean,'' he replied. "I don't see Stephen very often.'' Dan searched for an excuse to keep her on the line. "What do you say? Can we schedule the appointment now?''

"I'd rather not,'' she said. "But do call again after I've returned from the trip. It's good to hear from you. I've . . . we've thought about you even if we didn't call.''

As Dan hung up the receiver, he wondered why he hadn't told her he had been invited to Abbie's wedding.

AFTER ALL THESE MONTHS, Eileen Mills thought. She brushed the stray brown curls tickling her temple and forced her gaze from the window back to her desk top.

Has Daniel Page been thinking of me often? As often as he had been in her own thoughts the past few weeks? The phone beeped several times in her ear, reminding her that she was still clutching the receiver. She replaced it and tried to return to the account books in front of her.

She smiled, recalling the times she and Dan Page had met. He had called for an interview almost two years earlier. His visit to the potato farm had been planned for an hour and had evolved into a full afternoon and an invitation to stay for dinner with the family. Then there was the excitement of seeing the Mills family in print and living color when Dan personally delivered the magazine.

By that time her husband's condition had weakened so much he'd been unable to join them at the dining room table. The reporter's tact had been emotionally wrenching for Eileen when he had excused himself from the table and taken his plate and silverware and joined Duncan in the room down the hall that had been converted into a hospital room.

Over the months since her husband's death, she had replayed those times over and over again, analyzing her own reaction to seeing Duncan Mills and Daniel Page together. The journalist's warmth and sincerity had edged its way into her heart and grown slowly to fill the emptiness. She had welcomed each of Dan's visits and the opportunity to chat with him in the blue-and-white farm kitchen over steaming cups of coffee or fresh-brewed exotic tea blends. He was an easy man to talk to. Was it because he was an outsider, a sounding board, a person who had promised to not pass on the feelings she found herself revealing to him, the agony of watching her husband wither away before her eyes?

The afternoon of visitation after the funeral had changed everything.

Now, as she sat staring down at the open checkbook, tears blurred her vision. Dan was making a reentry into her life, a life she had tried so hard to stabilize, not just for herself, but for her children as well. They surely missed their father as much as she missed her husband.

Her grief had begun to recede and she was picking up the pieces. Could one of those pieces include the personable reporter from Boise? There was a tiny photo of Dan in the corner of the title page of each part of the magazine series. She fought the urge to go upstairs to her bedroom and look at his face. Involvement with a man so soon after losing Duncan would be inappropriate. *Involvement? How foolish to jump to such silly conclusions,* she thought. *The only reason he called me was to ask for an interview!*

Why was her heart pounding against her ribs? Why was her breathing erratic when she was sitting still in her chair? Why was she torn between calling him right back to cancel the appointment and anxious to move the date up to a day or two away? Eileen grimaced. There was no appointment scheduled. What was she fretting about?

When Dan called again, she would just keep her head about her and give him her regrets and make up a little white lie about being too busy to see him.

But would it be a lie? *No,* she thought. She had no time in her life for a man like Dan Page, who could turn her knees to jelly and upset her emotions with just a phone call.

CHAPTER TWO

EILEEN REMOVED the white wedding gown from its hanger. Rows and rows of gossamer Crystalette ruffles covered the full skirt of the dress while Schiffli embroidered roses decorated the bodice and the lower portion of the bell sleeves. A band of lace topped the high neckline, giving the gown a prim, traditional appearance.

She held it against her slender body and laughed. "I'm such a shrimp compared to you. Abbie, it's the most beautiful wedding gown I've ever seen." She handed the dress to her cousin.

"Do you really like it?" Abigail Hardesty asked, turning toward the long mirror on the motel bathroom's door. "Maybe it's too fancy. Maybe it's too traditional . . . maybe this is all a dream." She closed her eyes and leaned against the wall. "Maybe this is all wrong."

"Wrong?" Eileen exclaimed, frowning at the tall, auburn-haired woman. "Are you having second thoughts? Don't you love Dane anymore? How could you not love that man? He's so...so special, and for him I'm sure you are the moon and the stars."

Abbie laughed. "Dane says there's an old Danish proverb that says a deaf husband and a blind wife are always a happy couple. Neither of us fits that saying. Dane's oldest brother Knud says Danish people are a combination of bacon-and-eggs practicality and fairy-tale flights of fancy. When I first met Dane he was definitely bacon-and-eggs practicality during lambing, but right now we're both in the middle of a crazy flight of fancy.''

"I'll admit I'm more than a little surprised at the size of this wedding," Eileen said. "Whose idea was it to go all out?"

"We started off very simply, but it's gotten out of hand." Abbie shrugged. "We're paying for it ourselves. Dane insists it will be my first and last wedding, because it's going to be his last, too. He was married once before, you know."

"Yes, you told me. Did he have a large wedding then?"

"No, they went to Jackpot, Nevada," Abbie said. "Can you imagine anyone getting married in a place called Jackpot?" Suddenly her features turned serious. "Sometimes I wonder if...if he compares me with...her. Do you think husbands do that? I mean compare their different wives?"

Eileen smiled. "Maybe. But that doesn't mean they have regrets. Of course, Duncan and I had nothing to compare our marriage with so... Abbie, you're just being a nervous bride-to-be. You do love him, don't you?"

Abbie blinked, shedding shimmering tears. "I love him so much I'm afraid something might happen, something terrible like..." She paused. "Eileen, I never really understood what you were going through before Duncan died until these past few months. Sometimes I lie awake and try to imagine my life without Dane, without his love, without having his arms around me at night, and I get all teary-eyed. You know I've never been a crier...until I met him." She tossed the dress onto the bed and reached for a tissue to pat her eyes, careful to preserve her makeup. "You're so brave to be alone," she said, smiling at Eileen over the edges of the facial tissue.

Eileen smiled wanly. "I'm adjusting. I still miss Duncan very much, but I have a full life. The children keep me busy and the farm work is unrelenting. You know how that is."

"You're right," Abbie replied, reaching for the dress again. "Working the sheep this summer has kept me slim and trim as well as busy. I've had time at the loom to complete only one tapestry. Did I tell you about the room Dane is adding on to the house? He positively forced me to describe the ultimate weaving studio and now the room he's built to specification is almost complete." Abruptly, she stopped talking and clasped her hands around her slender waist. "No one will be able to count on their fingers for this bride."

Eileen laughed. "but they will anyway."

"When they reach nine months and there's no baby, they'll wonder," Abbie replied.

"Being pregnant when you get married is acceptable in today's society, Abbie. Are you being a prude?"

"Maybe a little bit," Abbie replied. "Do you think anyone ever breaks free from their upbringing, Eileen?"

"Probably not," Eileen said. "Why?"

"I just think babies should be planned for, that they should have a willing father as well as a mother. Not like poor Callie. Don't you wonder what her life would be like today if she and Bobby Joe had waited or taken precautions?"

"Second guessing and 'what ifs' can be dangerous," Eileen cautioned. "Pregnancies and babies should be left to the participants. Now, I'm going to get dressed." She removed an ankle-length, apricot voile gown from its hanger and held it up against herself.

Abbie scrutinized Eileen. "I'm glad I chose that color for you. It brings just enough color to your cheeks to make you appear healthy."

Eileen touched her cheek. "I *am* healthy."

"You're much too thin."

"But I'm gaining...a little each month," Eileen insisted.

"How much did you weigh when Duncan...passed away?"

Eileen glanced away. "I was down to ninety-five pounds."

"That's not very much for a five foot, four inch woman," Abbie said.

"I know, and I'm trying to eat regularly, but it's hard," she admitted. "Sometimes I can't get anything down. I'm better now. Really. I'm up to one hundred five pounds."

"Fully dressed or dripping wet?" Abbie asked.

Eileen shrugged. "Dressed."

"You'd better fatten yourself up so when some man takes a liking to you, he can find more than a bag of bones beneath your clothes."

Eileen paled. "There won't be another man."

Abbie covered her mouth with her hand. "I'm sorry, Eileen. That was thoughtless of me. I'm truly sorry. Isn't it time to get dressed?" She glanced at her watch. "Still almost an hour?" She tossed the dress onto the bed again. "When will Callie get here? What if she missed her flight? I'm so glad she accepted my offer to pay her expenses. She's entirely too proud for her own good. And why didn't she come with Aunt Minnie and Uncle Harry? What if her dress doesn't fit?"

Eileen dropped to the other bed. "Abbie, you're as nervous as a cat. Callie will be here any minute, so stop worrying. And if you think I'm thin, wait until you see Callie. Anyone who wears a size three dress can't be very big."

Abbie smiled. "I know. When I called her and asked her to come and be part of the wedding, she was very hesitant. I apologized for each and every harsh word I'd ever said to her from when we were kids to when I bawled her out for being on welfare." Abbie tossed her auburn head. "Callie couldn't even remember some of the things I'd said."

"Sounds like your guilty conscience has stayed with you longer than necessary," Eileen suggested.

Abbie's straight brows furrowed. "I convinced her we couldn't have the wedding without her, and Callie finally agreed, but she insisted on making it up to me sometime. I told her I wouldn't accept money, so she said she would think of something special that I couldn't give to myself."

Eileen reached for the petite salmon-colored voile dress that matched her own in style. "It's lovely and I know Callie will be beautiful in it with her dark hair and eyes. I used to think she looked like a little doll when we were children."

"Me, too," Abbie agreed. "I teased her too much, but I always thought she would grow up to be the prettiest one of us all. When I started to shoot up tall that summer between eighth grade and high school, I felt like a giraffe. Callie always stayed so petite and graceful. Her voice was beautiful and natural. Do you think she ever sings anymore?"

"You can ask her if you think the time is right," Eileen replied, wishing her cousin would stop her restless pacing. She hoped the reunion between Abbie and Callie would go smoothly. She herself was in no mood to referee an argument if one arose. "But please, Abbie, no squabbles. You and Callie can find more things to disagree about than any two people I know, especially when you've been like sisters ever since we were kids."

Abbie beamed. "I'm in no mood to disagree with anyone." She touched the gauzy veil attached to her headpiece. "I waited long enough to become a bride, didn't I?"

"No one knows when love will come," Eileen said as she began to coil her long brown hair on top of her head and position hair pins to anchor it.

"Yes," Abbie replied, "I wasn't looking for love when I met Dane. I thought he was a drunk and he wanted to run me off the place, and now look at the two of us."

"Love that is spontaneous and unexpected is the best kind," Eileen assured her cousin. "So relax and be patient. This day will be over before you know it." She peeked out the window. "Do you think Jordan and the twins are okay? They're probably driving everyone at the ranch crazy."

"You spoke to Dane's sister Anna just this morning. Didn't she say they were having a wonderful time exploring the place? If they are driving all the grown-ups nuts, it's because Anna and Aunt Minnie insisted they stay there," Abbie said, pacing the room again. "I'm glad we decided to come to town yesterday. A bride-to-be shouldn't let the groom see her on the wedding day... even if they have been sleeping together for months. Oh, Eileen, I hope Aunt Minnie doesn't suspect."

Eileen smiled. "It's your business, but I'm glad you decided to make it legal. People in love should get married. It's the natural thing to do and I'm sure you're doing the right thing." She sprang from the bed. "I hear a car. It must be Callie."

A minute later they heard a faint knocking. Abbie motioned to the knob and stepped back as Eileen opened the door.

In the entrance stood a black-haired woman in her late twenties, barely over five feet tall. Her large brown eyes were full of uncertainty. "Hi, have y'all been waitin' for me?" she asked breathlessly, her soft Southern drawl barely above a whisper. "My plane was almost an hour late taking off from Dallas, can you imagine? May I come in?"

Eileen took Callie's hand and gave it a squeeze. "Of course. We were getting a little worried. Come inside." Eileen closed the door behind her and stood aside.

Callie and Abbie stared at each other.

"Abbie, is that really you?" Callie asked. "I don't remember you being so tall." Her chin trembled as she held her hand out to Abbie. "It's been a long time, hasn't it?"

"Too long," Abbie murmured, holding out her arms to her cousin.

As Abbie and Callie embraced, the hurt of the past was erased. They separated, still holding hands.

"I'm sorry, Callie, so sorry," Abbie sobbed, "for every cruel thing I ever said to you."

"There's nothing to be sorry about," Callie said. "Any problems we have, we bring on ourselves. Trust me, I've learned the hard way the truth of that. Now you just stop this crybaby stuff or you'll have a blotchy face for your own wedding." She squeezed Abbie again and stepped away.

"We'd better finish dressing," Eileen said, while Abbie repaired her makeup again. Eileen hid the tucks that were needed around her waist with the chocolate velvet ribbon sash. Callie and Eileen stood on chairs and lifted Abbie's dress over her head and eased it down over her shoulders.

When Abbie stood in front of the mirror, her green eyes widened. "Is this really me? I look so..."

"Beautiful," Eileen said, zipping up the back of the dress. "Now the veil." Callie adjusted the net and lace over Abbie's head, allowing it to form a soft frame around her face.

Eileen stood back. "What jewelry are you wearing?"

Abbie smiled and lifted a gold chain from her small jewelry case. "My locket, of course!"

"Do you still have it?" Eileen asked. "I almost forget to bring mine and drove five miles back to the farm to get it." She retrieved the gold locket from her purse and fastened it around her neck. It fell to the vee of her neckline. She grimaced. "Once upon a time I had some cleavage. Do you think if I regained my weight, I'd get my breasts back too?"

"You'll never know until you try," Abbie replied, giving Eileen an encouraging smile.

Callie opened her battered blue suitcase and rummaged through her clothing. She turned, holding up her gold locket. "Remember the day we got these?"

"Yes," Eileen said. "That was the last time we ever met at that cave."

Callie tipped her head thoughtfully. "My folks sent me to Aunt Belle's cabin near Harlan, remember? They never did tell me why I had to go, but I went for the next three summers. That's where I learned to really play the dulcimer, so it wasn't all bad. And you, Abbie?"

Abbie laughed. "I'll never forget the reason I couldn't go traipsing through the woods that next summer. I broke my leg during a track meet and spent the entire summer with a cast clear up to here," she said, hiking her gown to her mid thigh.

"I went twice," Eileen said, "but going to a cave alone isn't much fun...and the cave and that little glen didn't seem as large as when we had been there together." She shrugged. "I had to go to work in the fields with my brothers. Daddy offered me a price I couldn't refuse."

Callie grinned. "What was your price?"

"A whole dollar a day," Eileen said, chuckling, "and I saved every one of them until I graduated. That money paid for my high school wardrobe and my daddy didn't say a word when I came home with an honest-to-goodness miniskirt. Remember those things?"

They all laughed. "Did you save it?" Abbie asked. "They're back in style. I always thought my legs were too long."

"And mine were too short," Callie added.

Eileen sashayed across the room. "Well, I thought mine were just right...but in winter my knees turned red from the cold, so I eased the hem down ... three times, until there wasn't a thread more to lower."

They laughed.

"Daddy never said a word," she concluded. "Well, we'd better stop this hen party and finish dressing." She turned to Callie. "Can I help you?"

"No, I can do it," Callie replied. "The clasp is bent a little. Bobby Joe got rough one time and ..." She busied herself with the chain.

"Let me," Abbie said, taking the chain from Callie's palm.

"I seldom wear it," Callie confessed, "but it brings back memories of the good times. I'll give it to Linda someday."

Eileen frowned. "And how is your daughter doing? I wish you could have brought her. Jodie and Jolene wanted to meet her."

Callie smoothed a strand of her straight black hair, then tucked it beneath the headpiece she wore. "It costs enough to fly one person out here, much less two or three. That wouldn't have been right and you both know it. As for Linda, the new doctor said that since her last operation, she should start growing and maybe in a few years she'll be up with her classmates."

"That's great," Abbie said, as she fastened the gold chain around Callie's neck and smoothed her hair. "You really do have beautiful hair, Callie, but isn't it a chore to care for?" she asked, lifting a handful of the waist-length shiny tresses.

"At times, but it's the only thing I have that no one can take away from me," Callie replied, as she busied herself with her shoes, then hurried into the bathroom and closed the door.

Eileen and Abbie exchanged glances, but when Abbie opened her mouth to speak, Eileen shook her head. "Give her time," she whispered.

Callie's features were composed when she returned to the room. "Life has been good to you two. I'm still paying my debt."

"Don't carry your guilt alone, Callie," Eileen said. "Bobby Joe is equally responsible, but I don't hear of him worrying about Linda or coming to visit Robbie. Don't lose heart. There are good men around. They aren't all like Bobby Joe."

Abbie laughed. "You're playing matchmaker, Mrs. Mills. You might have to eat your words."

"Do as I say, not as I do," Eileen replied primly, grinning as Abbie stood in the center of the motel room, checking her image in the mirror. "A woman can find her own happiness in the world without a man."

"But sharing her happiness with someone she loves makes it much more fun," Abbie said.

Eileen smiled and squeezed the others' hands. "You can never be sure about matters of the heart." Her eyes filled with tears. "This is truly a reunion of the Secret Society of Sisters and Friends," she said. "Two of us may be thousands of miles from the Rainbow Hills, but our promises can still hold true. We've got to swallow our pride and ask for help when we need it. We've all ignored that part of our pledge, haven't we?"

The other two nodded but remained silent. "Well, I have too," Eileen admitted, "but I promise to ask for help when I need it from now on. How about you two?"

They nodded again, but Eileen sensed the tension. "We're three liars, aren't we? We're great about offering help, but terrible about accepting it."

Abbie and Callie smiled, but didn't say a word.

"We're hopeless," Eileen concluded, "but I love you both so much. Even if we're too proud for our own good, let's get in touch more often. Okay?"

"Agreed," Abbie and Callie replied.

"Great." Eileen glanced at her watch. "Are we all ready? Uncle Harry will be here soon to drive us to the church."

A few minutes later a horn sounded from outside.

Eileen opened the door and waved to the two men in the car. "They're here," she exclaimed. "Uncle Harry and Moses Parish."

Within minutes, they had traveled the mile to the church and were inside the building. The ushers, including Eileen's son Jordan, had seated most of the guests and were waiting near the doors for late arrivals as the bridal party gathered in the vestibule. The organ struck the first note of the processional and the twins, Jolene and Jodie, started down the aisle. Their matching dresses were white taffeta with tiny apricot and salmon flowers. Around their waists, they wore chocolate-brown velvet ribbons. They were followed by Callie and then Eileen.

The sanctuary, filled to capacity with guests, was decorated with bouquets of pale yellow, soft orange and muted red silk flowers in wicker baskets. Brown velvet ribbons cascaded from the baskets. The autumn color scheme was continued in the bouquets of the wedding party. Abbie's bridal bouquet contained cascading white roses and tiny orange rose buds nestled in green.

Eileen pushed the memories of her own simple wedding from her mind as she took the first step down the aisle toward the altar, concentrating on the organ music. When she reached the altar she nodded at the groom and turned to watch Abbie and Uncle Harry come up the aisle. She hoped she wouldn't cry.

Memories of her own wedding intruded. They had been married in a small chapel a block from the campus of the University of Tennessee in Knoxville. Duncan has been the older brother of her roommate, Esther Mills. They had met in her junior year and it had been mutual love at first sight. Both had been raised in fundamentalist families and they had promised both sets of parents to be reasonable. But within the month they had become secretly engaged and set a wedding date, a frustrating date two years in the future when he would complete his masters degree in agribusiness and agronomy and she would complete her bachelor of science degree in business administration.

All their plans had come to pass except the one to spend the rest of their lives together.

She and Duncan had shared their lives for eleven years, but for the last three, his sickness had been the focal point of their existence. She could still remember the meeting with a specialist who had explained to Duncan and her what multiple sclerosis did to the nervous system, attacking the sheath that protected the message-carrying nerve fibers in the brain and spinal cord.

Duncan's first question had reflected his concern for his family. "Will I pass it on to my children?" he had asked.

"No," the physician had assured them, "but the predisposition may run in families. The disease is not inherited in the strict sense of the term. Factors in the environment, such as a virus to which a whole family might have been exposed can be influential," the physician explained. "People living in cold climates are more likely to have it, but ironically, cold itself seems to lessen the effects on the body."

"So my children are safe?" Duncan had asked.

The specialist had frowned. "Families, having the same genetic makeup and ethnic backgrounds, and living in the same area for generations may be more likely to have it than the public at large. The farther from the equator, the greater the possibility. Frankly, Mr. Mills, we don't know what triggers it. Research is still being done. I *can* tell you that no one ever died from MS." He told them of the problems the

MS person might have and discussed briefly the complications and side effects of the disease, then dismissed them with an encouraging smile.

Within months, Duncan had begun to show susceptibility to many of the disease's complications. Pneumonia was the first to strike, followed closely by a series of bladder infections. His sense of balance had eroded, his vision blurred, and his usual inexhaustible supply of energy had been replaced with unrelenting fatigue. Because of his inability to do the farm work, he had increased the credit line with the local bank and hired several extra workers. Some had taken advantage of the family's problems.

Then a strapping giant of a man named Hogan Waite had been hired as foreman and had taken charge of the operation with gusto. Duncan had expressed his confidence in Waite, and the two men had become fast friends in the two years Waite had stayed with them. During a period of remission for Duncan, Waite had received an offer from his sister in Alaska to join her in a fishing venture near Ketchikan. Waite had been hesitant to leave them, but Duncan had assured him his strength was returning and he would be able to take the reins of the farm again.

Less than a month after Waite's departure, Duncan had been hit by a debilitating kidney infection. It had been the end of the disease's only period of remission.

Eileen had received a sympathy card from Hogan a month after the funeral, writing that he would be glad to return if she needed him. She had declined, but thanked him for his concern in a letter and assured him that if he was ever in eastern Idaho again to stop by. She wrote that he would always be considered a special friend. One Tuesday morning, when she was trying to settle an argument between two workers about how to best repair one of the planters, Hogan Waite had appeared on her doorstep.

"I thought you might need me," he had said, his towering six feet six inch height carrying with it the authority she needed.

"You're hired!" she had exclaimed. He had suggested she return to the house and let him take over. She knew Hogan Waite would never be a romantic partner, but a treasured and loyal friend had been just what she had needed that morning.

Eileen's thoughts returned to the wedding as Uncle Harry released Abbie's hand and stepped back to seat himself beside a tearful Aunt Minnie. Dane Grasten stood impatiently beside his brother Knud, both of them wearing black formal wear. Eileen smiled as she watched Dane, who was oblivious to all but Abbie. Dane reached for Abbie's hand, and Eileen shifted her gaze to her cousin as Abbie's features lit up in a smile of loving adoration.

The minister began to read the wedding ceremony, and Eileen's gaze wandered over the people seated in the pews as the minister's voice continued in a heavy Danish accent. Eileen had given up on following the message word for word, knowing it was steeped with traditional instructions to the husband and wife.

The mood in the church and the smiles on the guests' faces as they watched the wedding warmed Eileen's heart. Everything was as it should be. Happy, loving, romantic, with visions of the future in evidence for all to share.

Several guests were standing along the wall in the back of the church. A man entered the rear door and an usher nodded his regrets as he motioned to a vacant spot against the back wall. The man shrugged out of an overcoat and draped it over his arm, then scanned the sanctuary.

Eileen blinked and leaned forward, wondering if her eyes were playing a trick on her. *Could that be...?* No, she must be imagining him. Why would Daniel Page be here at Dane's and Abbie's wedding? She remembered Dan's phone call and his comment about meeting Dane and Abbie at the sheep sale.

Disturbing memories from the afternoon of visitation after her husband's burial came back. She remembered how Dan Page had come to the farm, how he had chatted with the children and distracted them for a while, visited with Dane Grasten and Abbie, and then how he and Dane had taken her outside for a walk.

Eileen had accepted their arms, drawing strength from each man in a different way. Once, when they had paused between two plowed potato fields, she had lost control and started to cry again. Dan had put his arm around her shoulders and had drawn her close and she had rested her head against his chest.

The warmth of his arms and the firmness of his body had lulled her, and her thin arms had found their way around his waist. For several minutes she had given in to his embrace, soaking up his genuine concern and affection.

Then she had spoiled it all when, to her disgust, a stirring had begun to grow from deep within her. Upset at the thought of betraying Duncan's memory only hours after his burial, she had pulled away, refusing the shelter and solace Dan had offered.

Several weeks later she had read that such reactions were often a normal part of the grieving process, but that knowledge did little to erase the impact of the unexpected experience.

Although Dan had stayed in her thoughts for months, she had refused to call him, determined to work through the difficult period of adjusting to life alone. But strangely, Daniel Page had become an invisible source of strength in her early widowhood. His business card had been taped to the phone on her night stand. She had received continued solace knowing that help and a sympathetic ear were only a phone call away, but she had never given in to the urge to hear his voice.

Eileen didn't realize she was smiling until she saw Dan nod his brown head. She tore her glance away and concentrated on the ceremony, giving Abbie the wide gold wedding band when the minister asked. Her attention swung to the back of the church again. Dan Page smiled and this time she was the one to nod, her heart pounding wildly.

The ceremony progressed to a closing summary of marital responsibilities. Eileen glanced to the back pews again. "Oh, no," she murmured. Abbie, Dane and the minister glanced at her. She motioned for them to continue. She certainly didn't want to stop the wedding just because Daniel Page was gone.

CHAPTER THREE

EILEEN SEARCHED the sea of faces. Perhaps, she reasoned, he had come to cover the wedding, but why would the marriage of a sheepman and a weaver be newsworthy? Maybe he was doing a story on the century-old Lutheran church and the ethnic history of the area. Surely he wouldn't leave without speaking to her. Was he upset or angry at her refusal to set a definite time and date for the interview? She hoped not.

Her attention returned to the ceremony. She lifted Abbie's veil from her face and stood back, laughing with the wedding guests when Dane bestowed a passionate kiss on his bride's lips. The minister introduced the new husband and wife to the congregation and the sanctuary was filled with organ music as the bride and groom hurried down the aisle.

The next half hour was filled with picture taking, but Eileen's poses were mechanical. She kept thinking about Dan.

The receiving line formed in the fellowship hall. Eileen took her place next to the bride and listened to the names being given her, chatted briefly with each guest, then introduced each person to Callie. Her hand grew tired of being shaken and after several minutes, Eileen started performing the motions automatically. A glance down the line confirmed her suspicions that it was growing longer instead of shorter.

"Can a friend of the family kiss one of the matrons of honor?" a masculine voice said, interrupting her meandering thoughts.

Daniel Page took her hand. An inch or two shorter than six feet, he had the wiry build of a runner. Eileen fought an almost irresistible urge to rest again in his embrace. The image brought a pink flush to her cheeks and she hoped others would attribute it to the increasing warmth of the reception hall.

"If you want," she murmured, his lean handsome features filling her view.

"I do." Dan put one hand on her rosy cheek and touched her mouth lightly with his. The warmth of his lips on hers drew her forward, but he pulled away and moved on to talk with Callie before she could say a word.

She had trouble remembering the names of the next several guests but no one seemed to mind. Spirits were high as everyone became caught up in the marriage celebration. Finally, the receiving line disbanded for the buffet.

Eileen spied Jordan with several local boys his age leading their way down the long table heavily laden with delectable dishes. Jolene took her hand and tugged her toward the food.

"Where's Jodie?" Eileen asked.

"I don't know," Jolene replied, concentrating on filling her plate with strawberries.

"I'm right here," a small voice said directly behind Eileen. "Guess who's helping me?"

Eileen turned around to find Daniel Page helping Jodie select an assortment of cheeses, Jodie's favorite snack.

"Hello again," he said, catching Jodie's plate as it tipped sideways. "Rest it on the table," he suggested. "Why don't you change places with your mother so I can help her fill her plate?"

"Why?" Jodie asked. "She can do it herself."

Dan smiled. "She's too thin. I'm going to see that she fills her plate and eats every bite."

"She *is* sorta skinny," Jolene agreed. "She used to be kinda fat."

"Jolene!" Eileen scolded.

"Out of the mouths of little girls," Dan teased. "I can't imagine you 'kinda fat,' though," he said, reaching for a slice of turkey and dropping it on her plate.

They worked their way down the line. "We can come back for dessert later," Eileen said, glancing at Dan's full plate.

"Sounds good," Dan agreed but found room for one more slice of spiced meat roll he had dipped in hot mustard sauce. "These Danes sure know how to lay out a feast," he said. "I was raised on cabbage and boiled potatoes. I think I'll suggest to my editor I do a series on ethnic foods."

"I'm a southern-fried chicken cook myself," Eileen replied, "but this is a nice change of pace." She stepped away from the long table and surveyed the room. "There's one." She pointed to a small table across the room.

"Follow me," Dan said, and began working his way through the milling crowd. "Stay close."

She concentrated on the back of his suit jacket, admiring the stylish cut and quality fabric as she followed him. Was he fashion conscious? she wondered. Probably, she decided, since he was single and had no financial worries. Her two delinquent loans at the Shelley bank came to mind and she frowned. She planned to pay them off as soon as Hogan delivered the truck loads of potatoes.

They reached the table and sat down.

"We forgot silverware," she said.

He laid his hand on her shoulder when she started to rise. "Stay put. I'll get it."

She watched him work his way back through the crowd. What was it about him that made her feel at ease? Was it partly because he seemed to be in control of his life while her own was still unsettled? He collected the silverware and linen napkins and turned, searching her out in the crowd and smiling. Her pulse quickened. Whenever they had met, the atmosphere had been strained, yet each time she had sensed an invisible thread of communication between them, a sense of mutual caring.

"You look very serious," Dan said, laying the silverware and napkins on the table and sliding into his chair.

She started. "I was just thinking."

"About what?" he asked, pushing some cutlery toward her.

"Love," she admitted, then regretted her word.

His brow arched. "Love?"

"Don't misunderstand," she explained. "Our preacher loves to challenge us to stretch our minds. He often talks about the different kinds of love; between a man and a woman, between mother and child, what we feel for our parents and our relatives. He talked about love for our fellow man and how unselfish that must be since we have none of the emotional strings that complicate what we feel for our loved ones."

He smiled. "Very philosophical. And what kinds of love do you see in this room?"

She surveyed the crowd and for a moment her gaze fell on Abbie and Dane. "All of them."

Dan chuckled. She turned her attention back to him, expecting a comment but he cut a piece of turkey instead. As he chewed, he gazed at her. Eileen felt her cheeks warm under his perusal. "Please don't," she murmured.

"Don't what?"

"Stare at me."

"I'm sorry," he said, taking another bite of turkey. "I didn't mean to make you uncomfortable," he said. "You're a very attractive woman, and beneath that proper facade...well, never mind." He frowned. "I'm glad I came to the wedding."

"Where are the children?" she asked, realizing she hadn't thought of her children once since they had left the buffet.

He motioned to another table. "There's Jordan, eating with some local boys. The girls have found another set of twins." He pointed to a pair of dark-haired girls a few years older than Jodie and Jolene. "So we're stuck with each other," Dan said. "Now clean your plate."

Eileen smiled and gave him a mock salute. "Bossy." She finished most of her food. "I haven't eaten this much food in a long time. Perhaps my appetite is coming back."

"Good," Dan said. "I wouldn't want you to eat just because I forced you. How about some dessert?" Before she could reply, he left the table, returning a few minutes later with two small plates of assorted cakes and fruit salads.

"I'll be stuffed," she said, taking a bite of a wheat and cream cheese dessert salad. "This is very good."

Their knees touched beneath the table and Eileen pulled away. She glanced at him and found him staring at her. She pushed her plate away. "Is something wrong?" she asked.

"I was just trying to recall all the information from the interview I did with you," he said. "Are you agreeable to another go round?" He reached for her hand.

She nodded. "Yes, if you can wait until early November." She tried to free her hand but couldn't. Her left hand touched his hand. "Please."

He took both of her hands in his. "Your rings are gone."

"I...I removed them last month," Eileen said. "I began to feel like I was holding on to a—" She stopped. "I didn't mean it...like it sounds. I love Duncan. I always will."

"Of course, you will," Dan agreed, "but you did the right thing. Duncan would want you to live again. He was too fine a man not to. I'm glad I met him. He released her hands and reached for the plates, giving them to an attendant.

The members of a band were tuning their instruments across the room. One of the musicians played a Scandinavian song on an accordion and several of the guests began to clap in time to the melody. The other band members made final adjustments to their chairs and music stands and began to play the first dance tune.

Dan pulled her from her chair. "Let's move closer." She followed him to the crowd gathering in the open area of the hall.

Dane and Abbie Grasten danced around the room several times. The groom whispered in his bride's ear and she smiled. They parted and Abbie motioned to her Uncle Harry while Dane coaxed his white-haired mother onto the dance floor. Dagmar Grasten was in her mid-eighties, and as Dane whirled her around the floor they called to each other, then she said something else and laughed. The members of the crowd who understood the language applauded.

"What did she say?" Dan asked.

Eileen shook her head. "I don't know."

Knud Grasten volunteered a translation. "She says a woman is never too old for loving or dancing and my little brother asked her if she meant in that order." He chuckled. "Momma answered by saying 'Skaal.'"

"And what does Skaal mean?" Eileen asked.

"You see, each letter has a meaning," Knud explained. "*S* is for togetherness, *K* is for love, *A* is for many talents, the second *A* is for longevity and the final *L* is for luck. It's an old Danish custom to say 'Skaal' when you're drinking and fellowshipping with your friends or loved ones.'' He cut in on Dane as they danced by.

"Everyone dance," Dane ordered, catching Callie's hand and sweeping the shy dark-haired cousin away.

Other couples joined the dancers.

"Let's dance off the calories we consumed," Dan suggested. His arm slid around her waist.

Eileen tensed. "I haven't danced in years."

"It will come back to you," he said, as he took her other hand in his. "I must confess, it's been a few years since I've waltzed."

Eileen scanned the crowd. "They're dancing very fast for a waltz."

Dan laughed. "I think it's the dancers' choice. We'll take it slow like the traditionalists and shift gears later if we decide we can handle the faster pace."

"Abbie told me that Dane suggested a waltz for a starter to please the older people," Eileen replied. She looked around the floor at the gray-and white-haired dancers. "Do we qualify?"

He squinted at her upswept hairdo. "I don't see any gray."

She smiled. "But I do." Without thinking, she lifted her hand from his shoulder to his well trimmed sideburn. "You're getting a few. You'll have silver wings in no time." Her fingers graced his cheek. "How old are you?"

His green eyes darkened. "Does it matter?"

She sobered. "No." Her hand returned to his shoulder.

"I'm thirty-five calendar years old," he said. "I've lived at least fifty, but right now I feel like a teenager. Now let's dance before this romantic song ends."

He guided her across the floor. She stepped on his toe. "I'm sorry."

"Relax," he whispered as he pulled her closer, putting his hand protectively around hers and tucking it against his body.

Dane and Abbie danced by, nodding and laughing as they moved away. "They're very happy, aren't they?" Eileen said.

Dan nodded. "Let's hope their love lasts."

"Does it ever?"

"Didn't yours?" he asked, peering down at Eileen.

"Well, yes, we loved each other until the end but..." She bit off the words, unwilling to admit her inner conflicts and anguish.

"Just dance," he said, pulling her closer. And they did until the band took a break. "Let's get some fresh air," he suggested.

"The children..."

"...are fine. Be selfish," Dan said. "You're always thinking of others. Think of yourself for once." He guided her to the coat rack in the hallway. "It's getting dark already and it's probably chilly outside." He helped her into a long ivory mohair coat, then pulled on his own overcoat. "Ready?"

She nodded and accepted his hand as he led her outside.

The crisp fall air held the promise of frost. Overhead, the stars twinkled in a clear sky. They strolled across the street to a school and soon the dark shadows of the building cut them off from the rest of the festivities.

His hand fell to her shoulder as they walked. "What's new on the farm?" he asked.

She smiled. "It was a good season. The potatoes are all in the spud cellars. It looks like we have over fifty percent number ones. Our bank loans will appreciate that. The barley is on its way to the brewer's storage depot. The hay is baled and we have a buyer for most of it."

"Don't you use it yourself?" he asked.

"I sold most of the livestock," she explained. "We have ten calves we're fattening and Dane has given the children three ewe lambs that have been bred. I took six horses as part payment for the cattle. Four are geldings, but the two mares will be foaling next April. The children are very excited about that."

"Do you ride?" he asked.

"I used to, but we sold our favorite horses when Duncan..." She paused. "I'm sorry." She exhaled slowly. "Do you ride?"

"I did a few times when I was a kid," he replied.

"And where was that?" she asked.

"A small farm near Oak Valley, New Jersey," he said.

"New Jersey?" She turned to him and smiled. "I've never met anyone from New Jersey. Isn't it just the overflow from New York?"

He feigned injury. "I'm crushed. Much of New Jersey is filled with wonderful truck farming communities. Why does everyone think of us as an appendage of New York City?"

"How did you get to Idaho?" she asked.

"My folks owned forty acres and it was directly in the path of a new interchange on the turnpike. They saw the writing on the wall, took the money and ran to Weiser, Idaho, where they had friends. I was in college and for a while I felt like the kid whose parents classically sold the house and moved while he's in school."

He smiled. "When I graduated with a degree in journalism I came to Weiser for a month before beginning a job search. I was offered a position in the public relations department of a potato-processing plant. That's where I met my former wife. She was in finance...but that's another chapter in my life. Anyway, I still have a sister and cousins in New Jersey. If you can stay off the turnpikes and freeways, it's a great place to visit. I think I'm a true Idaho transplant now." He dropped his arm from her shoulder and shoved his hands deep into the pockets of his coat. "How did we get on the subject of my past? We were discussing your livestock. Do you still have the rabbit that raids your garden?"

She walked up the steps to the entryway. "Yes, and the chickens and geese. In spite of everything, it's been a very good season. The first frost hit a few weeks ago but we were almost finished digging spuds. We lost only a few acres."

"Now what do you do?"

"We sell the potatoes to the buyer with the best price."

"And then?"

"We pay off the line of credit and hopefully catch up on the other loans." She stepped away. "Enough about the farm. How about you? Are you busy?"

He followed her up the steps. She turned and leaned against the double doors of the school entrance. He propped his hand against the wall near her head. In the dark shadows she could barely make out his handsome features. He was close enough to be touched. She slid her hands behind her hips and rested against the glass panels.

"I rode the middle fork of the Salmon river in July," he said, his voice low and husky in the darkness. "I've interviewed the owners of two of the white-water rafting companies. I'm setting up interviews with some of the other women in my update article...but you know all about that."

As he stared down at her in the shadows, he tried to deny his own reaction to her. He couldn't understand the attraction between them. She was everything he wasn't: she had ties to the land, family responsibilities. She was a woman filled with determination and strength to survive.

Her fragrance drew him closer. She was a beautiful woman, a mixture of maturity and youth, a woman with love to give to the right man. *Am I that man? No,* he chided himself, *not in the least.* He was free and that was the way he wanted to stay; free to move about, to search out stories and write them for the readership of *Western Living*, to travel, to keep his relationships with women casual. What relationships? Since seeing Eileen again at her husband's funeral, he had had a grand total of two dinner dates and each had ended in a chaste kiss at the woman's door without even a tinge of desire on his part to pursue the possibilities.

She touched his lapel. "Is something wrong?" she asked. "You're so quiet."

He straightened. "I was just thinking."

"What about?"

"You."

"Good or bad?" she asked, wondering what he thought of her. "I'm just a woman...with problems...and responsibilities."

"And pride."

She smiled. "Callie and Abbie and I all have pride. Too much sometimes. We have this tendency to try to solve all our problems alone...too proud to ask for help..." Her fingers caressed the fabric of his coat. "But we manage to survive."

"Let me help if I can," he murmured, his warm breath brushing against her cheeks. "You don't have to go it alone."

"I'll manage," she replied, looking up at him. His lips parted, his expression neither a smile nor a frown.

"I want to kiss you," he whispered.

Her heart leaped at his words. She felt his fingers on her cheek, then he touched the sensitive skin near her ear. The warmth of his touch awakened the need for contact with this special man who had become her private source of strength.

Why not? she thought. *Would one kiss matter?*

"Yes," she murmured, but when his mouth settled on hers, she knew she had taken a risk greater than she had intended. The kiss deepened and she leaned against him. Some inner voice told her to withdraw. *Go away,* she thought, before losing herself in his arms.

Dan's voice broke the ecstasy and she tensed as he pulled her hands from his body. "Eileen, honey...we should stop...this isn't the time...or the place."

She whirled around, burying her face in her hands. "Oh God, forgive me," she sobbed. "I'm sorry...I'm sorry..." She wanted to run, to gather her children and race back to the safety of the farm, to submerge herself in her responsibilities...and memories of Duncan, safe from the temptations of being here in Dan's arms.

"Eileen, it's okay." Dan turned her around, holding her while she cried against his chest. He handed her a large white handkerchief. "It's clean. I just carry it for sobbing women I meet in schoolhouse doorways."

She accepted it and wiped her face. "I'm sorry, really. I don't know what happened. You should have stopped me." She refolded the damp handkerchief into a tidy square.

"I was busy coping with my own emotions," he said, chuckling.

She glanced up. "What...do you mean?"

He touched her lapels. "You were all buttoned when we started up these steps," he said, carefully refastening the coat.

Fleeting images materialized. He had opened her coat and she had helped him, encouraged him to touch her. His hand had rested against her breast for an instant before sliding between the bulky coat and the thin material of her dress. The heat of his palm had burned through the fabric. Her moan had been muffled against his throat when she had kissed his neck.

When she had tried to loosen his tie, the stubborn knot had become a barrier. Giving up the futile attempt, her hands had grown bold, exploring his conditioned body through his clothing, and she had pressed closer, closer.

The memories grew clearer and she dropped her gaze. "I don't know what got into me. Forgive me."

He cupped her chin and lifted her face. "You're forgiven, if there's anything to forgive," he murmured, kissing her lips lightly.

"He's...he's only been...gone..." Her eyes glistened.

"He's been gone for several months...I know...and you're still grieving," he replied. "I'd never take advantage of a grieving widow...but you're also a woman. Don't forget that." His mouth brushed hers again, then he stepped away. "Let's get back to the reception before they send out a search party for us," he said, reaching for her hand.

Later, after they'd returned to the hall and they were dancing again, he held her loosely in his arms. "Are you okay now?"

She nodded.

"Will you still let me interview you?" he asked.

When she gazed into his eyes she saw the potency of unfulfilled promises. "Yes, of course," she murmured, wondering at the wisdom of her decision even as she agreed.

CHAPTER FOUR

"WHERE DID YOU and that reporter guy go, Mom?" eleven-year-old Jordan Mills asked, as Eileen drove her family home.

They were still north of Idaho Falls and the traffic on Interstate 15 was light. The children had talked her into staying two extra days at Dane's and Abbie's sheep ranch.

"Spud vacation is still on," Jordan had reminded her. "We don't need to go to school until Monday."

Jordan had said little since the wedding. Dane Grasten had invited the boy to ride along with him when he delivered part of a band of sheep that had been sold to a rancher near White Sulphur Springs in the central part of the state.

"But what about you and Abbie?" Eileen had asked at the time. "You should be on your honeymoon, not driving sheep trucks."

Abbie had smiled. "We've delayed our honeymoon until next month," she had explained. "Business first...then we leave the country to romp and play in Australia. So let him go."

"We'll be gone overnight," Dane had explained.

Jordan had become sullen since the wedding, saying very little to either her or to his sisters. She didn't know why, but Eileen suspected Jordan had used the overnight trip as an opportunity to avoid her. Now as he questioned her, she knew she was about to find out what was bothering him.

The last reason for his mood she would have considered would have been the reporter from Boise.

"We danced . . . and went for a walk . . . outside," Eileen said. "He drove back to Boise right after the wedding. You know that. You were with us when he came and said good-bye."

"Why would anyone drive all the way from Boise to a dumb wedding?" Jordan asked. "He must be a real number one jerk."

"Jordan! Abbie's wedding wasn't dumb and Dan Page is no jerk, so watch your tongue, young man," she cautioned.

"What did you do outside?" Jordan persisted.

"We just . . . walked . . . and talked a little."

"You let him kiss you, didn't you?" he asked.

Eileen stiffened. "Why would you . . . say that?"

"I seen ya!"

"Saw."

"I went with Jim and Chris Garrod to their place to see their baseball card collection," he said, glancing at his sisters.

"You should have told me," Eileen chided.

"I couldn't find you! We came back by the high school and seen this man and woman." He shifted his gaze from his sisters to Eileen's image in the mirror. "Jim said they looked like they were wrestling, but Chris said they were making out."

"Making out?" Jolene questioned.

"Yeah. Chris says if you kiss a girl long enough she'll . . ."

"That's enough, Jordan," Eileen said.

"I kept quiet when I seen it was you," Jordan continued. "That coat Dad gave you looked like a white light in the doorway. I knew no one else could have a coat like the one *Dad* gave you. Did that reporter make you go with him . . . or did you wanna?''

"The reporter has a name," Eileen said, irritated at her son's accusations. "His name is Daniel Page. I call him Dan. You can call him Mr. Page unless he says it's okay to use his first name. Do you understand, Jordan?"

"Did he make you do it?" Jordan asked, ignoring her.

Eileen's mouth tightened.

"Did you and Dad do that kinda stuff?"

Memories of Duncan's lovemaking conflicted with memories of the passion-filled embrace on the school steps and she was unwilling to accept the contrast. "That's my business, Jordan." She glanced in the rearview mirror at her glaring son. "Of course, your father and I . . . I loved him very much. Don't you remember seeing your father and me kiss?" She smiled. "It was usually in the kitchen when I was trying to prepare breakfast and you children were hungry."

"Yeah, but that was different," Jordan said. "He was our dad. Moms and dads are supposed to do that kind of stuff."

She glanced at him again in the mirror, hoping he would drop the subject. His glare compelled her to reply. "Dan Page and I like each other. That's all. He'll never replace your father."

"That's for sure," Jordan declared. "I don't like him. He tries to act all friendly but I don't like him . . . *at all*."

"I think he's a nice man," Jodie said.

"Me, too," Jolene chimed in. "He's fun and he helps us and we think he's handsome enough to be on television."

Jordan punched Jolene's shoulder. "What do girls know? You're just little kids. He's a creep."

"Jordan!" Eileen exclaimed.

"You're lying. You like him, and you'll want to marry him, and you think we'll want him as our new dad," Jordan cried, flinging himself back against the seat. "Well, you're wrong. He'll never be my dad. I got only one dad. I'll never call anyone else dad and you can't make me."

Eileen glanced from her son's reflection to the highway and turned on her directional signal for the Shelley exit. She had no time to give a satisfactory reply to her son as she drove through town and onto the gravel road toward home. When they pulled into the garage, the twins darted away, but Eileen grabbed her son's arm as he left the back seat.

She took both of his hands in hers. "Just because a woman and a man kiss, it doesn't mean they intend to do anything more. Making out is not one of my intentions. And you're right. You'll only have one real and true father. I know you miss him." She squeezed her eyes shut for a few seconds. "Oh God, Jordan, don't you think I miss him, too?"

Her son's thin arms surrounded her waist and she held him. "Jordan, you don't need to worry about me trying to replace your father. And you don't need to hide your feelings. Cry. It's okay. Goodness knows, I do it enough."

He pulled away and squinted up at her. "When do you cry? I never see you crying."

"At night," she replied, brushing his brown hair from his eyes. *Oh, how much he looks like Duncan,* she thought. "In the shower. I guess that's my favorite place to cry." *Soon he will be taller than me and almost grown, able to assume some of the responsibility of the farm.* She dismissed the thought, determined to spare him the burden of growing up too soon.

"Darling," she said, squeezing his shoulders, "you're the spitting image of your father and no one can ever take that away from you. But he's dead. We each must face that. You'll have photos and good memories to keep him alive. Someday I might remarry...and when I do then we'll decide what to do about having a stepfather. Mr. Page and I are just friends, so don't start ringing wedding bells for us. One wedding is enough for a while."

Jordan brushed at his tear-filled blue eyes with the heels of his palms. "That's for sure. It was fun but I'd hate to wear one of those tuxes very often," he admitted. "It choked me."

"But you looked very handsome," she said.

"Ah, Mom." He pulled away and reached for two of the suitcases. Together they carried the luggage into the house. Jordan headed to the stairs.

"Jordan?" she called.

He turned. "Yeah?"

"Mr. Page is coming here the first part of November to do another interview," she said. "I wanted you to know I'm not keeping secrets. He's doing an update on that magazine article. Do you still have your copy?"

Jordan nodded. "That's the last picture of Dad I have where he doesn't look sick."

"Yes," Eileen agreed. "Mr. Page is a very good photographer, isn't he?"

Jordan frowned. "Yeah. I guess he isn't all bad . . . but he'll be a creep if he starts hanging around here."

As Eileen lay in bed later that night, her thoughts were jumbled, shifting from the wedding to the farm, her family and Duncan. His image blurred and faded to be replaced by her son's face.

At all costs, she must protect Jordan. He had already spent too much time fretting over the potato crop. Several times she had found him reading the industry trade publications in her office. She had insisted he play Little League baseball during the summer. League baseball had been the passion of his young life for several years but he had spent most games of the past season on the bench.

She glanced at the clock on the nightstand. It was an hour before midnight. Hugging the pillow tightly in her arms, she rolled to the empty side of the bed. The cold sheets sent a shiver through her and she turned back.

What was wrong with her? She felt out of control, troubled by a force she couldn't identify. The days passed quickly enough but the nights had grown endlessly long. She found herself filled with doubts and misgivings. Had she allowed herself to become too dependent on Duncan? Had she become too secure, too complacent, taking their lives for granted?

She sat up, pulling her knees up and resting her chin on them. A full moon brought a soft familiar glow to the room. Sometimes she hated it here with all the hopeless memories of a life gone forever. Her eyes burned and she left the bed.

In the shower, the hot spray gradually washed her tension away and when the tears began to fall, she gave in to the torment that raged inside her.

Duncan had brought this on her. If only he hadn't gotten so sick, if only he had kept his vow to grow old with her, if only they had been given a little more time, time to raise their family, time to pay off the mortgages and loans now coming due, time to love each other. But as the water temperature cooled and the tears stopped, she knew Duncan would never return to help her. Only she could pick up the pieces and bring new direction and strength to her life and the lives of her children.

DAN PAGE STUDIED the paragraphs he had written just that morning. How could he produce an upbeat sequel when so many of the women's lives had taken a turn for the worse?

At times such as these, he wished he held a more routine job, one that took him to an office from nine to five or to a factory where he would work the physical labor and go home exhausted.

Continually, he found himself staying in touch with the people he interviewed. Perhaps it was a weakness in his genes that sucked him into their trials and tribulations, their joys and triumphs. He received holiday cards from many of them and on occasion lengthy letters giving him updates on their lives.

He had done research on many professions and, as part of his philosophy, to walk in the shoes of the person he was interviewing, he'd worked for a day or two at many jobs. But journalism was his specialty: the written word. Not literature but crusty, hard-hitting factual reports about real people trying to survive in a world gone askew. He wondered if his own outlook had become jaded.

His one stab at entrepreneurship had ended in bankruptcy, but the memories were still bittersweet of those months running a newspaper. His editorials in the *Southwest Daily News* had hit hard at local issues, hit hard until he had stepped on the toes of his much larger competitor, who'd been closely associated with the political power structure of the area for decades.

"Page!"

Dan's head jerked up and he spied Gil Hadley striding across the room, weaving his way through the maze of computer terminals and desks toward him.

Dan glanced at his watch. He should have been in Gil's office five minutes ago. "Coming." Grabbing the sheets of computer paper, he almost ran.

Gil swung around the desk and into his chair, motioning for Dan to sit down. "How is it going?"

"I'm not getting what I expected," Dan said, sliding the first sheet toward Gil. It was heavily marked with changes.

"What did you expect?" Gil asked, scanning the first page.

"Success," Dan replied, running his hand through his brown hair. "Continuing, bountiful success."

"Aren't those women still making it big?" Gil asked.

"A few . . . damn it, Gil, this is crazy," Dan said, tossing the rest of the drafted article onto Gil's desk. "I'm finding failure mostly . . . and when their careers did show promise of advancement, some of them jumped ship." He frowned. "There's an instability here that I never expected. Read for yourself." He waited impatiently while Gil scanned the paragraphs.

Gil checked off the names as he read from a list lying on his desk, then tipped his chair back on its flexible base. "Where's that beautiful wife of yours? You haven't written about her yet. Don't tell me she's a failure as well."

Dan grinned. "Former wife. She received a promotion to a full vice presidency last month. No one but you knows she was once my wife. Thanks for suggesting I interview her as Vanessa Harcourt. You paid for her dinner last night."

"Still blond?"

"Not a sign of gray in that golden hair. Maybe she touches it up a bit. I wouldn't think of asking her. And that financial analyst's mind of hers is sharper than ever."

Gil peered across the desk. "Do you and Vanessa have one of these liberated divorces I've been reading about?"

"What do you mean?" Dan asked.

"You know, bedroom privileges, etcetera."

"No."

"Why not, if both parties are agreeable?"

"It's too easy," Dan said. "We split because of career conflicts. Stephen is reason enough to stay on a friendly basis with Van, but we're strictly platonic."

"That leaves only your spud lady," Gil remarked, hand-ing the marked-up draft back to Dan. "She's a widow now if I remember correctly. I suppose she's gone bankrupt by now in today's farm economy? Or remarried to have a man to keep the place going?"

Dan shook his head. "Neither."

"Did you see her at that wedding?" Gil asked.

"Sure did," Dan replied.

"Got something going with her? Helping the grieving widow adjust? You wouldn't be the first."

Dan frowned. "She's not the type. Damn it, Gil, I'd never take advantage of her or any other woman at a time like that."

Gil held up his hand. "Don't jump on me. I was only kidding. I would never have given you that assignment with all those women if I'd thought you would mess around with them . . . Vanessa being the exception, of course."

"Gil, you're pushing."

"Sorry. So how is the spud lady? Can she survive alone on a big place like that?"

"She's a strong woman," Dan said. "Not very big but a survivor and filled with pride to a fault."

"She always was your favorite subject, wasn't she? Are you doing an update on her, too?"

"Of course," Dan replied, rising from his chair. "I'm having dinner with her tomorrow evening, compliments of Gil Hadley and *Western Living* magazine."

THE NEXT MORNING when Dan stepped from the shower, the phone was ringing. Dripping water on the carpet, he grabbed an oversized maroon bath towel and headed for the bedroom.

As he tucked the receiver between his chin and shoulder, he wrapped the towel around his hips and dropped to the bed. "Yes?" *What could be wrong at this hour?* he wondered. Half past six in the morning. Perhaps Stephen was sick, or he'd been hurt. "Van, is that you?" he asked. There was silence on the line for several seconds.

"No," a feminine voice replied. "It's me, Eileen Mills. I hope I didn't get you out of bed."

He frowned. "Eileen?" He hadn't spoken to her since the wedding. They had agreed to a dinner appointment just after he had decided to head for Boise. He had said his good-byes and left, driving all night to reach his apartment. Twice he had succumbed to the urge to hear her voice and called but she had been out. And she hadn't responded to the messages he had left. "I was in the shower actually. I just got back from a four-mile run. It gets my blood pumping so I can meet the rigors of the day."

"I knew you must be a runner," Eileen said. "You're so . . . trim."

"I was going to confirm our appointment later this morning," he said. "It's so early. I was afraid perhaps that my son had . . . been injured."

"Is that why you called me . . . Van?"

"Vanessa is my former wife. She has custody of Stephen."

"I'm sorry to have alarmed you," Eileen said. "I wanted to be sure and catch you before you left. I'm never sure if you work out of an office or travel around the country when you're writing your articles."

"I do both," he replied, loosening the towel and drying his chest. He heard voices in the background.

"I'll call you back," she said and hung up before he could say a word.

He replaced the receiver, puzzled. Maybe she wanted to tell him something special. He hurried to his desk in the living room and checked her phone number in his Rolodex file. He finished drying off, expecting the phone to ring again.

When it remained silent for several minutes, he pulled her card from the file and dialed her number, but the line was busy. Perhaps she was trying to call him again. *Better stay off the line,* he decided. What did she want? Eileen's image grew stronger as he picked up the damp towel from his bed and carried it back to the bathroom.

He dialed the number again but it was still busy. He began to dress, then plugged in his electric razor. Halfway through his shave, the phone rang. He had it in his hand before the second ring. "Eileen?"

"Yes," she said. "I'm sorry. Mornings are hectic around here. My brother called from Kentucky. Then your line was busy."

"You must have called when I was trying to call you," he replied, glad she had kept trying. "What can I do for you?"

He heard a deep sigh.

"I can't have dinner with you tonight."

"Why not?" he asked, trying to suppress a surge of anger.

"I . . . I just don't think I . . ."

"You're the only woman I haven't interviewed, Eileen. The article would be incomplete without you."

He heard children's raised voices in the background, then a girl squeal. "I'll call you back," she said.

He finished shaving and splashed on a little after-shave lotion, then reached for a beige broadcloth shirt. As he knotted a cinnamon-brown woven tie around his collared neck, he wondered what had caused her to change her mind. *Is she still upset about what happened on the high school steps?*

He grabbed the phone and punched out her number. It was answered on the fourth ring.

"Mills farm," a young boy said. "This is Jordan speaking."

"Hi, Jordan, this is Dan Page. Is your mother around?"

"Oh . . . she had to go out to one of the spud cellars. She won't be back for a long time."

The boy's brisk manner irritated Dan. "I need to talk to her," he explained. "Would you please tell her I'll be out this morning about eleven?"

"She's gonna be busy all morning, Mr. Page," Jordan said. "You'd be wasting your time driving all the way from Boise."

"Well, you tell her anyway, please? Are you and the girls out of school today?" Dan asked, trying to be friendly to the boy.

"We catch the bus in fifteen minutes."

"Well, have a good day, and please give my message to your mother. Do you understand?"

"I understand English," Jordan replied. "I've gotta go now."

"Tell her."

"Sure."

CHAPTER FIVE

EILEEN HAD TRIED to get Dan Page all morning between trips to the spud cellars and a quick run into town for a spare part, but with no success.

She had left a message with the receptionist at *Western Living*, but the woman had said he would be out for the rest of the week. Eileen speculated that Dan had probably left on assignment once she had notified him of her change of mind about her own interview.

His presence, whether real or imaginary, had begun to have an effect on her and her family. She and Jordan had had words twice since the return trip from the wedding. During countless sleepless nights and at unexpected moments in her busy day, thoughts of Dan had interfered with her determination to nip this friendship in the bud before it had a chance to bloom.

Pleased with her accomplishments since rising at 5:00 a.m., she'd already crossed off several items from her list of things to do that day. Seeing Dan Page was not on the list.

She had negotiated the sale and delivery of sixty thousand boxes of fresh potatoes at five dollars and fifty cents per hundred-pound box to a broker from the east. The sale would empty one cellar and most of a second one. She would be able to pay off the line of credit hanging over her since spring.

Eileen had contracted before the growing season with a processor in Firth, Idaho for twenty thousand bags of culls to be made into instant potato flakes. The price was lower than she had hoped for, but still above the three dollars and seventy cents it had cost her to grow them.

With two cellars still to sell, an equipment loan delinquent, the house mortgage two months behind, and the fan motor on one cellar burned out, she was relieved not to have to see him.

She took a side trip to the bathroom to freshen up. As she was ready to leave, she glanced in the mirror. The dark circles had vanished from beneath her eyes. She had gained a few more pounds but still had several more to go before she reached her goal. Not every woman had to work so hard to maintain enough weight on her hips to keep her jeans from falling down. When she touched her cheek, the skin was warm and glowing, her complexion reflecting her renewed good health.

Removing the combs that held her hair away from her temples, she ran a brush through her wind-blown hair and carefully wove a single braid down the back. It was the best style she had found to keep it out of her eyes. She had toyed with the idea of having it cut very short, but couldn't make up her mind.

The doorbell rang. Eileen twisted the elastic around the tail of her hair, leaving several inches to fall free, and flung the heavy braid over her shoulder. It fell to the small of her back. Who could be here now to disturb her tight schedule? Most of her friends called before dropping by. The only door-to-door salesman who came by was the McNess man and he wasn't due until the first of December. Perhaps it was a lost traveler who had strayed from the interstate highway.

She skipped down the stairs, but her lightheartedness vanished when she flung open the door.

"Hello," Dan Page said, leaning against the porch post, looking handsome and debonair in a chalk-stripe, double-breasted brown business suit. He straightened and took a step toward her. "Did Jordan give you my message?"

"Jordan? Message? What message?" she asked, her heart pounding against her rib cage.

He gazed down at her and smiled. "You look like a school girl." Wispy curls tickled her temple and she brushed them away. Her eyes were bright and a touch of color highlighted her cheeks. "You look...wonderful," he said softly.

Her gaze swept down his suit and back to his face. "You...look pretty good yourself," she said, smiling. "My son...what was Jordan supposed to have told me?"

He looked puzzled. "That I'd be by this morning to see you...since you couldn't make this evening."

Her hand clutched the brass doorknob. "He didn't tell me."

"Perhaps he forgot. May I come in?" he asked.

She motioned him to enter. "Would you like some coffee? Tea? I have bread in the oven. I can't leave until it's out."

As if on cue, the oven buzzer sounded.

Dan followed her into the cheery blue-and-white kitchen and stood aside while she removed the three pans of yeast bread from the hot oven. The crusts were golden brown. As she brushed the tops with a stick of butter, she glanced over her shoulder and found him watching her. He smiled. She reached for a long sharp knife, sliced off a thick crusty heel, and spread a generous serving of butter and currant jam on the steaming piece of wheat bread.

"You probably grind your own wheat flour," he said.

"Yes I do," she said. "Disgusting in this day of store-bought white bread, isn't it?"

"I think it's great," he replied. "More moms should do this for their kids."

"Most moms work."

"This isn't work?" he asked.

She shrugged. "Of course, but I can adjust my schedule in order to bake. Most moms don't have the time or space . . . or wheat or the mill to grind it," she said.

"I suppose it takes more effort to return to the basics than it used to," he replied. "Are the results worth it?"

"Find out for yourself. Have a bite." She held the piece of bread out to him.

"How could I refuse?" He bit off a corner and chewed.

She took a bite from the other end. "Do you like it?"

"I haven't had a piece of home baked bread since . . . the last time I came to see you . . . and Duncan." He reached for a paper napkin and wiped his mouth. "I'm sorry."

"It's okay," she replied. "I'm much better now. I think I'm going to make it."

"What happened?" he asked.

"Right after I returned from the wedding I . . . had a few sessions in the shower." She glanced out the window. "Crying in the shower is therapeutic, you know."

"What were you upset about?" he asked.

Reluctant to divulge all that had happened, she said, "Jordan and I had several arguments."

He frowned. "About what?"

"His father, other boys' fathers, Dane Grasten . . . even you got caught up in it."

"Me?"

She took the knife and cut the heel into two pieces and gave him one, then poured two cups of coffee. "Sit down, please. I didn't expect you, but now that you're here, please stay."

"Am I keeping you from your work?" he asked.

She couldn't remember any of the chores still on her list. "Nothing that won't wait."

"I've called twice before and left messages, once with Jolene and once with Jordan," he said. "Did you get them?"

"No," Eileen replied, her amber eyes reflecting her surprise and dismay. "Surely Jolene would have told me... unless Jordan threatened her. Jordan has been difficult lately. I suspect he deliberately short-circuited your messages."

"Why would he do that?"

"He... he saw us... on the high school steps." His eyes held hers. "He was angry," she explained. "He accused us of *making out*."

"Not a bad idea," he teased, grinning boyishly.

"I didn't think he was old enough to know what making out involved," she said, frowning.

"Boys grow up fast," he replied. "Stephen has asked me some startling questions lately."

"And how did you answer him?" she asked.

"With the truth," he replied, then added, "as best I remember it from when I was his age."

"You have the advantage. I was never an eleven-year-old boy." She traced the blue-and-white pattern of the tile on the counter top. "Perhaps you're lucky to have your son only at visitation times." She sighed. "Sometimes I don't think I know how to raise Jordan anymore, to give him the guidance he needs."

"Take it one day at a time," Dan suggested. "You'll manage. You're a strong woman, even if you don't feel like one now. You're still adjusting and so is he."

She glanced at him. "Do you think that's all it is?"

He nodded. "Jordan and Stephen are less than a year apart. Maybe sometime they can meet and compare notes... see if they are getting the same answers from their parents."

"I didn't think boys thought about sex until they were older," she said.

"Boys begin thinking about sex as soon as they notice that girls have started to develop. You see, my dear," he said, cocking one brow wickedly upward, "boys are usually shorter than girls at the onset of puberty and the girls' breasts are at eye level. How could you expect them to notice anything else?"

Her eyes sparkled. "You're serious, aren't you?"

"Would I joke about something as serious as girls' breasts?"

She thought of her own regained cleavage. A blush warmed her cheeks.

"It's the male fetish of the ages, you see," he continued, his voice low and husky. "It's in our genes. It's passed down from generation to generation from our ancestors." He smiled and took a sip of coffee. "At least that's my theory."

She nodded. "Now that I think back to my older brothers, I believe you might be right. I'm the youngest and they were always talking about Mary Lou's or Bunny's or Anna Belle's bosom." She caught his engaging smile.

"Bunny? You actually know a girl named Bunny?" he asked.

"Of course, and Charity and Sugar and Honey and Missouri. I went to school with twins named Chastity and Purity. They told the rest of us all about boys and swore it came of practical experience. I told my momma and she said that's what parents get for naming their children silly names." She suppressed a giggle.

He started to chuckle and soon she joined him in laughter.

She started when the back door slammed.

Her six-foot-six foreman filled the doorway. She shot from the chair, embarrassed. Brushing the tears of laughter from her cheeks, she nodded. "Hogan, this is the reporter who interviewed Duncan and me last year. Dan Page, meet my foreman, Hogan Waite. He was a real savior around here this past summer. I couldn't have gotten along without him."

"I knocked but you two were laughing and didn't hear me," Waite explained. "I don't make it a habit of walking in."

It's a good thing, Dan thought as he rose from his chair and extended his hand. The man's shoulders were as broad as his waist and hips were narrow. His full head of dark hair and his piercing blue eyes made him a handsome giant. A full mustache hid part of his upper lip. Dan's gaze shifted to Eileen. Was it admiration he saw in her expression or affection? *Is this man responsible for her apparent recovery from the loss of her husband?*

Dan straightened. For a fleeting moment he regretted not inheriting his father's height. His confidence was bolstered when Eileen came to his left side and took his arm. "Dan is doing an update of his series on women in unusual occupations, Hogan."

The two men shook hands. "Don't break Dan's fingers," Eileen teased. "He needs them to type his article."

"So you earn your living by your fingers?" Waite asked, not quite smiling.

Dan's normally masculine hand was engulfed by the larger man's grip. "Yes, but I worked as a logger in Oregon," he said.

"You did? I spent ten years in the Cascades and another three in Alaska. Loved it. A man can't beat the Alaskan outdoors. Glad to meet you, Page. Mrs. Mills runs a good place here. Treat her kindly in those articles." He turned to

Eileen. "We have the trucks loaded. We're heading to Firth. I told the drivers we'd catch a bite in town, compliments of the boss lady. Is that okay with you? I won't turn in a bill if you disapprove. We'll be gone most of the day."

Eileen smiled. "That's fine. Drive carefully."

Waite was gone as quickly and silently as he had arrived.

"Where did you find him?" Dan asked, pouring his cold coffee down the kitchen drain.

"Duncan found him at a bar in town several years ago," she explained. "He's worked for us off and on ever since. He came back when he heard about Duncan's death. He's really a gentle bear of a man. Don't let his size intimidate you."

He turned. "Size? What size?"

She laughed. "Good, I wanted you to like him. Now, should we get started on the interview?"

"Sure," Dan agreed. "But can't I take you into town to lunch? It's the least I can do after intruding on you like this."

She shook her head, the curls near her temples waving in the air. "If you don't mind leftovers, I can heat some beef stew in the microwave and we can pig out on this bread. I'm trying to gain more weight. Abbie accused me of being a bag of bones."

"You look fine to me," he said as his gaze roamed up and down her trim jeans-clad figure.

Eileen smiled and quickly turned away. Suddenly she turned around. "I didn't know you were ever a logger in Oregon."

"Only for a week," he admitted. "I was researching an article." He shrugged and smiled sheepishly. "I just thought, for my own preservation, I'd better join his he-man world of the outdoors and gain his respect. I've gone white-water rafting several times. Would that have qualified, too?''

She covered her mouth and laughed again.

After lunch, Eileen took Dan on another tour of the property. "You were here in midsummer the first time," she said as they parked on a dirt lane. They were near a line of irrigation pipe which was suspended on wheels and ran down the edge of the field. "The crops are all in now, thank goodness. The ground is frozen," she explained. "We got a good price on our malt barley."

"And the potatoes?" he asked.

She studied the fields which had already been plowed and were waiting for next year's planting. "The spuds were great. Some of the fields were over half number ones. We had a lot of number twos because of their size not their quality, and even the culls were good culls."

"You're pretty proud of this place, aren't you?" he asked, turning in the cab of the truck and propping his arm on the back of the seat.

"Is that wrong?"

"Of course not," he said.

"The scriptures say pride goeth before a fall, so I try to not get too proud," she replied. "This was a year of trial for me... you know what I mean... and I made it, I actually made it." She rested her arms on the steering wheel. "There were times when I doubted I would, but now the crops are all in and I have buyers for most of them. I've covered my costs already and now I can begin to catch up."

She twisted the key in the ignition and the engine turned over. "I do prattle on at times," she murmured. They drove back to the farmhouse after Eileen showed Dan all the points of interest and soon they were back in the kitchen.

"What are you going to catch up on?" he asked, accepting a cup of tea.

"What?"

"In the fields," he reminded her. "You didn't finish what you were talking about."

"Oh, that." She played with her spoon. "It's nothing. Sometimes I'm afraid I've overlooked something that might cause a problem. But I'm ready...for almost anything. Now, ask me any questions you want. I'm at your disposal until the children come home and the workers return."

They spent the rest of the afternoon discussing potatoes, malt barley production, the good growing season just past, trends in agricultural experimentation, the rising prevalence of consulting services for monitoring crop moisture and other aspects of the potato business.

Dan's attention was riveted on the animated woman sitting across the table. *She's such a contradiction,* he thought. On the surface, Eileen appeared almost fragile. When those wounded amber eyes looked into his, he wanted to gather her in his arms. He wanted to shield her from all the forces that were lurking just out of sight, threatening to whisk away what little profit she'd managed to make.

She worked without the dependable paycheck most adults took for granted. She and other farmers borrowed in the spring and used their faith in the future and their knowledge of the seasons to convince the financial world to bankroll them on a gamble that could be wiped out by storms, hail, drought, pest infestation, unexpected freezes. At least the pricing structure of potatoes was free from government control.

Eileen stirred some honey into her tea and the tantalizing curls at her temple caught his attention. God, how he wanted to touch them, to caress the silky strands and brush them away and kiss the pale skin beneath, to hold her in his arms.

He didn't want her to think of him as a man with seduction on his mind, but the idea of seduction had begun to conflict with his desire to have her as a friend and confidante.

Her voice was warm and sincere, more feminine than any he had ever heard. Gradually, he stopped listening to her words as he began to wonder how she felt about him. He toyed with the idea of simply asking her. He wanted his son to meet her children. Recently he and Vanessa had had an argument about the wisdom of keeping Stephen in the military school.

Images of the Mills children meeting Stephen were quickly replaced with the reality of Eileen's devotion to the memory of Duncan. Dan had three research trips scheduled in the next two months while she would be tied to the land by her own responsibilities. With the ever-present helpfulness of the handsome hulk of a foreman named Hogan Waite, why would she want to make time for a reporter who ran four miles each day to diminish the effects of aging?

A movement across the table caught his eye and he smiled.

"What the matter?" she asked, straightening in her chair.

"Matter?" He frowned. Had she read his thoughts, he wondered.

"You were smiling. Did I say something strange?" She rose from her seat, aware that he had stopped listening to her several minutes earlier. Wanting an excuse to keep him for a little longer, she had continued talking about subjects as diverse as separation of church and state, the price of cattle, problems of children, and a recent television special on third-world nations. He had sat across from her, nodding again and again, appearing to agree with her on everything she had said.

"Actually, I wasn't listening," he confessed.

She smiled. "Does that mean this interview is over?"

He reached for his camera bag. "I haven't taken any photos. Could we go to the spud cellars? I'd like to get a few shots of you and the fruits of your labor. Do you mind?"

"Of course not, but there's no one there," she replied.

"Then it'll be just you and me and all those spuds."

"We'll have to be careful. Those spuds have eyes," she teased.

He smiled. "But no mouths, so they can't tell tales. We're safe from their gossip."

She laughed as she motioned him to follow her outside. The sway of her jeans-covered hips was partially covered by a gold-and-white-striped bulky knit pullover. The drape of the knit hinted at curves that had not been present the last time he had seen her.

Near the cellar, he took several action shots as she posed at the sorters, others at the entrance of the cavernous building, which had been built half underground, its earthen walls extending well above their heads. The building was filled with the pleasant aroma of fresh soil still clinging to some of the potatoes. A single string of light bulbs overhead provided illumination. The soft hum of the ventilation fans broke the silence.

He peeked into the cellar. "I wish we could have taken some photographs inside," he said.

"Did you know that you're looking at about seventy million spuds?" she asked.

"No wonder I feel as if I'm being spied upon," he replied. "That's no small potatoes!"

"Don't think we're a bunch of flakes around here." Her eyes danced with excitement.

"Not until you get processed. For now you're strictly a number one."

Her laughter filled the air. "I like you best when you're witty."

"I'm glad," he said, taking her hand. "I've enjoyed this day... learning more about you, what your working day is like. It's certainly different from the usual nine to five job."

"I enjoy it."

He put his camera and note pad onto a wooden box. "Eileen, about that night in Montana..." The words slipped out before he realized what he was saying.

She laughed again but her mirth was tainted with tension. "I've put it out of my mind, really." She jerked her hand from his.

"I haven't." He touched her cheek.

Eileen laid her hand against his chest. "I don't know what got into me that night. I don't want you to get the wrong impression of me. Sometimes I feel so awkward. Am I socially retarded because I went from a tobacco farm to a potato farm and I've been here ever since?" She glanced up at him. "My life doesn't sound very romantic, does it?"

"It's the people, not the location that make for romance," he said. His hand gripped her shoulders as he drew her against him.

"Dan, we shouldn't," she murmured but her arms found their way around his neck. His finger moved up and down on her cheek, caressing her smooth skin. She turned her face and his finger sought her mouth, tracing the outline of her lips.

"You're a beautiful woman," he whispered.

She looked up at him and her eyes caught the reflection of the sunlight, giving each one a tiny blaze. A rush of desire surged through them both as his hand cradled her head.

He tipped her chin upward. "I want to kiss you."

Her head barely signaled her acceptance as her lips parted.

"My conduct isn't the least bit professional," he admitted.

She touched his earlobe with her fingertip. "I don't care. Not this time." His mouth hovered inches from her lips. "Dan, oh, Dan," she sighed, closing the distance.

CHAPTER SIX

THE SOUND OF GIGGLING brought them slowly apart. When they turned and saw the eight-year-old twin girls standing by the sorter, Eileen leaned her head against Dan's chest for an instant before pulling free from his embrace.

She walked primly toward her daughters. Jolene edged toward her but Jodie stood still.

"We're hungry," Jolene said. "We were hoping you had baked cookies and we ran all the way from the bus stop and when you weren't in the kitchen, we went hunting for you." She gulped a deep breath. "We knew Mr. Page was here 'cuz of his car. Hi, Mr. Page," she called, clinging to Eileen's jeans pocket to keep her balance and waving to him from around Eileen's hips. "You were kissing him, hah?" she whispered.

Eileen tried to make the best of the situation. "Mr. Page was taking some photographs," she explained.

Jolene frowned. "Where's his camera?"

Dan laughed and laid his hand on Eileen's shoulder. "Give up, Mom. You've been caught in the act," he murmured near her ear. He turned his attention to the twins. "Hello, girls. I do have a camera." He motioned to the bag still on the box. "Have a good day at school?"

Jodie sidled away from the sorter and worked her way toward them, dragging her shoes through several soft patches of snow. "We had a test," she volunteered shyly. "I missed just one word and Jolene missed two. She was mad."

"A spelling test?" Dan asked. "What word did you miss?"

"Truth," Jodie replied, beaming up at Dan. "I spelled it t-r-u-g-h-t. Isn't that dumb?"

"We all make dumb mistakes," he said. "And you, Jodie. What words did you miss?" he asked, turning to the other girl.

The girls giggled.

"I'm Jolene. Can't you tell us apart?" Jolene asked.

Dan grinned. "I guess not. How does your mother do it?" He glanced at Eileen.

"It's a secret," Jodie said. "Shall we tell him, Momma?"

"That's up to you two," Eileen said, glad the subject had changed.

The girls whispered in each other's ear several times, then turned to him. "We'll tell if you promise not to tell anyone, 'cuz that would spoil everything."

"I promise," Dan said, holding up his hand in a mock salute.

"See this?" Jolene asked, pointing to a small brown birthmark an inch below her left ear. Dan stooped over to examine the mark, straightened, and nodded. "Well, Jodie doesn't have one, at least not in the same place." She giggled.

"And where is hers?" he asked.

Jodie jerked on Jolene's sweater. "Don't you tell. No one but you and Momma knows and you both promised never to tell!"

"Girls, that's enough," Eileen said.

"Momma has one in the same place and we promised to keep it a secret, too," Jolene explained.

"Oh?" Dan turned to Eileen.

She smiled. "I'll never tell."

Jolene beamed. "Our teacher in the third grade couldn't tell us apart and finally Momma made us tell her about my mark. Then she couldn't remember who had the mark." The girls broke out in laughter again.

Dan walked back to the box and retrieved his camera. "Girls, how about a few photographs? Maybe I'll put one in the magazine."

The girls posed for Dan as he suggested different activities for them, then he took several shots of the twins with Eileen.

In the distance Jordan got off a yellow school bus. Eileen glanced at her watch, surprised at the lateness of the day. "I've got to get to the kitchen and start supper," she said. She reached the house as Jordan was taking the steps two at a time.

Jolene and Jodie each took one of Dan's hands. "Momma, can he stay for supper?" Jolene called. "He's just gotta be hungry."

Jordan groaned aloud and disappeared inside. Eileen glanced at Dan as he and the twins approached the bottom step. "I'm sure he has plans for this evening?"

"Do you, Mr. Page?" Jodie asked.

"I had a dinner date but she stood me up," he replied, catching Eileen's gaze again.

"Was she a beautiful woman?" Jolene asked.

"Yes," he agreed.

"Why would she do that?" Jolene said.

"I don't know, but I'll ask her the first chance I get to talk to her about it," he promised.

"Gee, if you asked Jodie and me to dinner, we'd say yes wouldn't we?"

Jodie nodded.

"Someday we'll do just that," Dan said.

The twins darted inside, leaving Dan and Eileen alone on the back porch.

"You really are welcome to join us," Eileen said, "but if you have plans or work, we'll understand."

"I'm already packed for a trip so I can leave from here," Dan replied, "but if it would be awkward for you or the kids, I'd rather go."

"Please stay." She touched his sleeve briefly before dropping her hand to her side.

"I'll put my camera equipment away," he said, heading toward his car.

Inside the kitchen, she found Jordan munching on an oatmeal cookie and looking sullen.

"You invited *him* to stay and eat?" Jordan asked.

"I did and he accepted," Eileen said. "And I expect you to be polite."

"But this is the night that Mr. Waite eats with us."

"Oh, I forgot," Eileen said. "Well, I'm frying chicken and I have enough for everyone. Now, you get your chores done and then clean up. We'll eat at six-thirty."

Two hours later, everyone but Jordan was seated at the table.

"Where's your brother?" Dan asked Jolene.

"In his room," she replied. "He said he wasn't hungry."

Eileen stiffened and began to rise from her chair. Dan laid his hand on hers. "Maybe we shouldn't press him," he said. "But I did want to take some more photos around the table, with the family and the foreman, and all this fried chicken. City readers will be impressed with the down-home atmosphere and the rural readership will be delighted."

Hogan Waite rose from his chair, towering over the table. "Okay if I go get him?" He turned to Eileen.

"Please," she replied, knowing that Hogan had surely sensed the tension between Dan and Jordan. After he left the room, she turned to Dan. "I'm sorry. He's usually not like this."

"It doesn't matter."

"But it does. Jordan knows better than to be rude to guests."

"Perhaps he sees me as a threat," Dan said.

"How come?" Jolene asked, her eyes filled with curiosity.

Eileen motioned her daughters to silence as Dan left to get his camera bag again. Hogan returned to the room with the boy in tow. Jordan had changed into a blue knit shirt. His hair had been plastered down and water trickled down his temple. Dan busied himself with changing lenses on his camera. After several photos had been taken, he paused, then turned his attention to Jordan.

"How would you like to be in some shots all alone?" he asked the boy. "Maybe in your room, doing homework or working on a model or whatever you'd like?"

Jordan frowned. "Me?" A new trickle of water caught in his brown eyebrow for a second before plopping onto his plate.

"Sure," Dan replied. "I took some of your sisters, so it's only fair I give you equal treatment. Let's swing by the bathroom. Maybe we can find a towel and check in the mirror again. I want you to look your best since thousands of subscribers will be reading about you."

"Okay," Jordan grudgingly agreed, then shot from his chair and scrambled up the stairs.

Dan shrugged over his shoulder to the people still at the table. "Boy psychology," he said, sauntering after Jordan.

"I have some work to do outside," Hogan said, excusing himself. "Thanks for supper, Mrs. Mills. Great food as usual." He disappeared through the doorway and into the night.

"Can we go see what Mr. Page is doing with Jordan?" Jolene asked. "I hope he made him wipe his face. He looked yucky."

"He looked just plain dumb," Jodie.

"You have to force him to comb his hair on Sunday," Jolene added. "Why did he make it sopping wet?"

"That's enough, girls," Eileen said, "now, let's see what's going on upstairs."

When they entered the upstairs bedroom, Jordan was seated at his desk, an open book in his lap. Pictures of rocket ships on the pages matched those in the large colored posters on his walls. His hair was combed casually, his twin cowlicks threatening to reclaim their usual upright stance near his crown.

"We were just finishing up here," Dan said.

Eileen's gaze settled on the unmade twin bed. A muddy pair of jeans and three unmatched tube socks were draped over the foot board. The other bed was made.

"We shot the photos on the neat side of the room," Dan assured her. "Jordan tells me he's responsible for keeping the room clean...and says he's been busy...with school and chores. I told him I understood. We talked about Stephen and the military academy. Stephen has no choice in the matter. I'm sure Stephen would think Jordan had it made here on the farm." He picked up the camera and turned to the family. "How about one or two of the whole family? Mom and the children?"

Eileen touched her hair, then her lips. "I need . . ."

"You're fine," he assured her. "You sit in Jordan's chair and, kids, you gather around your mother. Jordan, you're the tallest. You get in the middle between your sisters." Dan waited while they arranged themselves and he took several shots before Jordan pinched Jolene and she retaliated with a stomp on his toe.

Dan followed Eileen back to the kitchen. "Let me help," he said. He wiped the table while she loaded the dishwasher.

"Do you have time for one more cup of coffee before you go?" she asked.

"Of course."

"I have trouble thinking of you doing domestic chores," she said, smiling over the rim of her cup and enjoying the precious few moments left in their day together.

He grinned. "If I don't do it at my place, no one does. I've learned the hard way to keep things clean. I hate coming home from a few weeks travel to green stuff growing in the sink." He put his cup down. "I've stalled long enough." He gathered his camera bag and suit jacket.

"I'll walk you to your car," she said, grabbing a cardigan against the chill of the autumn night air.

Outside, the glow of the single light fixture high on its pole in the yard faded as they walked around to the front driveway where he had parked his mid-size sedan.

"I always expect you to be driving a sports car," she said, in the darkness.

"Why?" he asked as he put the camera bag in the back seat, closed the door again, and leaned against it

She shrugged. "Swinging bachelor image."

"I'm not a swinger," he said, "just a man who lives alone and travels a lot."

She tried to make out his features in the darkness. "You must feel fortunate in your career, to be free to travel, to see the world, no one expecting you to come home."

"I like the job and love to travel, but saying that I see the world is a slight exaggeration. Coming home to an empty apartment has its pros and cons. Spending the day with you and your family reminds me of what I'm missing." He took her hand. "Sometimes I have this crazy fantasy about my son living with me."

"And your wife? Van...Vanessa, isn't that her name? Do you see her often?" She pulled her hand free from his grip. "I'm sorry. I'm prying."

"Van is busy with her own career," he said. "We were married for three years. We stayed together that long because of a baby that was born six months after we were married...and he wasn't a premature baby. We both live in Boise. I run into her several times a year. She was one of the women I featured in the first series. She has legal custody of Stephen but in reality she doesn't see any more of him than I do. She insists he's better off in a private school for boys. I think he belongs at home with his family...except he doesn't have one."

Eileen's heart went out to him. She stepped closer and touched his forearm. "You'll work it out. Didn't you tell me to take it one day at a time? You should do the same."

"Giving me a dose of my own prescription, spud lady?" His hands slid up her arms and settled on her shoulders.

She smiled. "I'm glad you came. I had a good day," she said. "I hope you did, too, in spite of Jordan."

"He's just a boy trying to figure out some of the cruelties of life," Dan said.

"I hope so. I want to be a good mother to him but sometimes I don't know what to do," she said. "I didn't think I'd ever feel that way about my children."

"Eileen?" His hands slid down her arms.

"Yes?"

"I'd like to see you again," he said.

She hesitated. "I'm very busy. You are, too."

"Everyone needs a break once in awhile," he replied. "I'll be gone for three weeks. I have several interviews to do in Riggins, Idaho, then I'm going to the Rogue River area in Oregon.''

"You won't be home for Thanksgiving?" she asked.

"Mom has asked me but spending it with them only reminds me that I don't have a family of my own."

"You're welcome to join us," she said.

"Maybe I'll talk Stephen into doing something." Dan's tone changed, and she sensed his loneliness.

"Bring him with you...unless...Vanessa has plans for him...and you. We eat about two in the afternoon. I mean it. You're both very welcome."

"Thanks. I'll keep that in mind. Maybe I'll call Stephen and see if he's made plans yet."

They stood together quietly, enjoying the serenity of the night.

She freed her hand from his. "I should go inside."

"Not yet," he said. "Thanksgiving invitation aside, if I call when I get back to Boise, would you have dinner with me?"

"It's a long drive. I could never..."

"I'd do the driving," he assured her. "I don't mind. I do a lot of rewriting while I'm on the highway. I keep a cassette recorder with me."

"The children..."

"Bring them along."

"No," she replied. "I'll work something out."

"Then you've accepted?"

She smiled. "I'm out of practice."

"You can practice on me. I'm harmless."

"I'm not so sure about that."

He laughed and pulled her into his arms.

Oh God, at last, she thought, sliding her hands inside his open jacket and around his waist. She pressed her cheek against his shirt front, enjoying the warmth of his embrace. "This is crazy," she murmured against his chest.

"Yes," he agreed, tipping her chin upward and smiling at her.

As his mouth settled on hers, she admitted that perhaps it was the sanest thing she had ever done.

The kiss was brief. His lips had barely covered hers when he stiffened slightly and withdrew. "Good night, Eileen, and take care," he said before turning away and opening the car door.

"Good night, Dan," she whispered.

He nodded from inside the car and started the engine. His parting words were muffled behind the window glass. She stepped away, her emotions sinking into disappointment as she watched the vehicle disappear into the darkness.

When she returned to the house, Jordan was leaning against the upstairs bannister. "Is he gone?"

"Yes. You should be in bed," she said.

"Why did you stay outside so long?" he asked.

"That's my business," she snapped. In spite of the flush she felt warming her cheeks, her embarrassment was quickly replaced by anger. "Jordan, what I do with Dan Page is my business and I don't answer to you. I'm thirty-three and you're eleven. Remember that. Now go to bed."

"I think . . ."

"Right now I don't care what you think, young man," she said. "Don't you try to tell me what I can and cannot do."

He whirled around and stomped to his bedroom, slamming the door behind him.

She hurried from door to door, locking the house up tight. Until Duncan's death, she had never worried about locking the doors but now, alone and responsible for the safety for her family, she had begun to lock the front door in case a stranger came. More recently she also locked it to keep out any of the employees who might enter while she was upstairs.

The heightening sense of energy she had felt outside drained away when she entered her bedroom. She twisted the knob and slid the safety catch into place. Other than when they had made love, she and Duncan had never locked their bedroom door. In fact, she had always wanted to keep the door open at night so she could hear the children if they needed her. Lately she had been unable to fall asleep unless the door was locked, barricaded against some unknown threat or danger that was driving a wedge between her and her children, her and the outside world. Only when she withdrew into her bedroom did she feel safe. She had to work through this new difficulty and knew it was one more part of her adjustment to accepting her widowhood.

Eileen showered and blew her hair dry, then pulled on a yellow tricot gown. She turned out the light but her eyes refused to close. Studying the shadows in the darkened room made matters worse, bringing all kinds of images to her mind. Would this be another night of sleeplessness? She had learned not to fight the insomnia. Sitting up, she turned the light back on and reached for a magazine.

The well-worn copy of *Western Living* lay beneath a current issue of a woman's magazine she had picked up at the grocery store. She browsed through page after page featuring a handsome healthy husband and two or three beautifully groomed children sitting at a table admiring a devoted wife and mother's creative effort to please and nourish her family. Angrily, she tossed the magazine to the carpeted floor.

She retrieved the dog-eared copy of *Western Living* and settled against the pillows, opening the magazine to the pages showing the Mills family. As she stared down at her husband, her eyes gradually filled with tears and his image blurred. She stared across the room, not seeing the pattern of the wallpaper.

A comment Dan Page had made worked its way into her consciousness. He had featured his wife in the series. Eileen didn't recall anyone named Page. Vanessa . . . his former wife's name was Vanessa . . . Van he had called her.

She retrieved the other issues of the magazine and searched for the first article in the series, carefully checking each woman's name. Finding no woman named Vanessa in the earlier issues, she grabbed the one which had featured herself. She groaned aloud as her gaze fell on the blond woman smiling back at her. Vanessa Harcourt . . . a rising executive . . . of course . . . in a potato processing facility in Boise. This beautiful, chic woman had once been Daniel Page's wife.

Eileen devoured the article, returning again and again to examine the photographs of Vanessa. Surely, Dan had taken the photographs. One showed the woman in her own living room, decorated in Queen Anne style furniture which looked much too elegant to ever be sat upon, especially by a young boy. Had Dan spent the evening with her? Alone? Had Stephen been there? Did they have a "modern" relationship?

She closed the magazine and turned out the lights. In the darkness, she lay awake thinking about Dan, acknowledging how little she really knew about him, but conceding that the attraction was growing between them.

From the first time he had come to their house, she had felt a strong desire to cultivate his friendship. Now she found herself torn between wanting him to be more than just a friend and fearing the consequences of such an involvement. Faithfulness and trust had been paramount in her marriage. Yet a tinge of uneasiness troubled her when she tried to keep the memories of hers and Duncan's marriage alive. Had they taken each other for granted? Fallen into a way of life that presented no challenges? But wasn't that what married life should be? Why should she have doubts now about a marriage that had lasted eleven years?

The possibility of becoming involved intimately with any man other than Duncan had always been reprehensible to her. Dan Page had made her aware of her vulnerability. Each time he had come into her life, she had felt as if he belonged there, as though it mattered little that she didn't know him because she had always known him. An invisible thread was drawing them together.

Crazy, she thought, rolling onto her side and curling into a comfortable position. *Lying here awake, fretting about a man who drifts in and out of my life, asking nothing, taking nothing.* Now that she'd resolved to accept her widowhood, how could this man disturb her so? All she wanted in her life was to be given a chance to succeed on her own, to prove to herself and to Duncan's family that she could make a go of the farm, to convince the banker in town that she was a good financial risk for next spring, to give her children the emotional support they needed in accepting their loss.

"But what about me?" she murmured aloud in the darkness, as she hugged a pillow and felt sleep begin to take her.

A WEEK LATER, the financial officer of the bank in Idaho Falls called her. All thoughts of Dan Page were swept away.

"Mrs. Mills, could you come in today?" Sam Ludwig asked. "We need to talk." The man was an old family friend who had often expressed doubts about Eileen's ability to manage the farm alone.

She scanned her calendar. "Couldn't it wait until Wednesday, Mr. Ludwig? I have a potential buyer for spuds coming this afternoon. I've already had to postpone his visit once.''

"You'd better delegate him to that foreman of yours," Mr. Ludwig said. "I'm afraid this is quite serious. It can't wait."

She straightened in her chair. "What's wrong? Something is wrong, isn't it? What is it?"

"I'd rather discuss this in person, Mrs. Mills, and yes, it's potentially quite serious. We have some checks to discuss."

She swallowed the lump in her throat. "Our accounts have plenty of funds in them," she replied, hating the rising tone in her voice.

"Can you be here at two?" he asked politely. "We'll discuss the problem then."

"Of course, Mr. Ludwig." As she hung up the receiver, Eileen searched for a logical reason for this mysterious problem her banker refused to discuss over the phone. She had tried to bring most of the loans current and still maintain a balance in the farm's operating account to cover the ongoing expenses.

She glanced at the clock. There were three hours until the meeting with the banker. Outside, she searched for Hogan and spotted him striding between the third and fourth potato cellar.

"Hogan," she called, waving to him. He didn't hear her and she called again. "Hogan, I need you!" This time he stopped and turned, then waved and came toward her.

"What can I do for you, Mrs. Mills?" he asked.

Eileen looked up at him, shielding her eyes from the sun with her hand. "I need you to cover for me this afternoon," she said, walking alongside him as they approached the house. She had to take two steps for each of his. Eileen explained the call from the bank briefly without giving the foreman too much insight into the matter. "Can you take care of Scott Patton for me? We've discussed the price range I'll accept. You can bargain harder than I can. Just don't go below five dollars. Will you do it?"

Hogan grinned down at her, touching her shoulder for an instant before shoving his fists into his jeans pockets. "Of course, Mrs. Mills. You can always count on me. The mister and me, we talked many times about you and the business. I'd never let him, or you, down when it comes to keeping this place going like he'd want."

"Thanks, Hogan," Eileen said, wondering about the series of conversation Hogan had hinted at several times since Duncan's death. Someday, when the time was right, she wanted to ask him more about them. "Tell the men dinner will be ready a little early, so I can leave by one o'clock."

"Sure, Mrs. Mills."

The four men around the kitchen table had barely taken their last bites of dinner when she whisked their plates into the dishwasher and shoved pieces of chocolate cake in front of them.

Hogan seemed to understand her preoccupation. "Come on, fellows, let's get out of here and give Mrs. Mills some peace." He herded the other workers out the kitchen door. "Everything will be all right," he assured her, glancing over his shoulder. "You just keep faith."

"Thanks, Hogan. I hope so," she replied, shoving the last of the dishes into the dishwasher. She slammed the door shut and turned the machine on.

Hogan lingered just inside the door. "If you don't ease up on that poor machine, ma'am, you're going to have a repair bill on your hands."

She paused, then turned to him and smiled weakly. "You might be right. Thanks, Hogan."

"For what?"

"Just for being here when I need you."

He saluted and clicked the heels of his work boots. "Just doing my job, ma'am." With a wave of his hand, he left her alone in the kitchen. Only the soft churning of the water in the appliance broke the silence around her.

A sense of foreboding filled her as Eileen ran upstairs to change. She searched her closet for an appropriate outfit to wear to the banker's office. Her gaze settled on a softly pleated, muted beige-and-gray woolen skirt with matching beige blouse and a white sleeveless pullover sweater.

She hurried into her last pair of new panty hose and a beige slip, then stepped into the skirt. While she fought with the zipper, she wracked her brain fruitlessly in search of the reason for the banker's call.

She twisted her hair into a loose knot on the upper back of her head and added a touch of red lipstick to give her pale features a little color.

As she tucked a few stray strands of hair into place, she surveyed herself in the mirror. "Bland," she murmured. "Elegant but bland." Today was not the day to look too meek. She searched the closet for a solution.

She spotted the brown velvet blazer she had purchased in a moment of madness a few years earlier. Slipping into the jacket, she reappraised her appearance and smiled. It added just enough color to her ensemble to give her confidence the boost it needed. At times such as this, she wished she had her cousin Abbie's height and outward appearance. Abbie always met her problems head on and seemed to thrive on new challenges.

Eileen preferred to plan ahead, to organize a plan B only after the preferred plan A proved inadequate. Her college professors and her husband had always praised her management abilities, but during the past few years she had been spinning her wheels trying to solve problems not of her own making.

Now she had no choice but to step into a pair of beige pumps and walk out the door, drive to the city and confront Sam Ludwig.

CHAPTER SEVEN

SAM LUDWIG'S PRETTY, young, black-haired secretary led Eileen into his office promptly at two o'clock.

"Sit down, Mrs. Mills," the rotund, balding man said, as he dropped again into his executive chair.

Eileen tried to relax and maintain her outward appearance of confidence as she sat down, yet all the while she felt as if she was perched on an unforgiving spring that might catapult her out of the man's office.

"I reconciled all the bank accounts earlier this month, Mr. Ludwig," she said, then wished she had not taken the defensive. "I mean I know they are in order and have the funds to cover..."

"Mrs. Mills, I regret to inform you that the last check you deposited, the one from that Eastern broker, was returned to us yesterday by his bank."

Her eyes widened in disbelief. "How could that be?"

He frowned. "The man closed out his account two weeks ago. You aren't the only grower left holding a bad check, my dear. Two other area growers are in the same position as well as several around Rupert."

"But I don't understand," Eileen said, refusing to accept the devastating news. "His other two checks cleared just fine."

Sam Ludwig nodded. "That's the way some of these fellows operate. They get you to trust them and then..." He snapped his fingers and she flinched. "He was good looking, wasn't he?'' Ludwig didn't wait for her response. ''Women tend to fall for that line more than men and...''

She shook her head. ''No, you're wrong. He paid me five dollars and fifty cents a hundred,'' she explained. ''That was twenty cents more than any of the other brokers offered.''

''Perhaps that should have been a warning.''

''But that last check was for one hundred twenty thousand dollars,'' she said. ''I can't just loose that much money. I can't survive! The bank account will be overdrawn! I need that money!''

''Mrs. Mills...''

''Don't Mrs. Mills me,'' she exclaimed. ''That creep of a broker has my potatoes. No, he doesn't! He's sold them to those Eastern restaurants and by now they've been served to their customers and... My spuds probably don't even exist anymore! He owes me. How can he be allowed to cheat us? Can't we sue him...or throw him in jail...or something?''

''A Rupert grower was the first to get taken by this broker, Mrs. Mills,'' Sam Ludwig said quietly. ''He did press charges but the law enforcement agencies haven't been able to find the man. He's disappeared. His own wife and family are looking for him, too.''

''But he must have millions of dollars from the sale of the potatoes. Millions! He can't just...get away with this.''

''For now, we must work together to correct the problem and make the best of the situation. For the moment, our records show that your account is overdrawn by ninety-six thousand dollars. Of course, we'll work with you, but we can't let this overdraft remain for long.'' He tapped the financial statement lying on his desk. ''What would you like to do about this matter, Mrs. Mills?''

Eileen's shoulders ached. To relieve the pressure she pulled away from the chair back. "What are my options?"

"You have several," he said cautiously. "We can reverse some of the payments you made on the line of credit, or the payments on the house...but of course that would make the house mortgage seriously in arrears. If you could find the collateral, we might consider another loan to cover this problem. Of course, that might affect next spring's line of credit." Ludwig glanced up from the financial statement. "Perhaps you should consider selling."

"No!"

"Now, now, Mrs. Mills," the banker said, raising his chubby hand and waving it in the air. "I didn't mean the entire farm. Just a section or two of land. Or perhaps you can lease some of the fields to your fellow growers. Dallas Odell is expanding."

"Dallas Odell?" Eileen rose a few inches from her seat then dropped back down. "Odell is the last man I'd consider selling to. He's an outsider. He came in here and bought out farmers and paid them as little down as he could get away with, then he makes the annual payment as late as possible. Duncan told me all about him. Thank you, but no thanks."

"Perhaps you're right," Ludwig conceded. "Oh, not about Dallas Odell, he's one of our best customers, but about leasing the land. That would not bring funds into your account until next spring...and you need money right now. Well," he said, glancing at his diamond encrusted gold pocket watch, "I have another customer waiting." He rose from his chair and extended his hand.

She accepted it, hating the warm sweaty palm that pressed hers. "How long do I have?" she asked.

"We can hold off until next Tuesday," he replied. "That gives you a week to think about it, contact some of your other financial sources, but Mrs. Mills?" He smiled.

"Yes?"

"Don't write any payroll checks on Friday," he cautioned. "The bank couldn't honor them under the circumstances."

EILEEN MILLS APPLIED the brake briefly then accelerated as she passed a large supermarket in Idaho Falls. *I should use up the food in the pantry before spending any more money on groceries.*

"That fat old Mr. Ludwig is making me paranoid," she murmured under her breath. *How can pinching pennies on food bring back the thousands of dollars I've lost?*

Perhaps Hogan had negotiated a favorable price with Scott Patton from the potato processor in Boise. Better to find out what happened there before grasping for other straws.

As soon as Eileen drove into the yard and parked, she was out of the car, into the house, and racing up the stairs. On the landing she collided with Jordan.

"Oh, I'm sorry," she exclaimed feeling sheepish. Breathing hard, she tried to catch her breath while her son did the same. "Are you all right?" she asked.

He straightened. "Sure," he said and started to pull away. "Mr. Waite said you'd gone into town. What for?"

She patted his shoulder. "It's nothing. Just a matter with Mr. Ludwig at the bank in Idaho Falls."

"Did you pick up my new football shoes like you promised?" he asked. "When the store called yesterday, you said you'd get them on your next trip in."

"I'm sorry, Jordan, I forgot," she said, unwilling to burden him with the actual problem.

"I gotta have 'em by Friday," he pleaded. "We have another game and the coach says I can't play unless I have new ones because my old ones are falling apart. Didn't you remember?"

"I forgot, that's all," she replied.

"You're always forgetting...since you came back from Aunt Abbie's wedding...always!" His features grew sullen. "It's that reporter guy. You're always thinking about him, aren't you?"

"Dan?" she asked, surprised how easily his name slipped out. "Of course not, and I haven't seen or heard from him for two weeks. He's gone out of state on an assignment."

"Good."

"But he may come for Thanksgiving."

Jordan groaned aloud.

"I asked him to bring his son. He's about your age."

Jordan squinted up at her. "Now I suppose you expect me to like him, too? First you try to make me like Mr. Page like a father and now you want me to treat his boy like *my brother?* Well, I won't! He's probably a creep, too."

She sighed. "All I ask is that if they come, you remember your manners and treat them like welcome guests."

"Even if they're not?"

"But they are." She glanced at the calendar again. "I'd almost forgotten how close Thanksgiving is. I'd better think about baking pies and bread and..."

"Are you gonna do extra stuff just because they'll be here?" he asked begrudgingly.

"No, young man," she replied. "Don't we always have extra stuff, as you call it, on Thanksgiving?"

"Yeah," he admitted. "Will Mr. Waite be eating with us?"

"Yes, and Grandpa and Grandma Mills, and your Uncle Thomas and Aunt Esther with their two boys, and any of the men who work for us who don't have families to be with.''

"Gee, why so many?'' Jordan asked. ''I figured since Dad...won't be with us...you'd just forget the whole thing.''

"Oh, Jordan,'' she murmured, pulling him close and giving him a tight hug. ''I want this to be a special holiday. We'll all miss your father, but that doesn't mean we have to stop celebrating holidays that were so special when he was alive. Would he want us to do that? To sit here, all alone, feeling sorry for ourselves? Do you really think he'd want us to be that sad?''

"Nah, I guess not,'' Jordan said, pulling free from her embrace. ''I'm glad we're gonna have a turkey and all that other stuff. I told J & J you'd probably just skip it, but they said you wouldn't. I guess they're not as dumb as they used to be.''

"Jordan,'' she cautioned.

He grinned. ''I like it when everyone comes...even if that reporter guy comes...and even if he brings his boy. Does he really go to a military school and get to shoot guns and wear a uniform?''

"I believe so,'' she said.

"That must be great,'' he said. ''A guy wouldn't have to worry about matching his tube socks or nothing.''

"Perhaps you can compare notes on school.''

"Maybe.'' He darted around her and raced down the stairs and out of sight.

Children, she thought, *how quickly their moods change. One minute sullen and defiant, the next carefree.* She could recall her own mood shifts in her youth and that memory always helped her accept them in her own children. She deliberately tried not to think of the holiday and Dan's visit, as she went upstairs and changed into jeans and a blue flannel shirt. Her problem with the bank was paramount now. Perhaps Hogan had a solution waiting.

Eileen found him in the machine shed working on the conveyor belt of the sorter. It had given them problems during harvesting.

"Hogan," she called.

He crawled out from under the chassis and stood, wiping grease from his hands. "Yes, ma'am. How did it go?"

"So, so," she hedged. "Did Patton take the spuds?"

She held her breath while he unbuttoned the flap of his plaid flannel shirt and retrieved several sheets of folded paper.

"He offered us five-twenty-eight a box," Hogan said. "I started at five-thirty-five and let him work me down to five-twenty-eight." He laughed, his deep voice filling the building. "He never knew I was willing to go lower."

Her mood brightened. "Five-twenty-eight? Really?"

"I told you he was interested. He liked the quality. Said we had some of the best spuds he'd seen this year." Hogan handed the papers to her. "He said to call him later today and confirm it if you want to do business. Is it a go, Mrs. Mills?"

"Oh, yes, Hogan. It's definitely a go." She smiled, her eyes shining with moisture.

"You look pretty happy, Mrs. Mills."

"Happy? I'm so happy, I could kiss a frog," she exclaimed. "But they're all in hibernation, so I'll kiss you instead. Bend down here." With that, she planted a firm kiss on his cheek and ran from the building, leaving the surprised foreman alone.

Inside the house, her hand shook as she listened to the ringing at the other end of the phone line. "Calm down," she whispered, then clamped her mouth shut when a woman's voice answered.

"Boise Processing & Agribusiness," the woman said.

"Mr. Patton, please. Tell him Eileen Mills is calling."

"One moment, please," and Eileen was put on hold.

She tapped her foot restlessly. Three minutes later, she was about to hang up when a voice came on the line.

"Patton here. Help you?"

"Yes," Eileen said breathlessly. "This is Mrs. Mills. You spoke with my foreman Hogan Waite this afternoon."

"Why of course. How are you, Mrs. Mills? Sorry to have missed you. Duncan and I did business in the earlier years but somehow we let our business dealings drop. It's a shame. And I'm so sorry about his . . . passing. Great guy, really a fine man."

Eileen listened impatiently as the man reminisced about the times he had met Duncan. Finally, she interrupted. "Mr. Patton, about the offer you made this afternoon?"

"Oh . . . sure," he said. "I reckon we should conduct our business before . . ." He cleared his throat. "Your potatoes are very good quality and we'd be sending them to our chip plant in California. We want the best number twos you can deliver. F.O.B. at our plant in Boise. We'd like twenty-five thousand boxes."

"How about thirty thousand boxes?" she replied. "They are more like oversize number ones; uniform and top quality. They'd make wonderful potato chips, Mr. Patton. I could let you have them all for five twenty-five."

He laughed. "You drive a good bargain, Mrs. Mills. Thirty thousand it is. When can you deliver?"

Mentally, she counted the trucks she would need. "Monday. We can have them in Boise by 2:00 p.m. Monday. Mr. Patton?"

"Yes?"

"I would appreciate it very much if you could expedite the payment," she said. "I'd like my foreman to pick up a check."

He paused and she held her breath. "I think I can do that, Mrs. Mills. You tell him to come see me after the trucks have been weighed."

"Thanks, Mr. Patton," she replied. "It's been a pleasure doing business with you. Remember the Mills Farm next fall."

"I'll do that. Bye bye now, young lady. No one need worry about the continued success of the Mills operation."

"Thank you," she said and replaced the receiver in its cradle. She closed her eyes. She had pulled it off and kept one of her promises to Duncan. She had saved the farm . . . for now.

Early Tuesday she would take the check to the bank in Idaho Falls and deposit it, after showing it to Mr. Ludwig. It would wipe out the overdraft and leave enough to cover the operations for several weeks. She would talk to the financial officer at the bank in Rupert and explain that the equipment loan payment due the first of December would be a week or two late. Somehow she would find a way to cover that obligation, also.

On Friday when she prepared the weekly payroll checks for the four remaining employees, her mind was on the upcoming holiday. Would Dan accept her invitation? What would Duncan's parents think of the reporter and his son joining the Mills family at their table? She hadn't considered their reaction when she had invited Dan and his son. *Peace,* she prayed, *just give me peace. I can't carry many other burdens, Lord, but for now, just help me make it through this next week.*

TUESDAY MORNING, the phone rang as Eileen grabbed her purse to leave for Idaho Falls. Anxious to reach the bank as soon as it opened, she considered ignoring the caller, but wondered, what if it were Dan? Grabbing the receiver, she exclaimed, "Hello!"

"Mrs. Mills, this is Sam Ludwig at First Falls Bank," the caller said. "I cautioned you about issuing payroll checks on Friday unless you cleared your overdraft. Did you really think we could honor these bad checks?"

Her gaze fell on the check and deposit slip in her hand. "Oh, My God." How could she have been so forgetful? "Mr. Ludwig, I'm on my way in with a deposit. Please don't return the checks!"

"I'm sorry, Mrs. Mills, but the return item clerk processed them as usual yesterday. Because of the caution flag on your account the operations officer brought the notices to me before his assistant put them in the mail. Really, Mrs. Mills! This is almost criminal, don't you realize?"

Her heart thudded against her ribs. "Please, Mr. Ludwig, listen to me. I sold thirty thousand boxes of spuds and picked up the check yesterday. I was on my way out the door. It's all going to be deposited into the operating account. Please, can't you stop the return of those checks? My employees will be...be devastated." *Not half as devastated as I am,* she thought.

"I'm sorry, Mrs. Mills. They came in through a weekend deposit from a grocery store chain and were processed automatically by the operations center personnel and forwarded to us Monday morning as are most of the bad checks we handle."

"They aren't bad checks!"

"Then where are the underlying funds?"

"In my hand," she admitted, her voice quivering. "Mr. Ludwig, I'll be there in a half hour. Please hold those notices and I'll pick them up when I make the deposit." Before he could reply, she slammed the receiver down and ran out the door.

Speeding all the way into the city, she arrived at the bank as a vice president was unlocking the front doors. She made the deposit, cashed a check to cover the payroll checks, then went to Sam Ludwig's office. His secretary was on the phone. Eileen glanced at her, caught enough of the conversation to know she was on a personal call, and walked into Ludwig's office unannounced.

She slapped her receipt and a copy of the check down on top of the financial reports he was reading. "One hundred fifty-seven thousand, five hundred dollars, Mr. Ludwig. It's on deposit now, so your bloody blooming bookkeeping department can wipe out my overdraft. Now what do ya'll think of that?" To her surprise, he smiled. The drawl of her Kentucky heritage had crept back into her speech.

"I suppose now I'm to reply 'ya'll come back now, ya heah?'" he said, reclining in his swivel chair.

She blushed. "I'm sorry. I lost my temper."

"Sit down, Mrs. Mills," he said, motioning to the chair with the unforgiving springs. He pushed the intercom. "Janice, bring in two cups of coffee and the fixings."

A few minutes later a silver tray and service appeared. "Thank you, Janice." He motioned to Eileen. "Cream? Sugar?" When she shook her head, he offered her a cup.

"You've been under a strain, Mrs. Mills," he said. "After thinking things over I'm putting through a request to have the NSF charges reversed, but be more careful next time, and trust us. Be more open with me if you're having financial difficulties. We're here to help you, not to make matters worse, but we have to know what's going on if we're to provide that help."

"Thanks, Mr. Ludwig," she said. "A week ago, I didn't know I had a problem." Her gaze fell on the NSF notices. "May I have them?"

He handed the small pieces of paper to her. "What are you going to do with them?"

"First I'm going to replace the checks with cash to each employee and hope they understand, then I'm going to keep the notices in my desk so each time I open the drawer I'll be reminded to make sure I have funds in my account before I write checks. Thank you for reversing the charges." She took another sip from her cup. "Good coffee," she said.

"Thank you," he replied. "Janice makes far too many personal phone calls but she makes terrific coffee."

Within the hour Eileen was back at the farm, handing an envelope to each employee and having them sign for the receipt of cash. She explained to each that a mix-up at the bank had caused the problem and the men seemed to accept the situation. She assured them her bank would send a letter to each of their banks upon request.

Eileen spent Wednesday baking pies and breads for the holiday dinner the following day. Early Thursday she pushed the large roasting pan into the oven and glanced at the clock.

As she tidied up the kitchen, her thoughts turned to Daniel Page and an idea came to her. He had complimented her on her baking skills. Why not send him and his son home with a care package? She gathered two quilted Kerr half-pint jars of last summer's blackberry jam and a jar of apple butter, selected the nicest loaf of bread and slid it into a plastic wrapper, then put several cinnamon rolls into a foil package.

Rummaging through her sewing room, she found a brown wicker basket she had bought years earlier for a project and never completed. She hurried back to the kitchen and arranged the items in the basket and tied a yellow ribbon on the handle. Pleased with the results, she set it aside and returned to the dinner preparation.

By one in the afternoon, the Mills relatives had arrived. Hogan Waite and two of the other employees made their entrance shortly before two. When the blessing of the meal was given by George Mills at his wife's nudging, there were only two empty chairs at the large table.

George Mills, seated at the head of the table, began carving the golden brown turkey and ladling generous servings of meat and cornbread dressing to each extended plate. As he sat down and the other dishes of food worked their way around the table, he looked at Eileen, his blue eyes much like Duncan's. "Who else were you expecting, my dear?"

"A friend of the family," she replied. "The invitation was tentative. He and his son may have made other plans."

"He's that reporter guy who took Mom and Dad's pictures," Jordan volunteered.

"Yeah, his name is Mr. Page," Jolene added.

"He's nice," Jodie said shyly.

"Friend of the family?" Geraldine Mills asked, her silver hair shining with a faint blue sheen.

"Yes, just a friend," Eileen insisted. "He's been here a few times to see if we were doing okay. That's all."

"He went to Aunt Abbie's wedding," Jordan said.

"Jordan! That's enough. Eat or leave the table, do you understand?" Eileen said, her face flushed with anger and embarrassment. She shot a warning glare to the twins when they started to giggle. "Now let's enjoy this meal," she directed, ignoring the glances being exchanged between her in-laws.

Perhaps it's just as well Dan and his son haven't come, she thought, hiding her disappointment as the meal progressed. She didn't want to explain to others a relationship she didn't understand herself.

"We have pumpkin and mincemeat pies," Eileen said, as the table was cleared of the main course.

She put the last piece of pumpkin pie on a dessert plate and handed it to Jolene. The doorbell rang and she started, almost dumping the pie into her daughter's lap. "I'll get it," she said, wiping her hands on her apron. Controlling the urge to run, she ignored the curious glances of her guests.

When she opened the door, Daniel Page was leaning against his favorite porch post, wearing gray flannel slacks and a maroon, long sleeved pullover sweater. A checked, maroon-and-white, button-down collar peeked out above the neckline of his sweater.

"Hello," he said, smiling and sending her heart into a spin. "Sorry I'm late."

CHAPTER EIGHT

"ARE WE STILL invited?" he asked, straightening and taking a step toward her.

"Yes," she replied breathlessly. "You brought Stephen?"

"He was reluctant, but when I explained the alternative was boiled wieners and a can of pork and beans, he reconsidered." Dan turned and motioned toward his car.

A sandy-haired boy left the car, hitching up his new blue jeans as he walked stiffly toward them. Mostly arms and legs and in the middle of a prepubescent growth spurt, the boy paused several paces from them. He scanned the rambling white farm house, but Eileen couldn't read his reaction. She met his curious gaze directly, sensing his discomfort.

"Hello, Stephen," she said, smiling.

"Good afternoon, Mrs. Mills," he replied, and she almost expected him to click his heels and salute her.

She accepted his outstretched hand and shook it. "I'm glad you wore jeans," she said. "Perhaps my son and daughters will show you around the place after you eat. We have some four-wheelers you can ride."

"Really? All-terrain vehicles? Gee. I've always wanted to—" He chopped off his words. "That would be nice, Mrs. Mills, if my father agrees."

Dan chuckled. "Of course it's okay with me, Stephen. Today is a day to forget the rules and regulations and enjoy ourselves."

"Thank you, sir," Stephen said, returning his attention to Eileen. "The stability of the four-wheel design is a vast improvement in recent years," he said. "Although more expensive to purchase, they are much safer to operate than the three-wheelers, you know. Aerodynamically, they are less likely to tip over and—" He smiled and his boyish charm surfaced. "I've read articles about them."

He had inherited his father's eyes and smile.

"Jordan's father taught him how to operate it safely and if he ever does otherwise, he looses all privileges," she replied.

"I'm sorry about the loss of your husband, Mrs. Mills. My father told me about...everything," Stephen said, nodding sagely.

Eileen resolved to make the boy's visit as informal as possible, sensing his need to unwind.

"Why don't you come inside," she suggested, suddenly aware of the chill in the afternoon air. She glanced toward the sky. "It looks threatening. Snow was predicted a few days ago but it didn't get here." A few giant flakes began to swirl through the air and light on the edge of the porch near the toes of her black pumps. "We're having dessert but I'll warm your dinners in the microwave."

"Sounds fine," Dan said. His hand reached out but dropped before touching her arm. "You look lovely today. The color and style become you."

She touched the winter-white woolen crepe of the shirtwaist dress. "Thank you," she replied, her gaze clinging to his.

"I wasn't sure if we should dress up or down," he said.

"You're both fine," she assured him. "We dress up for Easter, Thanksgiving and Christmas, but not very up."

He laughed. "Good. People should be comfortable at home."

"Yeah," Stephen agreed, "and not have to sit up straight with your feet on the floor and all that kinda...I wish I could wear jeans all the time."

Dan laid his hand on his son's shoulder. "This is neither the time or the place for that subject."

"You're both fine, really," Eileen assured them. "Jordan is wearing jeans and a sports shirt. The girls opted for dresses, but just for today. Tomorrow they'll be back in jeans as usual. Now, won't you come inside and join us?"

Dan glanced over his shoulder at the cars parked in the yard. "You have other guests?"

"Mills relatives," she said, "so you might be subjected to an interview yourself. I told them you were a family friend."

He smiled. "I'll try to remember that."

Inside, Eileen made the introductions and motioned Dan and his son to their places to her immediate left. Her spirits were soaring as she entered the kitchen and began to fix two plates, but her heart stopped when she heard her daughter's voice coming from the dining room.

"Isn't he handsome, Grandma?" Jolene asked.

Geraldine Mills cleared her throat. "Shush, Jolene, it isn't polite to talk about Mr. Page when he's right across the table."

"Even when he is?" Jolene persisted.

"Yes, he's handsome," Geraldine Mills conceded. "Now let's all finish our dessert."

"He kissed..." Jolene's voice rang out crystal clear. "Ouch! She kicked me!"

"Jodie, you mustn't kick your sister," Geraldine scolded.

"Momma said we shouldn't talk about that," Jodie said.

Eileen carried the plates into the dining room and set them down in front of Dan and his son.

Stephen and Jordan frowned at Dan. Most of the Mills relatives stared at the twins, but Geraldine's gaze was on Eileen.

"It's been only six months," Geraldine scolded.

Eileen's heart stopped. "Yes," she said.

"Six months is hardly long enough," Geraldine pronounced.

"Gerry," George Mills cautioned. "Eileen is mature enough to decide for herself when to get involved with . . . another man."

"I'm not involved," Eileen said.

"It's her business," her sister-in-law Esther interjected.

Eileen looked at her appreciatively.

"Motherhood should be her first priority," Geraldine said firmly, staring across the table at Dan. She dabbed at the corners of her eyes. "My poor Duncan . . . hardly gone."

Eileen stiffened. "He was gone a year before he died."

"Eileen, really!" Geraldine exclaimed, rising from her chair.

"It's the truth," Eileen cried. "He was so weak, he could barely make it from his bed to the wheelchair. I loved him. I'll always love him, but what am I supposed to do? Wear black for the rest of my life?"

George Mills motioned his wife back down into her chair. "I'm sure our son would want you to go on living, Eileen. Gerry should not have pried into your personal life."

"I think it's disgraceful," Geraldine murmured under her breath.

"I think it's healthy," Dan said, taking Eileen's clinched fist and prying her fingers open. "She took off her rings a few weeks ago. That was a step in the right direction. And she's right, we're not involved. We're friends, and if others don't interfere, we'll stay friends. I think the world of Eileen and I would never be a party to a compromising situation. She deserves better than that."

Geraldine eyed Stephen, who was sitting across from Jodie. "Have you also lost a spouse, Mr. Page? Are you a widower?"

"I'm divorced."

Geraldine huffed in disdain.

"My son's mother and I are still friends," he added.

Geraldine smirked. "I've heard about friendly divorces."

Dan's eyes narrowed. "The fact that we decided to dissolve our marriage does not mean we love our son any less. Stephen's emotional well-being is uppermost in our minds and he deserves two parents if possible, two parents who love him. Your grandchildren are less fortunate. They have only one parent left to love them."

He pushed his chair back and stood up. "If Eileen meets a man who interests her, that's her good fortune, and if that man happens to be me, then it will be my good fortune also, but what we do is our business and no in-laws or children or other well-meaning relatives have any right to stand in our way." Suddenly he stopped and closed his eyes for several seconds before surveying all the faces staring at him. His mouth tightened. "Why the hell am I explaining all this?"

"Profanity isn't necessary," Geraldine said tersely.

"I came here for a good home-cooked meal and to enjoy being with Eileen's family," he said. "What do I get? A raking over the coals and a warning to keep my distance from your daughter-in-law. Well, damn it, I'll touch her if I want to."

"Dan, please," Eileen said, rising again and turning to him, her face pale. "Too much has been said already."

"Sit down, you two," Thomas Cameron suggested. "You've made your point, and frankly, I agree." He took a bite of mincemeat pie and swallowed. "Let's enjoy the time we have together and stop all this family squabbling." He returned his attention to his slice of pie and ignored the others.

A tense silence filled the room for several minutes.

Finally, George Mills cleared his throat. "Mr. Page?"

"Dan . . . please call me Dan."

"Of course...Dan. Page is an unusual surname," George said. "What is its origin? Are you from around here?"

"The name is French," Dan said.

"It sounds English to me," Geraldine challenged.

"All I know is what my grandfather told me," Dan replied, meeting her gaze directly. "The name has been anglicized. He came to United States with a bundle of grape cuttings from the Bordeaux area of France, determined to start his own vineyard. When he couldn't arrange passage to California and ran out of funds, he sold his cuttings to a man who took advantage of him and his inability to understand the language. He met the daughter of an Irishman who took him home to her father's farm in New Jersey."

He smiled, recalling the story from his youth. "They fell in love. She taught him English and he taught her how to enjoy life. So instead of becoming a famous vintner, my Grampa Etienne settled in southern New Jersey and grew tomatoes. My son is named after his great-grandfather Etienne LePage. He was a wonderful man. I'm proud to have known him."

"New Jersey?" Geraldine's carefully plucked eyebrow raised slightly.

"Yes, ma'am, New Jersey. I grew up on that same commercial vegetable farm. It no longer exists, I'm sad to say."

"Really?" George asked.

"It became part of a turnpike interchange," he explained. "That prime agricultural land that would grow almost any seed you'd want to drop into it is now covered over with asphalt and concrete. My parents sold out and are now retired on five acres near Weiser, Idaho. I live in Boise.''

"And what do you do there?" George asked.

"I'm gainfully employed as a journalist for *Western Living* magazine," he replied. "I've been with the magazine for five years. My bank account is more than adequate. This fact surprises even me since I went through a bankruptcy in Texas several years ago."

"What happened?" George asked, ignoring his wife's mumbling.

"I lost my shirt trying to run a small-town newspaper in west Texas. My integrity got me in trouble with the local political scene...but that's another story. In spite of that, I've never missed a single one of my child-support payments. You can ask my former wife if you feel the need to do a security check on my past or my character. I'm thirty-five years old and my health is good enough to enable me to run four miles a day. I'm an early riser and a hard worker and I've planned for my future."

"Oh? How do you mean?" the older man asked.

"I've made a few sound, nonspeculative investments to ensure my security when or if I decide to retire, but I believe I have a few good years yet."

George nodded, then winked at Eileen who had covered her mouth. "You're a wise man to prepare for the future," he said. "Gerry and I passed this family farm on to Duncan and Eileen years ago and I've never regretted it for a minute. We take at least one cruise each year, preferably in January. Last year we went to Tahiti. This year we might try a trip to the Caribbean."

"George has invested in a mushroom venture on one of the smaller islands," Geraldine explained. "I was against it but he can be very stubborn at times."

"Mushrooms?" Dan asked.

"Yes, a mushroom farm that uses large greenhouses and sugar cane pulp for a growing medium." George frowned. "It's very complicated, but if it works...well, if it comes off the way it was explained to me, we won't have any financial worries in our old age."

"We don't have any worries now," Geraldine said.

"Sounds interesting," Dan commented.

"Want to buy into it?" George asked.

"Not at the moment," Dan hedged. "Why mushrooms?"

"Potatoes, mushrooms...it seemed logical."

"Logical, indeed," Geraldine snorted.

Before another word could be uttered by anyone, Eileen rose again. "Why don't you all go into the living room? I'm sure there's a football game on television. I'll bring in some coffee. Esther, could you help me?" she asked, avoiding Dan's gaze.

"Love to," Esther said, quickly shooing the others out of the dining room. In the kitchen, Esther grabbed Eileen's hands. "How long have we known each other?"

"Since university."

"And haven't we shared secrets we've told no one else?"

Eileen smiled softly. "Including my engagement to your brother for a year, and my pregnancy with Jordan for six months before I would admit it to George and Gerry. Why?"

Esther dropped Eileen's hands and clapped her own together. "Then tell me who this wonderful man is? Where did you meet him? Anyone who can stand up to my mother has more guts than I have."

She hugged Eileen, squeezing her tightly. "Now while we pretend to make coffee, tell me all about him. I loved my brother dearly but I know you went through hell these past few years. They must have been a terrible strain on both you and Duncan. Never once did I hear you complain. I don't know where you got your strength to keep going!'' Her eyes filled with tears. "He wanted to spare you, honey. He told me so several times, but he didn't know how."

Eileen's eyes shimmered as she faced her outspoken sister-in-law. "I know. Once he said he wished he was brave enough to take his own life. That's when I sold all our rifles. I was terrified to leave him alone even for a few minutes. Sometimes those last three years seem a million years ago... and sometimes I wake up and feel as if I'm trapped in them still. It's not easy. Perhaps that's why Dan and I get along so well. He was there. He knew Duncan and me when the times were at their worst. He came to the funeral. He..." She wiped her eyes. "He has this wonderful habit of being here when I need someone to talk to. He's willing to just listen. Do I make any sense?"

"You might if you tell me more," Esther replied. "I realize now that I met him at the funeral, and I assumed he was a friend." She hunched her shoulders and peered into Eileen's eyes. "You'd better tell me the whole story."

While the coffee brewed, Eileen explained how she and Dan had met and about the recent interview. "So you see," she said, smiling, "he's right. We're just good friends."

"But there could be more?"

Eileen didn't reply.

Esther grinned. "If you want my opinion—"

"You'll give it anyway," Eileen said. "You always did, from that first day at the university when you tried to tell me how to arrange my side of our dorm room."

Esther laughed. "You listened, then did it your own way. Well, my dear, you're my favorite sister-in-law and..."

"I'm your only sister-in-law," Eileen reminded her.

"So? My opinion is…that your relationship is much more proper than it first appears. It must be judged not on the time you've been a widow, but the period of time your friendship had been developing. Oh goodness, that sounds terrible. What I mean is even though you were married when you first met him, the two of you…lordy, it's getting worse isn't it?"

"Is that why sometimes I feel so guilty?" Eileen asked. "But Esther, when he kisses me I forget all about the hard times and the children and the farm, and it's as though we've left this old planet and been swept away to the ends of the universe…and that's just from a little old kiss or two."

"Well, honey, you know what's in your heart," Esther said. "Frankly, I like him. You have my blessing." She reached for the pot of coffee. "You get the mugs and follow me. If we don't get in there soon, the game will be all over or else my mother and your Dan may get into it again." She paused. "Are you okay now?"

Eileen nodded. "Talking to you makes it all seem so simple."

"Honey bun, love is never simple," Esther retorted, leaving Eileen alone to ponder her sister-in-law's parting words.

As the game finished and the empty mugs were gathered onto the serving tray, George Mills lifted the drape and peered out the window. "It's snowing pretty hard. I think we should head for home. You know how the drifts can block us in. Gerry?"

His wife nodded, and as he bundled her up in a white imitation fur coat, she turned to Dan. "I'm sorry, Mr. Page. I miss my son very much. He was so young. Sometimes I still find it difficult to accept the fact that he's gone."

"Especially on holidays such as this," George added. "Life can be cruel, but we still love Eileen like a daughter and we want her to find happiness again."

Dan accepted George's hand. "I understand, folks. I met Duncan twice. He was a fine man."

Geraldine squinted, pointing her enameled finger nail at Dan. "You were at the funeral, weren't you? Now I remember you."

George edged his wife toward the door then whisked her out. The other Mills relatives left soon after.

"Can we still try the four-wheelers?" Stephen asked.

"I'm afraid not," Dan said. "The wind has picked up and it's getting darker. We had better head for home ourselves."

Stephen groaned aloud. "Can we come back?"

"The first weekend you're with me again," Dan promised.

"Boise is a long way," Eileen said. "You're welcome to stay. We can make room."

"Thanks, but we should get on the road, in case the storm gets worse," he replied.

She nodded. "If you must. One section of the road into Shelly is notorious for drifts. It's about a mile from our gate, so drive carefully." She took the wicker basket of bread and jams from the buffet. "This is for the two of you. If you get snowed in, you won't get hungry." Their hands touched as he took the basket.

"Thanks." Dan wanted to kiss her but under the circumstances, thought better of it. "I'll call and let you know we made it home. Thanks for the meal. It hit the spot for two single guys. Stephen can have a hollow leg at times." He studied her face, memorizing each feature. "Bye." He turned away so he wouldn't give in to her invitation to stay.

Eileen remained on the front porch, clutching the collar of her coat up around her ears, until the glow of the red taillights disappeared in the swirling snow. For a fleeting moment she had hoped he would turn the car around and return. When she accepted the finality of his leaving, she reluctantly turned toward the house. The subfreezing wind whipped her skirt against her thighs. She mouthed a silent prayer that they would have a safe journey or if not, then they would find shelter from the storm.

Inside, she organized a work detail. "Jordan, you load the dishwasher and girls, you clean the living room. Jolene, run the vacuum. Jodie, bring in any glasses or cups we missed. Hurry now, so we can finish before the Snowman special comes on TV!"

Soon all evidence of the holiday dinner was gone. She glanced at the clock. *Dan and Stephen are still on the road,* she thought, knowing the phone would not ring for hours. She peeked out the kitchen window. The storm was quickly becoming a full blizzard. Perhaps he would stop and get a motel for the night.

Would he spend the rest of the holiday with his son and his former wife? It seemed natural for him to want to give Stephen the togetherness of a family. Hadn't he said as much to her father and mother-in-law? She shook the disturbing thoughts away and joined the children.

"Jordan, did you enjoy getting to meet Stephen?" she asked.

Her son grunted an unintelligible reply and returned his attention to the show on the screen.

Eileen was too tired to speculate on how he actually felt about meeting Dan's son, but she recalled having seen them sitting on the floor during the football game and discussing the wisdom of several plays. Perhaps Jordan had taken to Stephen better than he had Dan Page. She settled into the corner of the comfortable sofa. As she reached for a magazine, the doorbell rang.

"Someone is lost in the storm," Jodie said, sidling closer to her twin.

"No, it's Grandma and Grandpa," Jolene volunteered. "They bought a pizza and came back to share it." She beamed.

"You're both wrong," Jordan said. "It's a snow monster like Big Foot and he's come to get rotten little sisters." He towered over them, forming his hands into claws. "I'm gonna let him in," he threatened. The girls shrieked and broke into giggles as they rolled away from him in opposite directions.

The bell rang again.

"Be quiet, children," Eileen said. "It's probably Mr. Waite or one of the other men."

"They would have come to the back door, Mom," Jordan said.

"You're right," Eileen said. "I'll get it." As she approached the door and turned on the outside porch light switch, she caught movement. She reached for the baseball bat she kept in the corner of the room and clutching it in one hand, she cautiously opened the door.

Dan Page, wearing a bulky green parka covered with snow, greeted her with a bemused smile. He held the care basket in his bare hands, its yellow bow now drooping from the wet snow. A trembling Stephen stood beside him.

"Remember that drift you warned me about? I was so concerned about it that I overcontrolled and ran into its twin on the other side of the road and bounced into a ditch. I'm hopelessly stuck and I think I've damaged the control arm. I need a tow truck."

"Oh, Dan." Eileen dropped the bat and threw her arms around his neck. "Are you hurt?" she cried, kissing his cheek.

He grinned. "I got a goose egg on my forehead. Thank goodness we were wearing seat belts."

Her hands flew over his face, confirming the lump. Blood stained her fingertips. "You're bleeding!" Her palms pressed against his cheeks. "Are you sure you have no other injuries?"

He nodded. "I should run into snowdrifts more often. Can we come in?"

Her hands fell away. "Of course. You must be freezing."

Stephen picked up the bat, stomped the snow from his shoes, and followed Dan inside. His lips were bluish and his nose and cheeks red from the cold. He handed the bat to his father and blew on his hands, rubbing them together.

Eileen grabbed his hands. "They're like ice. Stephen...Dan, you might have frozen to death out there. Jordan, why don't you take Stephen upstairs and show him where the bathroom is? Take a hot shower, Stephen, and we'll find you some dry clothing."

Jordan motioned impatiently to the shivering boy, who followed him up the stairs, the twins trailing along behind them.

"And now you," Eileen said, turning her undivided attention to Dan's condition.

"I'm fine," he assured her. "Is this your secret weapon?" he asked, extending the baseball bat.

Embarrassed, she took it and propped it back against the corner of the room. "That's in lieu of a shotgun or a ferocious guard dog," she explained. "What can I do for you?"

"Don't ask," he warned.

She blushed at his insinuation. "Seriously," she said.

"I'm serious," he insisted, "but not now. If I can dry my hair and warm my hands, I'll make it." He shed his parka and she was relieved to see his street clothes were dry.

"Of course," she murmured and raced down the hallway to the linen closet. When Eileen returned, she found him already in the hall bathroom, running warm water on his hands. He washed the blood from an abrasion on his temple, then accepted the towel and rubbed his hair dry and ran a pocket comb through it several times. Eileen lingered against the door of the room, watching him in the mirror. He turned, sliding the comb into his hip pocket.

"I knew something was wrong," she murmured. "I wanted to call but I knew you couldn't possibly be home. I had said a prayer for your safety." She retrieved a small bandage from a metal canister and tore the wrapper open. "It's bleeding again. Lean down."

He leaned against the lavatory and bent his head.

"Does it hurt?" she asked, as she pressed the tape and gauze against his skin.

"It smarts a little," he admitted, "but I think I'll live."

She stepped away. "If only I'd known you had had an accident."

"Did you care? Enough to pray?" He stepped away from the lavatory.

"Yes," she whispered.

"I don't think anyone's ever said a prayer for me before. Thanks. It warms me, right here." He made a fist and put it against his chest. He edged her into the middle of the bathroom, reached around her and closed the door, locking it before releasing the knob. "If this is the only place we can have some privacy, so be it." He reached for her hand and she came toward him, touching the front of his sweater with her finger tips.

"All that talk at dinner," she said. "It must have embarrassed you. I'm sorry."

"It was much worse for you," he replied. "Now our involvement is out in the open."

"But we're not involved," she said, resting her forearms against his chest as he pulled her closer.

"We could be." He trailed a finger down her cheek and across her lips.

"No." She shook her head slowly. "It's too soon."

"Then I'll wait." His hands cupped the back of her head. "But I'm going to do what I want to do every time I see you." Holding her head immobile, he claimed her mouth with his.

CHAPTER NINE

EILEEN'S ARMS WENT around his neck. He released her head, pulling her hard against his body and the confirmation that he desired her sent a surge of anxiety through her.

"Dan, I'm so confused."

"Don't talk, just feel," he replied.

"Oh, believe me, I feel...too much. You make my insides churn and I think my heart is going to explode if it beats much faster."

"Then don't waste time," he murmured. "Kiss me again."

She savored the rough texture of his beard near the corner of his mouth. Her mouth opened and her tongue sought his, tentatively, almost shyly.

His hands ran down her body, cupping her hips through her skirt and pressing them tightly against his body before moving upward again. While she rested her head against his shoulder, trying to catch her breath, he removed the rubber band from her single braid and loosened her hair. He combed it with his fingers before burying his face in its fragrance.

She turned her head, seeking his mouth again. Their lips parted and they savored each other's warmth.

"Oh God, Eileen, I want to make love to you," he whispered hoarsely against her cheek.

"No, we can't," she replied, stiffening in his arms. "This isn't right."

"Why not?"

A knock sounded against the locked door and the knob was shaken from the outside.

"Momma, are you in there? We hunted everywhere and couldn't find you," Jolene called.

"Hey, Dad, come out. I've finished my shower and Jordan loaned me a pair of pj's," Stephen said, tapping the door again.

"What are you doing in there?" Jodie asked.

"They're kissing," Jolene said.

"No, they're not," Jordan exclaimed.

Inside the bathroom, Eileen opened her mouth to reply but Dan touched her lips with his fingers. "I know the reasons," he said and she joined in as he listed them. "Stephen, Jordan, Jolene and Jodie."

He laughed. "Be right out, children," he called. "Your mother was just helping me warm up against the cold. She bandaged the cut on my head. Go watch television."

Dan glanced into the mirror and rubbed a trace of lipstick from his mouth. "It's not my shade," he said, smiling at her in the mirror before turning and spinning her around. "Let me fix your hair."

She felt his fingers forming a braid again.

"Where's the rubber band?" he asked.

"You took it off," she chided. "Where did you put it?"

"Beats the heck out of me." He held the end of the braid with one hand and opened the cabinet doors with the other, slamming them shut again when his search proved futile.

"There it is," Eileen exclaimed. "About to slide down the drain!"

He grabbed for the elastic just in time and quickly wrapped it around the end of the braid. In the close confines of the bathroom, she watched his bowed head in the mirror as he worked on her hair. When he finished, he glanced up and caught her studying their reflection.

He pulled her back against him and one of his hands found its way to the underside of her breast, caressing it tenderly through her bodice. "Someday," he promised. "Someday we'll finish this."

In the mirror, her pupils were dilated, her cheeks flushed with unfamiliar desire. Before she could speak, he repeated his vow, "Someday," and unlocked the door.

They reentered the living room and Jolene leaped to her feet. "Can Mr. Page and Stephen spend the night?"

"It's snowing like crazy," Stephen said.

"Stephen can sleep in my room," Jordan offered.

"What about Mr. Page?" Jodie asked.

"He can sleep with Momma...just like..." Jolene suggested.

"No!" Eileen said. "I mean, no, that's not a good idea." She brushed an imaginary piece of lint from her skirt.

"I can take the sofa," Dan volunteered. "If that's okay with your mother."

"That would be fine," Eileen said. "I'll get some linens and a blanket and pillow." She turned to go but stopped when she heard laughter and giggling behind her. "What's so funny?" she asked, turning to confront four laughing children and a grinning Dan.

"Your hair, Mom," Jordan said, frowning heavily. "What happened to your hair?"

She touched her hair, feeling the irregular lumpy braid.

"I never did learn how to do that properly," Dan confessed. "In fact, I never learned to braid at all."

"If you want a thing done right, do it yourself. I'll fix it later. Now, children, run upstairs and get ready for bed. I'll be up in a little while and say good-night."

"Will you tuck us in?" Jodie asked.

"And kiss us good-night?" Jolene added.

"Of course," Eileen agreed.

"Me too?" Dan asked.

The children waited for their mother's reply.

"You can take care of yourself," she said, feigning aloofness as she hurried from the room. She heard the children laughing and talking as she gathered a pillow and bed linens for Dan. When she returned to the living room, the children were gone and most of the lamps had been turned off. He twisted the maroon pullover up and over his head and carefully folded it, then laid it on a nearby chair.

The intimacy of seeing him undress shook the bonds of her self-control. She tossed the bed linens to the sofa and hurried up the stairs, mumbling a hasty, "Good night," over her shoulder.

JORDAN FROWNED at the boy in the other twin bed. His mother had stuck her head in the door and said good-night. Thankfully, she had refrained from kissing him. He still liked an occasional hug—but not in front of his friends.

And he wasn't sure if Stephen Page was a friend or not.

"Thanks for letting me use your pajamas," Stephen said, punching his pillows a few times and settling in.

"I can only wear one pair at a time," Jordan replied.

"I thought we were gonna have to walk all the way to Idaho Falls," Stephen said. "My dad wasn't sure we should come back here." He propped himself up on an elbow and brushed his sandy hair from his eyes.

"We have people stay over all the time," Jordan said.

"But not my dad."

"No, not your dad."

"You don't like my dad, do you?" Stephen asked.

Jordan's mouth tightened.

"Why not? He's a good guy."

"How do you know?" Jordan challenged. "You don't have to live with him."

"But I sure wish I did," Stephen said.

"I think you're lucky, to live away from your parents. You're your own boss and you can do what you want to without asking permission all the time and having to do chores and..."

Stephen laughed. "You gotta be kidding. That military school has more rules than...than the army!

Jordan frowned. "But you get to wear uniforms...and you get to shoot guns. You told me you had your own rifle! Did you lie?"

"'Course not, but the rifles are locked up and we get them only when we have range practice or competitions, and we use stupid wooden rifles when we have drill." Stephen nodded sagely. "They don't really trust us 'cause we're just kids." He looked around the room. "My room could never get this messy. I'd lose all kinds of privileges. Someday I want to be a slob just like you are." He dropped back to his pillow.

"I ain't a slob," Jordan mumbled.

"And we can't ever say ain't," Stephen added. "We get punished if we don't speak correct English."

The sneer in his voice caught Jordan's ear. "Can I sit there?" he asked, motioning to the foot of Stephen's bed.

"Sure." Stephen sat up, crossing his legs beneath the blankets to make room for Jordan. "Do you miss your father?"

"Yeah. Sometimes I get so mad I hate everyone," Jordan admitted as he sat down. "But I only cried once. That was when Mr. Grasten came with my Aunt Abbie. Mr. Grasten is a great guy. Sometimes I wish he was my dad. 'Course he's already my uncle, but he lives a hundred and seventy miles from here so I don't get to see him much. He has this great big sheep ranch and they take sheep wagons up to the mountains and live in them all summer. He promised me that when I'm older I can be a sheep herder for him."

"I can't imagine my dad living in a sheep wagon," Stephen said. "I think he prefers living in the city."

"That's one reason why he shouldn't hang around my mom," Jordan said. "City dudes don't belong on a farm."

"But my grandpa and grandma Page lived on a farm in New Jersey," Stephen protested. He squinted at Jordan. "I don't think my dad thinks much about farming when he's around your mom."

Jordan curled his lip. "They're always touching and hugging. It makes me wanna puke."

Stephen chuckled. "Adults do that a lot. You watch television out here in the sticks. If you watch the actors real close, you can learn how to kiss a woman."

Jordan stiffened. "I don't want to kiss a woman."

"You will someday. You gotta be ready when girls come on to you. When's your birthday?"

Jordan glanced at the calendar. "September twentieth."

"Really?" Stephen beamed. "Mine is September twenty-fifth. I'm twelve already, but look." They flipped the pages of the calendar backward. "For five days we're the same age. That's crazy, isn't it?"

"Yeah," Jordan replied, sizing the other boy up with new interest. "But I still think your dad should leave my mom alone."

Stephen shook his head. "I don't. If Dad and your mom start hanging around together, I could come stay here." He sighed. "I could leave that stupid school and it would be like having two homes, a mother in Boise, another mother here, and a dad. I think that would be great."

"Well, I don't," Jordan insisted. "I ain't got but one dad and he's dead." Tears filled his eyes and he dropped his gaze. "I just want one mother and one father."

"Sometimes you gotta take what you can," Stephen replied. "When my parents got divorced, I hoped and prayed every night that they would remarry...but they never did. Once, when I was a little kid, Dad stayed over and I was sure they made up, but I was wrong."

"Mom sleeps alone," Jordan said.

"If she and my dad ever start sleeping in the same room, you'd better get ready to have a stepdad," Stephen warned. "If that happens, we could be stepbrothers. Would that be so bad?"

Jordan shrugged. "'Course not, but couldn't we be friends without your dad hanging around my mom?"

"Sure, but I don't think that's what's gonna happen."

"Do you think they want to get married?" Jordan asked.

"They might. You'll have to watch 'em and let me know. I wouldn't mind having your mom for a second mother. She's nice."

"Well, I don't want your dad for a second father," Jordan said stubbornly. He stood up and jumped to the floor and to his bed and turned out the lamp.

The boys lay quietly in the darkness.

"What's wrong with my dad?" Stephen asked.

"Nothing," Jordan replied, not wanting to hurt the other boy's feelings. "My father was the greatest guy in the world and no one can take his place around here. That's for sure. We'd better get to sleep before Mom comes in here again and nags at us." He rolled up in the blankets and pulled them over his head. Through the layers of warmth he heard Stephen call him.

"When I go back to the academy, would you write to me? Some of the kids get letters from their friends."

"Sure," Jordan said. "That way we can both keep track of what's going on around here."

"Deal," Stephen said.

EILEEN GLANCED at the red glow of the digital clock on her nightstand. She had been tossing and turning for an hour, listening to muffled voices coming from her son's room. When the glow coming from under his door was gone, she had turned once more but sleep still eluded her.

Her thoughts drifted back over the events of the day. The embrace in the bathroom quickly overshadowed all the other memories. Dan's touch had ignited a flame and his promise had branded a vision into her mind forever. *No,* she thought, *this can't be happening.*

Her recent habit of locking up the house as a final night-time ritual had been forgotten by the sight of Dan settling down in her living room. She left the bed and pulled on her cream-colored fleece robe, tying the belt tightly around her slender waist, then lifting her loosened hair from inside the robe. She finger-combed it away from her face and tried to calm her emotions.

Sliding her feet into sheepskin slippers, she made her way through the dark hallway and down the stairs. She paused by the bottom step and looked across the large living room, her eyes searching the sofa for movement. Seeing none, she hurried on. In the kitchen, she touched the doorknob and was surprised to find it safely locked. Careful to make no sound, she made her way across the living room to the front door. It, too, was locked.

A movement caught her attention. Dan had turned in his sleep. Silently, she approached the sleeping form. He lay on his back, the blanket up to his chin, his arms forming ridges beneath the blanket. His face was hidden in the darkness of the shadowy room.

She knelt beside him, yearning to touch him. Afraid she might be discovered, she started to rise again.

A hand snaked out and grabbed her wrist. "Did you come to tuck me in?" he whispered. He turned onto his side and lifted the blanket, inviting her into the narrow space between his body and the sofa back.

"No," she whispered.

He pulled her off balance and into his arms.

"I can't stay here," she whispered.

"Just for a few minutes," he murmured near her ear. "I'm lonely down here all by myself."

She slid her arm around his waist and was relieved to find him fully dressed. "Oh, Dan, what am I going to do about you?"

"Enjoy me while you can," he replied. "So what if there are four children sleeping in the house? Can't we still cuddle?"

She muffled a giggle against his chest. "For just a few minutes. That's all," she insisted as they snuggled in each other's arms.

"That's more than I thought I would get," he said.

"I was checking the doors," she explained.

"I locked them," he replied. "It's the city syndrome in me."

"Thank you," she said simply, warming to his nearness. "Can you stay tomorrow?" she asked.

"For the morning. Perhaps Stephen can get his ride on one of the four-wheelers. Are they safe?"

"We've always been very firm with Jordan," she replied. "No hot-rodding. If he even hints at breaking a rule, he loses all privileges. We use them for irrigating and for checking the place when the snow is heavy. They're better than a snowmobile. Any vehicle can be dangerous, if abused."

He kissed her forehead.

"Will you stay for lunch?" she asked.

"Yes, but I'll have to call a tow truck and get my car to a garage in Idaho Falls. I'll get a rental car. I have to get Stephen back to his school Saturday afternoon and head back to Oregon early Sunday morning."

"And I seldom go anywhere except into town for spare parts," she replied. "Our lives are quite a contrast, aren't they? Mine is as routine as yours is exciting."

"Even the excitement of new places and people can get monotonous at times. You're good therapy for me." Dan nuzzled her hair. "This visit has been good for my son too. He's too uptight for a twelve-year-old."

"Because of the military school?"

"A little, but mostly because he's Stephen. The poor kid inherited my cynicism and his mother's discipline and drive. He's a straight A student but he needs a chance to laugh and have fun. When he plays sports at school, he plays to win and forgets to have fun. I worry about him. That damned school has more rules and regulations than the real military. If I had my way I'd yank him out and stick him in a public school. He needs it. The kid is not the least bit streetwise."

"Public schools have their problems, too," Eileen warned, sensing the anger in his voice. "Stephen will work out his problems. Most kids do. Jordan has been under a tremendous strain this summer and fall, but he's adjusting. Did you notice he actually suggested that Stephen stay in his room and borrow his clothing? Maybe he's getting over his jealousy."

Her hand moved up his back, massaging the muscles she could feel beneath his shirt. "Relax," she murmured. "You can't sleep if you're all tense."

A strand of hair fell across her face and she rubbed against his chest, reluctant to remove her hand from his back.

"What's wrong?" he asked.

"My nose itches . . . my hair . . ."

His fingers sought the wayward strands, brushing them away from her forehead and tucking them behind her ear. "Nose itches, kiss a fool," he teased.

She gave him a light peck on his mouth. "Wish granted."

"My wishes are more complex than a chicken peck," he said.

"Oh, really?"

He reached for her belt and deftly untied it. She stopped breathing when his hand slid beneath the fleecy fabric. "I expected flannel," he whispered, "not this gauzy stuff." Halfway up her back, he touched bare skin and she exhaled.

"My nightgown is not gauzy stuff," she said. "It's tricot, and if I'd known we'd be together I would have worn my Doctor Dentons."

"Doctor Dentons?" His fingers found the rounded slope of her shoulder. As he caressed her satin skin, she trembled.

"Doctor Dentons have feet in them," she explained. "Mine are red, with a zipper from my . . . up to my neck."

"They sound like the sleepers Stephen wore when he was a baby. Are you kidding? Do they have them for grownup women?"

She nodded. "I used to wear mine when we went camping or hunting. They're very warm, and much safer when a woman is around someone with creeping fingers."

"I resent you calling my fingers creeping. I'm caressing you. Can't you tell the difference?"

He traced her collar bone. Her breathing quickened and she knew she was playing a dangerous game.

"Is the front as low as the back?" he asked, raising himself on one elbow. Her body rolled beneath him. He gazed down at her. "I think you're ravishing." His head dipped and he touched the skin between her breasts with his mouth.

Her hand tightened on his shirt. "How do you know?" she asked. "It's so dark in here you can't see me."

"I have a good imagination," he replied. "I've seen your hips when you wear jeans. They're rounded like a woman's should be. Your waist is small, especially considering you've had three children." He slid his finger beneath the thin shoulder strap of her gown and eased it down. Cupping her breast in his palm he caressed its fullness with his lips.

"I'm not very well endowed," she whispered.

"You're perfect." His mouth opened against her skin. "You're so warm," he murmured. "So warm." Bathing her skin with his tongue, he encircled her nipple. When finally he took it in his mouth, it was hard and responsive.

She moaned, burying her hands in his hair as she guided his movements and urged him to seek her other breast.

He complied, savoring it, rolling it between his teeth before gently sucking it into full erection. His hand slid down over her hip and thigh. As he kissed her throat, she pressed harder against him, wanting to explore the depths of arousal with him.

His fingers began to gather the skirt of her gown, and her bones turned to jelly. The erotic sensations surged through her, and she had to force herself to deal with the full ramifications of what they were doing.

Attuned to Eileen's emotions, Dan's hand stopped. His breathing was as ragged as hers when he smoothed her gown and replaced the shoulder strap. Holding her tightly against him, he rolled over, bringing her to the outside of the sofa cushions.

He tossed the blanket over the back of the sofa and adjusted her robe, folding one lapel primly over the other.

"Thank you," she whispered. "I didn't intend this to go as far as it did. Please believe me."

"I know you didn't." He smoothed her hair back from her face. "When I make love to you, we'll be alone, with no fear of intrusion. And the lights will be on because I want to see you when I love you, to see the passion in your eyes. There are enough secrets hidden in a woman's body without compounding them with darkness. I want to discover your secrets, learn how to bring you pleasure, hold you when we find satisfaction in each other's arms."

"Oh, Dan," Eileen murmured, pressing her face against his chest, her thoughts and her body suddenly alive with the images his words evoked.

"I half expected you to ask to come to my room," she said after they were silent for quite a few minutes.

"I wanted an invitation," he replied.

"I just couldn't."

"I know," he said. "I wouldn't compromise you in front of your children."

Reluctantly, she withdrew from his arms and sat up, perching on the edge of the cushion. She felt his fingers in her hair, smoothing it down her back.

"I should braid it again . . . or cut it all off," she said.

"No. Long hair is sexy."

"But it's a nuisance."

"I can see that, especially when you're busy during the day, but at night . . ." His hand sought her cheek. "Don't cut it until I've made love to you at least once."

She took his hand in hers and cupped it in her lap. "You sound so sure . . . that we'll . . . be lovers . . . someday."

He sat up and turned her around. "Do you believe in visions?"

"I used to. . . now I don't know."

"I had one the first time I saw you," he said, tightening his grip on her shoulders. "I know, Eileen, you were a married woman and I was a stranger."

"Please, Dan, don't say this. It sounds as if we've plotted for this to happen. I didn't!"

"Perhaps predestined, never plotted."

"But when people realize you and I met a year before Duncan passed away, they'll think we . . ."

"Damn the gossips," he said, shaking her.

"They're real. I'm not sure this is."

"Then we'll give them nothing on which to speculate," he said. "Now, you'd better get upstairs before all this talk of good behavior goes out the window. Good night, Eileen."

Her hand slid from his and she backed away from the sofa. He ached with regret as his gaze followed the glow of her robe and she ran up the stairs in the darkness.

CHAPTER TEN

THE HOUSE WAS QUIET the next morning when Dan Page awoke. Had it all been a dream, or had he held her in his arms, caressed her, explored the slopes of her body?

He tried to concentrate on the problems of the coming day and ignore the responses of his own body. His careless driving had damaged the car. If he had been paying attention to road conditions instead of thinking about Eileen, the accident might never have happened. The car would be out of commission for several weeks, just when he needed it most. He had planned to drive south from Oregon to do a story about the rice-growing area of central California. Stephen would be spending the Christmas holiday with his mother and Dan preferred to keep busy rather than dwell on the family he no longer had.

He stretched and smiled. The stories that intrigued him most were those involving people close to the soil: people who fed the world but who did so with little recognition; people with inner strength and determination to survive regardless of the indifference of urban society. He had lived in both worlds and wanted them to be in harmony but at times he wondered if they were destined for a collision course.

Folding the blankets, he carried them down the hallway and stuffed them into a linen closet along with the pillow he and Eileen had enjoyed.

In the hall bathroom, he ran his palm over the bristles of his beard. Rummaging in the medicine chest and under the vanity, he searched for a razor. Even a throwaway plastic one would do, but he found none. A swish of mouthwash would have to do until he got home to his own toothbrush. He pulled the maroon sweater over his head and down over the rumpled shirt. Accepting the limitations of his morning grooming, he went to the kitchen.

As he enjoyed the aroma of perking coffee, Dan searched the cupboards for a cup. He glanced at the large, apple-shaped clock on the wall. Eight o'clock. *So much for early-rising farmers,* he thought, smiling as he envisioned Eileen asleep.

Suddenly the sound of an engine caught his ear and he looked up. In the distance a snowmobile was breaking trail through the pristine white. Stopping at the farm entrance a quarter of a mile away from where Dan waited, the snow-mobile's operator shoved a rolled-up paper into a holder attached to the post just beneath the official mailbox.

Dan considered trudging through the drifts to retrieve the paper and discarded the idea. The news was probably negative anyway.

A knock on the kitchen door brought his head up with a start. He unlocked the door and pulled it open. Eileen's foreman Hogan Waite filled the doorway.

"Mrs. Mills here?" Hogan asked, frowning.

"She's still asleep."

Hogan's gaze scanned the empty kitchen behind Dan's shoulder.

"Can I help?" Dan asked.

"Doubt it."

Dan motioned for the man to enter. "I'm sure she will be down soon. We were up late . . . talking."

Hogan's blue gaze returned to Dan's face and the small bandage still on his temple.

"I wrecked my car," Dan added. "It's stuck about a mile from here. My son and I walked back here last night."

"Where's the boy?"

"He's in Jordan's room."

Hogan squinted at Dan but didn't say a word.

"I spent the night on the sofa," Dan added, wondering why he felt an explanation was needed. "Want a cup of coffee?"

Hogan nodded. "Sure. Mrs. Mills and I usually discuss the day's activities about this time. She never sleeps this late."

"She was tired," Dan said. "Yesterday was a trying day."

"Yeah," Hogan agreed. "That talk at dinner got out of hand. I felt sorry for Mrs. Mills. She's a sensitive woman. I'm surprised to see you still here after all that was said."

Dan wasn't used to feeling defensive. "I had planned to leave. I certainly didn't wreck my car on purpose."

Hogan took a sip of coffee. "I can get one of the tractors and try to pull you out."

"Thanks," Dan replied. "I'd planned to call a tow truck this morning."

"Those things cost bucks. We'll try this first," Hogan said.

They heard footsteps on the stairs and Eileen appeared, looking beautiful in a heather bulky-knit sweater and jeans. A single neat braid held her hair in place. Her eyes were bright but her warm smile froze when she spotted Dan Page and Hogan Waite sitting at the small kitchen table.

"Good morning," she murmured, her gaze swinging from Dan to Hogan and back to Dan. "I overslept."

"Good morning," Dan said, pulling a chair out for her.

"Page was telling me about his accident," Hogan said.

"Yes. Could you . . . ?"

"We've already made the arrangements," Dan said. "Someone has to take charge when the lady of the manor is sleeping in."

She blushed, then smiled. "I'd offer you Duncan's shaver but . . . I gave all of his clothing away. . . last month."

"That's fine," he replied, wanting to put her at ease.

She turned her attention to Hogan. "Is everything all right outside? Did the storm do any damage?"

He shrugged. "We were ready for the storm, but I'm still keeping an eye on one of the cellars."

"Which one?"

Dan broke in. "I thought you had sold all your spuds for this year."

"All but one cellar and part of another," she explained. "One of the buyers had to back out due to financing. I'm looking for another buyer."

"Oh." Dan watched her exchange glances with Hogan, and wondered what was going on.

"Breakfast, guys?" she asked. "The children are on their way down. I promised them scrambled eggs and hash-browns."

"I've eaten," Hogan said. "The temperature in the full cellar goes up and down. If it keeps heating up, we'll have to move the spuds and find out what's causing it."

"Why would the temperature go up?" Dan asked.

"Probably a few rotting spuds," Hogan said. "It happens."

"They get cut and the wound decays instead of healing over," Eileen explained. "Or maybe a few are frozen. They were caught in the field when the frost hit in October. We tried to find them all but if some slipped through, they could cause problems."

"Yeah," Hogan said. "Once I saw a whole cellar collapse into a pile of stinking spoilage."

Eileen made a face. "I've heard about that happening. This business couldn't handle a loss like that."

"What's the latest word from the attorney on that other matter?" Hogan asked.

Dan stared at Eileen as she busied herself in the kitchen.

"He's still investigating," Eileen said. "I might have to take a loss. It's going to hurt. I had plans for that money...but we'll manage. It's been a good year."

"What money? What situation? What happened?" Dan asked.

"It's nothing," Eileen said, giving him a brilliant smile. "Just part of doing business."

Before Dan could inquire further, the room was filled with noisy children who were anxious for breakfast. He let the subject drop, but only for the moment.

"Let me help," he said, taking the bacon and scrambled eggs to the table. "Stephen, have Jordan show you where the toaster is. If we eat, we work. Anyone who doesn't help now gets to clean up after breakfast. Girls, can you set the table?"

"Sure, Mr. Page," Jolene said.

A whirl of activity surrounded Eileen, leaving her with only a pan of potatoes frying on the stove to worry about. What a difference Dan's presence made! Her children were helpful, but usually needed a nudge to get them moving.

After breakfast, Dan left with Hogan and one of the other men.

"Why don't you kids go out and play while I clean up here?" Eileen asked.

"Can we give Stephen a ride on one of the snowmobiles?" Jolene asked.

Jordan laughed. "You certainly can't. You're not old enough. Dad always said we had to be at least ten."

Jolene stuck her tongue out at her brother and he tried to grab it. She attempted to bite his finger and came perilously close to succeeding.

"Children, stop that," Eileen cautioned. "Jordan, if you'll give Stephen a lesson in operating the four-wheelers, and if you let the girls sit behind you, and stay close in the yard and on flat ground, and don't go any faster than..."

"Ah, Mom, you put so many restrictions on us, it's no fun," Jordan said, but the sparkle in his blue eyes told Eileen that he was enjoying himself.

"You know our rules," she reminded him. "Safety first, fun second. No exception."

"Don't worry, Mrs. Mills," Stephen said. "I assure you I'll be very careful and not damage the vehicle or injure Jordan's sisters. I've had a good time. I like it here." He ducked his head briefly then met her gaze directly. "I wasn't sure I would."

She touched his shoulder. "I'm glad. You're welcome to come back any time." She returned her attention to her own children. "Stephen has to leave right after lunch."

The children groaned in unison as they left the warm kitchen.

Shortly before lunch, the men returned.

"We have it out," Hogan said.

"But I can't drive it," Dan said. "I'll have to call a tow truck. Can I use your phone?"

"Sure," she replied. "Use the phone in my office. It's the second door past the hall bathroom. It will be quieter in there."

Dan found the room, looked in the yellow pages of the classified section, selected a garage at random, and dialed the number. As he waited for an answer, his gaze fell to the desk. He tried to ignore the papers lying scattered on the desk, but the words on several bank notices leaped out at him. He scanned the top notice of insufficient funds, his eyes widening when he read the amount of her overdraft.

He whistled softly. The owner of the garage came to the phone and Dan concentrated on telling the man his location. As he listened to the estimate, Dan lifted the top notice and read the one below. Skimming through the stack, he counted five notices in all. How in the world could Eileen be so jubilant about the successful season when her bank account was overdrawn for such a staggering amount?

He thanked the man at the garage. "I'll be out there at one. Sorry to disturb your holiday weekend."

"Happens all the time," the owner assured him.

Dan replaced the receiver and turned, the bank notices still in his hand.

Eileen was standing in the doorway, her attention on the pieces of paper he held.

"Did you make your call?" she asked, not looking at his face.

"Yes." He waved the slips in the air. "What are these?"

"Nothing. I've taken care of them," she said.

Her stiff stance said more to him than her response. "A bank doesn't issue these without cause."

"That's my business. You have no right to rummage through my records."

"I wasn't rummaging. They were out in plain view."

"I told you I've taken care of them," she insisted. "Now please give them to me." She held out her hand.

"How does one take care of an overdraft of ninety-six thousand dollars, Eileen?"

Her chin protruded slightly. "I sold some more potatoes."

"And what caused the overdraft in the first place?"

"That's personal," she said. "My attorney recommended I keep the case confidential."

"You won't explain?" Dan dropped the notices into her open palm.

"No."

"Eileen, if I can help you, let me."

She opened the center drawer of the desk and jammed the notices inside, then slammed the door shut. "It's my problem. I'll solve it myself."

"If your account became overdrawn that much at one chunk, you must have already used the money," he said, guessing the sequence of events that might have taken place. "Did you pay off some loans?"

She ignored his question.

"Most farmers are in debt," he persisted. "Are you?"

"I've taken on no new debt since Duncan's death."

"Did Duncan leave you with loans you can't pay off?"

"Duncan didn't mean . . . he couldn't have foreseen . . ." She whirled away, her back rigid.

Dan wracked his brain for the right words. "We talked about debt ratios during the early interview. Duncan said he was tight but manageable. Was that true, or did he minimize the situation?"

"Sort of."

"Sort of true, or sort of understated? What is your debt ratio? Don't bankers restrict their loans to forty percent of your assets?"

"I'm a little above that limit," she admitted.

"Did he borrow when land values were inflated?" he asked. "Has the value of your assets declined?"

"Hasn't everyone's?"

"How many loans do you have?" he asked.

"Several."

"On the land, equipment, the crop, the house? What, Eileen?" He spun her around to face her. "Which ones have been used as collateral?"

"All of them."

"Are they delinquent?"

'Some are...but I can handle them," she said. "The banks have been very understanding. I already have a commitment for next spring's line of credit...and I'm letting two of the seasonal men go. Hogan is going back to Alaska in a few weeks. He'll be gone for three months, and Ben likes to go part-time in the off season. So, you see, I'll be here alone with the children for a while and we'll get along just fine. Jordan is a big help."

"An eleven-year-boy can't take the place of his father," Dan said.

"No one can."

"Perhaps not," he said pensively. "Farming is hard enough for any man but a woman alone..."

"Just because other farmers have lost their places doesn't mean the Mills farm is going under. I promised Duncan...I'd never...let that happen." *Only I never considered brokers who skipped out on their obligation.*

"Maybe Duncan was asking too much of you," he said gently. Dan tried to take her into his arms, but she pulled away.

"I'll keep my promise...and I don't need your help or sympathy. I can do it by myself." Eileen walked stiffly out of the room, leaving him feeling stunned.

Their tense lunch together consisted of turkey sandwiches and soup.

"How come you two aren't talking anymore?" Jolene asked. "Did you have a fight?"

"Your mother has some problems and I offered to help," Dan said. "She's declined."

Eileen said nothing.

"Can Stephen come for Christmas?" Jordan asked.

Dan shook his head. "His mother is taking him to Acapulco for the holidays. She promised him last summer. They're flying down with some friends."

"Can't they change their plans and go later?" Jordan pleaded.

"No," Dan said. "Van . . . Stephen's mother doesn't like last-minute changes and this trip was Stephen's idea. His mother tries to keep her promises." His gaze shifted to Eileen, but her bowed head hid her features.

"If he wasn't going there, could he come here, Mom?" Jordan asked. "Stephen said his dad was coming here anyway."

"That's enough, Jordan," Eileen exclaimed. She glanced at Dan, then at his son. "Of course, they would be welcome, but I'm sure they have already made other plans."

"I didn't," Dan said, "but I'll come up with something." He rose from his chair. "Stephen, go get ready. The wrecker will be at the car at one. We should be there so he doesn't have to wait around."

"I can drive you," Eileen said.

"I've already made arrangements with Hogan," Dan replied.

As they waited outside on the porch for Hogan to bring one of the farm trucks around, Dan turned to Eileen. "I'm sorry," he said. "I was out of line to inquire about those notices."

She shrugged nonchalantly.

As he heard the sound of the truck's engine start, he touched her arm. "About last night . . ."

"Another mistake," she said. "Perhaps we see too much of each other."

"Three times in six months? That's too much?" Dan grabbed her shoulders and stepped between her and the yard, blocking the view of the laughing children. "Look at me, please."

Slowly, she raised her head. The wounded expression in her eyes tore at his heart. "It doesn't have to be this way."

A tear trickled down her cheek and he wiped it away with his finger. "Maybe I walked back into your life at the wrong time," he admitted. "I don't know. But even if you did rebound from Duncan's death right into my arms, I was there because I wanted to be. I know the risks, but damn it, I care about you."

She shook her head. "You'll get over it."

"I don't want to get over it," he persisted. "Maybe I'm falling in love with you, I don't know. I worry about you, as a woman struggling alone, as a friend. It scares the hell out of me when I see you playing the brave, determined widow, all stiff and uncompromising, trying to fulfill the promises you made to Duncan on his deathbed."

"Don't talk that way," she cried.

"Well, damn it," he hissed, "I've made you a promise, too, and I intend to keep it. It's just as important as all the other promises that have been made around this godforsaken piece of lava ground."

"A promise to make love is just a promise for sex. I don't need it. You can find it somewhere else," she said.

"That's not what I meant and you know it." Dan pulled her against him. "Do you hear me?"

"Yes," she murmured, her chin trembling. "Sometimes I feel so inadequate." Her arms slid around his waist and tightened.

"We all do at times, sweetheart," he replied, rubbing his hand up and down her jacketed back.

"I had visions, too, at one time," she sobbed. "When I was a child in Kentucky and dreamed of getting away, when I got a scholarship in spite of my poor education. I was so proud each time I got an A in one of my college courses. I wanted to take my grade notices back to that school board and wave them under their noses and let them know that I was intelligent enough to make it in spite of the system back home."

"Don't torture yourself, Eileen," he said.

"But it's true," she said. "I was as much of a dreamer as Abbie. We used to talk about our futures when we were kids, when we would sneak away to this little secret cave where we could be alone and we would promise to help each other and we had such grand plans for our futures. I thought I had it all when Duncan and I came west to start our lives together, but now those visions have vanished...gone forever...and here I am alone, with three children to raise and I don't know if I can do it right and keep this place going and...and sometimes I even question if I actually loved Duncan or just took advantage of his offer to escape my home town." She looked up at him. "Is that why I lost him?"

"No, of course not, but maybe questioning your love and loyalty is your way of justifying your loss." He shook his head. "Sometimes there are no easy answers." He cupped her chin in his hand. "You have a friend at the end of the phone line. Call me."

She smiled through her tears. "You're seldom home."

"Then I'll call you." His lips brushed hers. "I promise."

She touched the day's growth of reddish beard on his cheek. "I didn't mean to turn into a crybaby."

"Everyone needs a release at times. You can't hold it in. If you do, it will eat away at you."

She touched his mouth with her finger. "Yes, Doctor Page."

"Is the patient listening?" he asked. "Really listening?"

"She'll try." She smiled gamely. "Will you spend Christmas with us?" she asked.

"If I'm welcome."

"Yes, oh yes."

"Then I'll do my best to drop in . . . if I'm in the area, I promise." He grinned, shaking his brown head. "I'm accumulating quite a string of promises. Maybe if I take them in reverse order and keep them, I can get back to my first promise to you. That's the most important one . . . for both of us. I can't envision when or where but if you'll hold that vision inside, in your mind, in your heart, it will come true."

He held her face close to his, his palms on her cheeks.

Her hands touched his. "I wish I had more confidence," she whispered.

"Then I'll give you some of mine," he said.

"If only it were that easy, Dan. It's my sack of problems and it's up to me to carry them."

"If you change your mind and want my help, call me. Two heads can be better than one, and if you won't let me help you, at least think of me." His mouth was hard against hers when he first kissed her, but gradually his lips softened, caressing hers until she trembled against him.

"Goodbye, sweetheart." He turned away before she could see his face again. In minutes he was gone.

JORDAN SIDLED UP to his mother. "Mom, remember that A I made on my math paper?"

"Yes, dear, it was great," she replied absently. "Keep up the good work."

"Is your phone bill all paid for this month?" he asked.

"Yes, dear."

"Can I call Stephen long distance?"

"Yes, dear...what?" She turned to him. "Call Stephen? Why?"

Jordan shrugged. "Just to talk. I have his number at the military academy. He can only get calls from seven to eight on Mondays and Thursdays."

"Okay, but set the microwave timer first and your limit is fifteen minutes," she said.

He nodded. "Thanks, Mom. You're a fox."

A fox? Hoping the term was a compliment, she glanced at her watch, then returned her attention to the book she'd been reading.

In the kitchen, Jordan dialed Stephen's number and waited impatiently for the woman who answered the phone to send for him. He glanced at the kitchen clock. Four minutes had passed by the time Stephen answered.

"Did you ask your mom?" Jordan said.

"Yeah, but she refused to budge an inch," Stephen said.

"Can't you try again? We only have two weeks vacation," Jordan said. "What's so great about flying to Mexico if you don't want to go?"

"Yeah, but she says it was all my idea to go in the first place." Stephen took a deep breath and exhaled loudly in Jordan's ear. "She's right. I guess we'll have to try for next summer."

"Geez. Well, start saving your money, okay?" Jordan asked. "That way if she or your dad won't bring you, you can ride the bus. Do you get an allowance?"

"Yeah, but she makes me save half of it," Stephen said. "What good is getting an allowance if you can't spend it? It sounds stupid to me, but I'd never tell my mom that. She'd kill me if I did. All the people at her company think she's a financial wizard."

The buzzer on the microwave sounded. "I gotta go," Jordan said. "Send me a card, will ya?" he asked and hastily said a final goodbye.

"ARE YOU SURE you'll be all right, Mrs. Mills?" Hogan Waite asked, tossing his battered suitcase into the back of his older model pickup truck. "I could tell my sister I can't come this year."

"No, that isn't necessary," Eileen said, extending her hand.

He accepted it, giving it a slight squeeze. "You people are like family. It doesn't feel right leaving you alone."

"We'll be fine, I'm sure," she replied.

"Keep an eye on that cellar, ma'am," he warned, glancing over his shoulder. "Something going on there. I think we should have re-sorted the spuds. We might have found the problem. I wouldn't want to come back and find out you had lost them all."

She laughed. "That won't happen, Hogan. The buyer is coming right after Christmas. He's bringing his company's own trucks and the cellars will all be empty when you come back. Have a good trip. Drive carefully to Seattle and enjoy the flight to Alaska."

She stepped back and watched him climb into the cab of the truck. He waved once as he shifted the gears into reverse, then drove away.

Completely alone for the first time in months, Eileen listened to the silence. Uncertainty and misgivings filled her as she thought about carrying the full responsibility of the farm. Was she really capable? Why not? Hadn't she kept the books for years? Worked alongside Duncan and the hired help during spring planting and fall harvesting? Of course, she was capable and it was silly of her to think otherwise. A duck quacked and flapped his wings. One of the mares grazing in the alfalfa stubble whinnied.

Feeling less isolated and much more confident now, she turned toward the suspect cellar. Should she hire some temporary help and discover once and for all the reason for the temperature fluctuation?

The distant ringing of the phone in the house interrupted her and she ran to the back porch and into the kitchen.

"Hello?"

"Hi," Daniel Page's voice said. "How is your day going?"

She had heard from him only once since his departure in November. "I'm fine. Where are you calling from?"

"John Day, Oregon."

She laughed. "What are you doing there?"

"Research. Did you know the place was named after a crazy man?"

"No, and I can't say that I care either."

"I'm crushed," he said. "To think I took time out from my busy schedule to call this spud lady I know in the next state and she expresses her lack of interest in my work."

"Dan, you're as crazy as this John Day person...but I'm glad you called." She twirled the phone cord around her hand.

"Have you missed me?"

"A little."

"Crushed again."

She glanced at the calendar nearby. "Christmas is only four days away," she said. "If you're in Oregon, I suppose you're too far away to...be in the area?"

"Well," he hedged, "I do have these gifts cluttering up the back of this rental car, and I need to return the car and pick up my own vehicle, so I might...drop by."

"Gifts? Who are they for?" she asked, feeling herself being caught up in the holiday mood.

"A couple of pretty little girls," he explained. "Funny, they look just alike...except for this birthmark...rumor says their mother has one too, only they won't tell me where."

She laughed.

"Their brother is almost the same age as my son, so I got him some sports equipment. A boy can always use a basketball, can't he? I noticed a hoop without a net mounted on the side of an old milking barn."

"He will love that," she said. "His basketball has a hole in it. He's talked a lot about Stephen. He's still a little uncertain about you, but he and Stephen have become friends. They've exchanged letters and I let him call long distance once. He could only talk for fifteen minutes. How much mischief can two boys make in fifteen minutes?"

"Time will tell," he replied. "Now about his skinny little mother..."

"Skinny? I'm not skinny!" Her hand touched the regained fullness of her breasts. "I've gained a few more pounds."

"In all the right places?"

"And what are the right places?" she asked.

"I'll tell you when I get there," he promised. "I'll try to get there on Christmas Eve as early in the afternoon as possible."

"Plan to spend the night," she suggested.

"Spend the night? Are you sure?"

She laughed. "I cleaned out a spare bedroom on the first floor. It should be more comfortable than that lumpy sofa."

He chuckled. "That lumpy sofa has good memories for me."

She sighed. "Well, you're stuck with the official guest room. It's more private, too. The door locks from the inside."

"Will you come tuck me in?" he teased.

"We'll see. Now I suppose you have work to do," she said. "I know I do. Farm chores are never done for long."

"I suppose not. Yes, I have an appointment down the street from my motel in thirty minutes. I'll see you on Christmas Eve, sweet lady."

CHAPTER ELEVEN

EILEEN SAT at the desk, staring at the reconciled balance in the checking account and wondering how she could stretch the amount to cover the two loan payments due a few days after Christmas, keep enough in reserve for unexpected emergencies, and get a check into the mail to the mechanic's shop for rebuilding the engine on one of the spud trucks. *Wouldn't it be lovely to just order a new truck, like Duncan used to do?*

"Never count your chickens before they hatch," she murmured aloud. *Daddy's old adage is right* she thought. Until the buyer's trucks arrived a few days after Christmas and hauled away the last of the spuds, she was reluctant to consider the various uses she had for the money. She knew it would be gone quickly.

If only Duncan had not taken out that last loan, the loan he had felt was necessary when he could no longer work in the fields alongside his men. He had replaced one of the harvesters with a new model with automatic features that would enable fewer employees to do more work. They had sold the older harvester to a neighbor. That money had quickly been consumed by day-to-day expenses and Duncan had also purchased a new spud truck.

The phone rang. "Yes?" she said, her thoughts still on the debts hanging over her.

"Mrs. Mills, this is Quincy, Harold Quincy, from Western Provision. I'm calling about the spuds we were scheduled to pick up next week."

Eileen was enveloped by a foreboding cloud. "Of course. Why? You are coming, aren't you?"

"Well, Mrs. Mills, we're swamped here under spuds. Our workers are going twenty-four hours a day, seven days a week, but frankly, we've overbought. We had contracts with most of our growers and of course those get our first attention. You know, Mrs. Mills, this was a bumper year for spuds."

"Of course I know that," she said, "but why is that a factor in your coming for my spuds?"

"Our buyer was overzealous when he offered to buy all you had," Quincy explained.

"But he said..."

"Did he give you a written order?"

"No, but...I thought his word was good, that he represented your firm and that you would...stand behind his commitment." Thoughts of the unscrupulous broker from New York surfaced.

"We do, I assure you we do," Quincy said.

"Mr. Quincy," Eileen said, running her hand across her forehead, "do you want my potatoes or not? If not I'll have to start looking for another buyer immediately."

"We would like to have them if you can wait a week or two before we pick them up," he said.

"Two weeks? How firm is that date?" she asked.

"Well, we might have to bump it again if the plant stays swamped like it is now. You see, one of our lines has been down. One of the machines..."

"Mr. Quincy, I have my own problems here, too. When could you come?"

"I'm sure we would have them out of your cellars by the end of January," he said.

"End of January!" she cried. "That's more than a month past the date we agreed on. I need that money." She clamped her mouth shut and took a deep breath. "I'll need a deposit, earnest money, something to show your good faith, Mr. Quincy."

"Now, now, Mrs. Mills," Quincy replied. "Have we ever had to resort to a deposit before? Your husband and I have done a lot of business together over the years and we made our agreements over a handshake or a phone call."

"But a handshake means very little right now."

He snorted in her ear. "I must say, your husband was a lot easier to do business with than you are. I realize you're inexperienced in all this and—"

"Mr. Quincy," she cut in, "what you and my husband did in the past is irrelevant. I need a commitment from you, either in the form of a deposit or in writing. I turned down two offers after your buyer was here. It's costing me money each day I store the spuds. Are you willing to do what I request?"

He cleared his throat. "Under the circumstances, why don't we consider our deal off," Quincy said. "If you haven't found a buyer by late January, I'll probably be willing to take them. Of course the price may drop and . . . well, frankly I can find other growers who are more cooperative. Goodbye, Mrs. Mills."

She replaced the receiver and dropped her head into her hands, trying to relax enough to stop the pounding in her temples. *What have I done? Screwed up the only opportunity to empty the cellars?*

The phone rang again.

"Mrs. Mills, this is Idaho Farmers' Equipment Leasing calling. We just want to confirm that you'll be bringing your account up to date on the pivot systems by the end of the year. We've extended both payments twice now and . . ."

"Yes! I'll get the money to you somehow," she almost shouted. Before the man on the phone could respond, she slammed the receiver down and ran from the room. As the kitchen door banged behind her, she heard the phone ringing again.

She didn't stop running until she collided with the rear of an empty cellar. The jarring of the hard dirt wall brought her back to reality. The world was closing in around her. Feeling the utter defeat of everything she had tried to accomplish since Duncan's death, she gave in to tears. Just a year ago, she had sat beside Duncan's bed and made promises to him, holding his weak hand, nodding, her heart breaking as she watched him stop and rest, his strength so depleted that even talking was difficult for him. Now he was dead.

Tears streamed down her face as she sank to the dirt floor of the cellar and sat in the darkness, succumbing to her misery.

Why am I here alone? Why won't the creditors leave me alone, just for a little while? Why can't I sell the place and leave? Why can't I just walk away from all this? Do I have to keep these promises I made?

Sobs continued to wrack her body until there were no more tears to shed. Her head throbbed. She felt as if her skull was about to explode and she wished it would. Perhaps then she would find peace.

JODIE'S SHRILL SCREAM and Jolene's laughter awoke her. Disoriented for a moment, Eileen sat up, rubbing the arm she had rested her head on when she had lain down on the cellar floor.

Pushing herself to her feet, she vowed not to let anything or anyone push her to the depths of despair she had found herself in just hours ago.

It's not worth the price, she thought. *The children need me. Who will take care of them if I don't? Who cares about them and loves them as much as I do? What if I do lose the farm? Won't life go on for us? Somewhere else if not here?* She had a university degree, so she could always get a job. Thoughts of herself, at thirty-four years of age, competing in the job market for the first time, against young women like Janice at the bank in Idaho Falls brought a smile to her face. "I can make good coffee, too," she said aloud. "If you can do it, Janice, so can I."

Brushing the dirt from her clothing, she walked out of the cellar and into the bright winter sunlight. Her daughters waved to her from the kitchen porch and she waved back.

No one will push me down again, no one, she vowed. If she walked away, it would be because she wanted to and for no other reason.

Christmas was three days away. She had work to do. Daniel Page would be coming. She would enjoy his company and forget all the pressures for a few days.

EILEEN FROWNED at her daughters as they sat at the kitchen table, stringing popcorn and cranberries on long needles attached to lengths of quilting thread.

"I'll feed the horses and ducks," she said. "You come get me when Dan . . . Mr. Page arrives. Promise?"

"Sure," Jodie said.

"Why do we have to call him Mr. Page?" Jolene asked.

"And what do you suggest?" Eileen asked.

"Dan like you do. I tried Daddy once but it didn't feel right," Jolene said.

"No, that wouldn't be right," Eileen agreed.

"Calling him Mr. Page makes me feel like I'm talking to the principal at school or to Jordan's scout leader," Jolene said, hunching her shoulders as she aimed her needle at the next cranberry. "You know what I mean."

Eileen nodded. "Yes, I know, but children shouldn't call grown-ups by their first names."

"Why not?" Jodie asked.

Eileen cocked her head. "I don't really know... I guess it's just a rule I've always lived with."

"But we've never had someone like Mr. Page around before," Jolene said.

Eileen smiled. "That's for sure, girls. Just keep calling him Mr. Page. Okay?"

The girls nodded.

"But when we talk about him in our room, we call him Dan," Jodie said, grinning at her twin sister.

The girls returned their attention to their task. Eileen watched them work for a few more minutes, then hurried outside to complete the chores early so she could clean up and be waiting when Dan arrived.

As she leaned against the feed trough, watching the horses muzzle the measures of oats she had given them, her thoughts turned to Dan. Her heartbeat increased. What did she feel for him? Friendship? More than friendship? If more, then what? Could she be falling in love with him so soon after losing Duncan? Perhaps it was only a physical attraction between two lonely adults.

They had known each other for almost two years. Admittedly, most of that time had been on a casual basis. Yet, as she thought back to that very first meeting, when he had knocked on her door and introduced himself as the reporter whom she had talked briefly with on the phone, she'd felt an attraction, a kinship, an ability to communicate, without words. More than once they had responded to each other's needs before the other had spoken aloud.

She continued to mull over this ability to sense each other's feelings while she fed the rest of the stock.

Disappointed that the girls had not called her, she put the feed buckets away on their hooks and washed her hands in the old milking barn. What if Dan didn't come? She caught her image in a broken mirror still hanging on the wall above the stained sink.

Patting the wayward strands of hair into place, she leaned closer. Her eyes were bright, her cheeks flushed from the cold air. Her weight gain had removed some of the shadows in the hollows beneath her cheekbones. Perhaps if she hurried, she could shower and change her clothing and hairstyle before Dan arrived. She had sewn a red velvet skirt just for this evening, and bought a creamy silk blouse with a scoop neckline which highlighted the fullness of her breasts.

She ran across the yard and back porch, and into the warm kitchen. "I'm going up to shower. Tell Dan I..."

Dan was sitting at the table, wearing faded jeans and a sports shirt with sage-green and white stripes, and attempting to follow the instructions the twins were giving him to make the arrangement of his string of popcorn and cranberries match theirs.

"You gotta do it right," Jodie warned.

His name stuck in her throat. A surge of emotion raced through her as he rose from his chair and turned. He had mentioned once the secrets of a woman's body and at this moment she was glad to be able to conceal hers.

He smiled and her heart stopped. "Hello," he said.

"Hello," she said, unable to control the tremor in her voice.

"I was going to look for you," he said, "but the girls put me to work."

"I see," she whispered. "I wanted to...tidy up...before you got here."

"You look fine to me," he replied, stepping close to her.

"I'm glad you were in the area," she murmured.

"So am I," he said.

His shoulders hid the girls from her sight. "Would you kiss me?" Her voice was so soft he had to step closer to hear her.

"If you insist," he whispered, his arms settling loosely around her waist. His kiss was light, yet the promise in his eyes told her more than his words.

She scattered kisses on his cheek before searching out his mouth again. "You do strange things to me," she whispered, resting her head against his heaving chest.

"Momma," Jodie said with a giggle, "you and Mr. Page are silly. Aren't they, Jordan?"

Eileen jerked away from Dan and whirled around. Jordan was just inside the kitchen door, staring at them.

Dan took Eileen's hand and led her to the table. "Sorry, kids, but your mother and I haven't seen each other for quite a while. We missed each other."

Jordan went to the sink and filled a glass with water. "Aren't we gonna eat tonight?" he asked, matter-of-factly.

"Of course," Eileen said. "It's all ready, but the girls and I want to shower and change our clothes. You two guys can visit while we're gone." She ushered the twins up the staircase, trying not to think about the wisdom of leaving Dan and her son together.

In the kitchen, Jordan peeked beneath the foil that was covering two trays of food on the counter.

"Does it look good?" Dan asked, trying to make conversation.

Jordan grunted as he retrieved a toothpick with two melon balls on its spear and popped the fruit into his mouth.

"Have you and Stephen stayed in touch?" Dan asked.

"Yeah."

"What do you talk about?" Dan asked.

"Nothing." The boy grunted something under his breath and left the room without a backward glance.

So much for trying to be sociable, Dan thought. He left the kitchen. In the living room, he admired the holiday decorations. The gold star atop the Christmas tree touched the ceiling and tilted slightly. The tree was decorated with lights and traditional ornaments handmade by the children.

Dan smiled, thinking back to his own family's Christmases. They had been traditional American affairs mixed with French and Irish customs. When he and Van had married, she had always insisted on an artificial tree each year, with color-coordinated ornaments that harmonized with the damned Queen Anne furniture she had begun to collect. Her yuletide style was not at all appropriate for an inquisitive toddler like Stephen.

Vanessa would have considered this room quaint to say the least, but he liked it. Its warm mood was perfect for his bone-weary body and spirit.

The rustle of velvet caught his ear and he looked up. Eileen was descending the stairs, a vision of Christmas. She had pulled her cinnamon-brown hair back from her temples and fastened it with a garnet-jeweled comb high on the back of her head, the rest of her hair falling free down her back.

An old-fashioned oval-shaped locket, suspended on a gold chain, rested against the creamy skin of her breasts an inch above the scooped neckline of a while silk blouse. The blouse's long sleeves gathered at her wrists. His eyes were drawn downward to the deep red full skirt that accented her small waist. The skirt fell to her ankles but above the hem was a six-inch inset of contrasting holiday colors in a diagonal Seminole pieced design.

He came to the landing. "You look lovely."

"Thank you," she murmured. "Just a little something I whipped up because I was expecting a gentleman caller," she said, in a distinct Southern accent.

"If you're trying to seduce me, you're succeeding, ma'am." He bowed slightly and assisted her down the final step. "I'm forever grateful I was in the area today." He kissed her cheek lightly, inhaling the subtle fragrance of her cologne.

The twins raced down the stairs, skidding to a stop inches from where Dan and Eileen were standing. Their skirts were miniature designs of Eileen's but in dark forest-green velvet.

"You two young ladies look almost as pretty as your mother," Dan said, bowing again to each of them.

"Will you kiss our hands like they do in old movies?" Jolene asked. When he complied, they giggled.

Jordan came down the stairs behind his sisters. He had replaced his shirt with a green knitted pullover sweater. "Can we eat?" he asked. "And don't try to kiss my hand," he warned.

After dinner they all gathered around the tree.

"When does everyone go to bed around here?" Dan asked.

Jolene, who had been rearranging the packages beneath the tree, leaned back on her heels. "We get to stay up late tonight."

"How can Santa Claus come if you're all still up?" Dan asked.

"Santa doesn't come here anymore," Jodie explained. "Momma takes care of all that stuff. She says she can only afford to spend so much, so we don't ask for much."

Eileen laughed. "That is a matter of opinion, my dear."

Dan feigned disappointment. "Modern youth," he said with a deep sigh. "No imagination at all."

Jordan slouched in a corner chair, listening but not saying a word.

Dan rose from the sofa. "Jordan, can you help me bring in some things from my car? Someone here has to believe in Santa."

Jordan shrugged and followed Dan out the door. When they returned, they were laden with packages. As they arranged the new gifts around the tree, Jordan turned to his sisters. "These three are mine and you aren't to touch them."

The twins sorted out the rest of the packages, stacking them according to the names on the tags. Jolene turned to her mother. "There's only one here for you, Momma, I mean from Mr. Page. And it's so little." She shook the gold-foil-wrapped package.

"Never underestimate the value of a small package," Dan said. "I have more but not for Christmas," he said. "We can look at them tomorrow after the excitement is over."

Jordan frowned. "He's spending the night?"

"Your mother invited me to stay. . . yes," Dan replied.

"Does he have to sleep in my room?" Jordan asked.

Eileen stood up. "Dan will be sleeping in the guest room down the hall."

"That's your sewing room," Jodie said. "What did you do with all your stuff?"

"I moved it into the room across the hall," Eileen replied.

"But that was the room where...Dad...stayed...when he was...too sick to go upstairs," Jordan said.

"Yes," Eileen said. She brushed at her skirt. "It's time to go to bed. All of you," she insisted.

"Me, too?" Dan asked.

"Yes, you too," she replied. "I have Santa work to do for about an hour and I can't do it if curious eyes are looking on. Off with you all."

The children ran up the stairs without a protest, but Dan lingered. "You didn't really mean me, too," he said.

She smiled. "Yes, I did."

"But..." he said, "I thought you'd at least tuck me in."

Her face was expressionless. "Perhaps later."

He glanced over his shoulder at her once more before accepting her wish to be alone. He had expected some quiet, private time with her after the children had been sent to bed, time to talk intimately, to hold her in his arms. He knew that to expect full intimacy with her tonight would be wishful thinking, but he was willing to wait until the time was right.

In the guest room, Dan undressed and slid between the sheets, but when he turned out the lamp, sleep would not come. He turned the light back on and reached for the first book his fingers touched on the shelf above the headboard.

It was a historical novel set in early Idaho. It wasn't a bad writing job, he decided, finding himself becoming engrossed in the plot and characters. He glanced at his watch. An hour and a half had passed and the house had grown quiet.

He returned his attention to the book, trying to stifle the urge to get dressed and go upstairs and find her. He yearned to be with her, console her, yet he was honest enough to admit that tonight there was only one thought paramount in his mind.

He adjusted his position and sat up higher against the pillows. The blankets fell to his waist and he left them there as he tried to concentrate on the story unfolding. The room grew warm and he shoved his left leg from beneath the blankets and pulled it up, resting his fist on his bent knee.

Images of Eileen asleep upstairs intruded and he pushed them aside. He heard movement in the hall outside his door and glanced up. A soft tap sounded against the wood.

"Come in," he said.

The door opened and Eileen stepped inside, closing it softly behind her. She was wearing the white fleecy robe. Her eyes were dark, her cheeks flushed.

Excitement raced through him and he tossed the book onto the floor. "Lock it," he said.

She leaned against the door. "I did."

CHAPTER TWELVE

EILEEN QUESTIONED her own good sense as she looked across the room to where Dan reclined against the headboard.

Even when she had extended the holiday invitation, in the back of her mind she had known she would be here, seeking him out, for the pathway that had brought her to him had no exits, nor did she want to look for any.

She had talked with her brother in Kentucky earlier in the day and when sleep continued to evade her as she lay in her bed upstairs, she had recalled the advice he had given her.

"Do something selfish this Christmas, Eileen. Give yourself a gift that no one else can give you. We worry about you out there, all alone with those children. Sell out and come home."

She had assured him she was fine. "Home is where the heart is," she had replied. "My heart is here."

Now, as she admired Dan's nude shoulders, the lithe muscles flexing in his arms as he tossed the book aside, a smoldering flame reignited, a flame she had banked each previous time he had come too close.

Only one man had made love to her before. Would this be different? Her gaze caressed him, gliding across the scattering of hair on his chest, following it down his stomach. When the bed clothes hindered her visual exploration, she returned her attention to his face. The surprise she saw there made her smile.

"I didn't expect you," he said.

"I'm breaking my own rule."

"Don't stay...if you'll have regrets."

"I want to stay," she assured him.

He started to leave the bed, but she raised her hand. "Let me come to you." Her gaze fell on the blanket. "Are you naked?"

He settled against the pillows. "Yes...and you?"

She loosened her grip on the lapels of her robe, allowing the garment to fall far enough to reveal her bare shoulders, but she clutched the robe tightly across her breasts. "The lights?"

"No," he insisted. "I told you once before I wanted to see you when we made love. Don't be embarrassed."

She sat on the edge of the bed. "This is difficult for me, Dan. I'm not used to..."

"I know, love," he said, his hand touching her covered knee.

Her grip relaxed and the robe fell to her hips. He inhaled sharply. As they looked into each other's eyes, he reached out and touched the swell of her breast. She trembled.

"Am I...attractive to you?" she asked.

"How could you have any doubt?" His fingers touched the throbbing pulse in her throat.

She bit her lower lip. "Dan, I want you to know that I'm here because I want to be, and I don't expect anything from you, no obligation, no commitment, and I won't be hurt if you..." She dropped her gaze. "I'm making a terrible mess of this, aren't I?"

The creases around his mouth deepened. "One could get the impression that you aren't used to initiating an affair," he said.

She looked pained. "Is that what we're about to have?"

"If you deny me the possibility of feeling committed or concerned about the consequences of tonight, then yes, you bring it down to a casual affair at best."

"That's not what I want," she said.

"What do you want?" he asked, turning her chin toward him.

"I . . . want you . . . to love me, at least for tonight," she explained. "I want you to hold me, to shut out the world for a little while. Is that asking too much?"

"It's probably not asking enough," he said.

"What if we don't . . . do it right, if I can't . . . I don't always . . . we might not be able to . . ."

"Be able to satisfy each other?" he asked.

She flinched at his bluntness.

"Why don't we let that come naturally?" he suggested.

She sighed. "I suppose by now, you're out of the mood. We've talked our time away, haven't we? Perhaps I should go back upstairs and forget . . . everything."

He shook his head. "You underestimate me. No, I'm not out of the mood. I've been in the mood every time I've seen you and when I've called you on the phone and when I'm thinking about you. Do you actually think I would let you go back upstairs after you cared enough to come to me? Oh, sweetheart, don't you think I have my uncertainties, too?" He pushed the blankets aside.

The sight of his arousal shook her confidence and she shot to her feet, her robe falling to the floor. Her body ached for his touch, yet she couldn't bring herself to look at him.

The soft glow of the lamp accented the curves of her torso. She felt his fingertip caress her lower abdomen.

He started to chuckle. "Is this the secret birthmark?" he asked, touching the dark spot just above her pubic bone.

"Yes," she replied, smiling. "Now you know why we don't talk about it."

"Sit down, please," he said.

Feeling embarrassed about standing naked before him, she dropped to the edge of the bed and reached for her robe.

"No," he said, "if you're cold, come under the covers with me, but first let me do what I've wanted to do all evening." He reached behind her and removed the garnet comb that held her hair away from her face. Using his fingers, he smoothed her hair around her shoulders, framing her face. The lamplight brought an amber glow to her hair that matched her eyes.

"I want you more than any woman I've ever known," he said, pulling her down beside him and cradling her in his arms.

"I have no doubts about our satisfying each other," he said, as he fanned her hair away from her face. His lips sought the pulse point in her temple, then explored their way down her cheek to the corner of her mouth. When finally his mouth claimed hers, she responded eagerly.

"Yes, Dan," she murmured. "I want you so much, so much." Her tongue found his, and he let her explore the moist interior of his mouth before she pulled away, breathing hard. She raised herself on an elbow and gazed down at him. "You make me feel so . . . womanly . . . so sexy. I'd forgotten how good that feeling is." She ran her foot up his leg and down again. Her breasts rested against his chest and she warmed to the role of seductress.

Her hand began to explore his body, searching out the sensitive spots of his tanned skin. "You have a beautiful body," she whispered. "Is it because you're a runner?" Her head dipped and she ran her tongue across his nipple, glancing at his face and smiling when he reacted immediately.

Sitting up, she lightly touched the muscles of his thighs before that part of him she now longed to have inside her.

Gingerly, she caressed him, watching her own hand as she learned more about him.

When she returned to lie beside him, she whispered, "I'm glad you insisted the lights be on. Now there are no secrets."

"No secrets," he agreed. He leaned over her, covering her throat with tiny warm kisses until he found her breasts and bathed each one with his tongue.

She buried her hands in his hair as she encouraged him, guiding him to more sensitive spots as he worked his way down her body. Her stomach was flat when his lips touched it before moving to kiss the birthmark. Lifting her hips, he buried his face against her inner thigh. She reached for him, desperate to fill the emptiness within her.

"I hate to bring this up, but we should take precautions," he said, his breath uneven. "I have something if you don't."

"It's okay," she said.

"Are you on birth control pills?"

"I've just finished my period," she said, her cheeks warming at the discussion of intimate matters. "This is my safe time."

"Good," he murmured, kissing her again. "I don't want us to have regrets later because we were swept away with our passion." His features became solemn. "Come with me, Eileen. I know this is right, the time, the place, us. Come with me."

His mouth sought hers and she responded, arching against him as he rose above her. His entry was gentle, his movements a mixture of torment and ecstasy. Panting, she moaned aloud as shards of desire ricocheted through her and she began to move beneath him, eager to participate fully in their lovemaking. Her palms stroked his hips then moved up his back, memorizing each muscle and bone beneath her fingers.

Before he could catch his breath, she cried out his name, trembling and convulsing against him, around him, into his heart and soul. He slid his hands beneath her hips and held her against him as he sought his own peace in the depths of her body.

They lay spent in each other's arms for several moments. Slowly, he pulled the blanket over them and pulled her against him, her head on his pillow, her hand on his chest.

"Merry Christmas, sweetheart," he said.

"Merry Christmas, Dan," she whispered.

"You gave me much more than I'd hoped for," he said, kissing her lips again.

She stirred. "I didn't think I could do this," she murmured. "I thought I'd be spending the rest of my life alone...celibate. I'm glad I took this first step with you. I may never have a second chance, and now I'll always have this memory of tonight." Her fingers followed the muscles over his ribs.

He stopped her hand. "We'll have other times, Eileen, I promise." He chuckled. "Promises and visions. Are they the keys to our lives?"

"Without them, where would we be?"

"Lonely and cynical individuals." He turned onto his side and peered down at her, resting his head on his hand. "What's to become of us now?"

She glanced away. "Why...nothing."

"Nothing? How can you be so fatalistic?" he asked.

"I want you to leave here when you have to, to return to your reporting travels, free to do whatever you please." She frowned. "Isn't that what you want? Isn't that what modern men really want? Commitments and obligations can stifle a career and when you meet other women, you can be free to..."

A pained expression crossed his face. "Do you know so little about me, Eileen?" He dropped back to the pillow. "If I smoked, I'd say it was time for a cigarette." He stared at the ceiling.

She rolled away from him and he didn't try to stop her, shaken by the unexpected callousness of her attitude to their lovemaking. She left the bed and put on her robe, pulling the belt tightly around her waist and tying it into a double knot.

"Feel safer now?" he asked.

She stiffened. "I must go back upstairs. The children might need me."

"I wouldn't want to come between you and your children," he said, watching her fiddle with the ends of the robe's belt. "Oh, hell," he growled, grabbing for the end of her belt, yanking on it and pulling her off balance. He caught her as she fell against him and rolled across the bed, trapping her beneath him.

He pushed the curls away from her temples. "Sometimes you look like a wounded doe," he murmured. "I want to change that expression to one of a woman in love, a woman who has discovered the joy of being loved by a man again, a woman who can believe in commitment and the future. Maybe we did jump the gun a little, but I have no regrets. Now you're trying to protect yourself by shutting me out. Don't do that. Don't be afraid of intimacy."

Her eyes glistened. "I don't know what to do next. I want to see you again, but I don't want you to feel obligated."

"Sweetheart, don't you recognize the difference between obligation and commitment?" he asked, trailing his fingers down her cheek to her mouth. She opened her mouth to speak, but he stopped her. "No, don't make it worse. Of course, I'll come to see you and someday I want to take you away from here, away from the pressures of running this farm, and let you taste the rest of life. There's a great big world out there and I want to share it with you."

"But . . ."

"No buts," he said, outlining her lips with his finger. "No buts, no time schedules, no plans. Just visions and promises for now. Tomorrow I want to enjoy you and your children. My only regret is that Stephen is not here with us. I have this crazy fantasy of us as a family when he's here. Can't you play along with me? Think of us as a special family when we're together, even when it's just for a few hours."

"Of course," she murmured. "Oh, Dan, I . . ." She bit off the words. Sliding her arms around his neck, she pulled him down. "Kiss me once more." His lips caressed hers, rekindling the passion they had shared.

He smiled down at her. "Now if you'll tuck me in, we'll say good-night and you can return to your bed upstairs."

"I thought we might make love again," she murmured.

He chuckled. "You're a woman of passion and I'd like nothing better, but something tells me we should go slow."

"I feel rejected."

"Never," he said, kissing her lightly once more. "Think of it as a sample of times to come."

Reluctantly, she slid from the bed and adjusted her robe again, then playfully tucked the blankets around his shoulders. "Good night, Danny boy."

"Danny boy?" he said, laughing.

"You're just one of the family, now," she said, smiling.

He sat up and the blankets fell to his hips again. "I didn't envision myself as one of the children."

"And what do you prefer?" she asked, edging toward the door.

"To be your lover." He had hardly uttered the words when she flew out the door, closing it firmly behind her.

As Eileen ran up the darkened stairway, Dan's words rang in her head. When she saw the light streaming from her open bedroom doorway, she stopped abruptly, recalling how careful she had been to leave her room in darkness and her door closed.

Jodie sat cross-legged in the center of the king-size bed, looking lost and frightened and clutching a white stuffed bear.

Eileen ran across the room to the bed and scooped her daughter into her arms. "Jodie, darling, what's wrong?"

"I had a dream," Jodie said, hiccuping twice. "It scared me and I came to tell you about it, but you were gone. Where were you, Momma?"

"I . . . I went to say good-night to Dan," Eileen confessed. "I stayed longer than I had expected to."

"I was afraid," Jodie said, scooting onto Eileen's lap. "I thought maybe you'd gone away . . . like Daddy did."

"No, darling," Eileen said, hugging her daughter. "I'm here and all is well. I won't leave you."

"But Daddy did." They sat together quietly for a few minutes as Eileen stroked her daughter's hair. Suddenly, Jodie pulled away and smiled up at Eileen. "I decided you had gone to Mr. Page to tuck him in. Did you?"

"Yeah, did you?" Jordan sneered from the doorway.

Eileen flinched, her memories of being with Dan still warm in her mind as she watched her surly son approach the bed.

"How come he didn't come up here?" Jordan asked.

Biting her tongue to suppress the impulsive retort to her son, Eileen brushed Jodie's brown hair from her eyes and kissed her cheek. "Yes, I tucked him in."

"I like Mr. Page, Momma. Jolene and I have talked about him, and we both really like him. Do you like him a lot, too?"

"Yes," Eileen said, sighing deeply. "I like him a lot."

"Are you gonna marry him?"

Eileen shook her head. "No, I'm not going to marry him, but that doesn't mean I can't like him and enjoy his company. Now why don't you go back to your room?"

"Let's go downstairs instead," Jodie said. "We can open some presents. We can be really quiet."

Eileen laughed. "Absolutely not, young lady. Back to bed. Now! Jolene might get worried if she woke up and found you gone. Three people awake at this hour is enough, don't you think?"

Jodie kissed her mother's cheek and scampered off the bed and out of the room, the bear bouncing behind her. Jordan turned to leave as well.

"Jordan?"

He frowned at Eileen.

"Stay a moment so we can talk," she said.

He shook his head. "I'm tired."

Staring at her clenched fists in her lap, she tried to think of a way to reach him. "Please, Jordan," she said, but when she looked up again, the doorway was empty.

In her private bathroom, she slipped into her gown. She wondered if Dan was still awake, if he had heard their voices, if he was aware of the conflicts their relationship was causing. He would be able to get in his car and drive away from all this while she would be surrounded with inquiring eyes and unspoken questions for weeks to come. But he was leaving her with memories, wonderful loving minutes of passion and joy to savor during the quiet times when she was alone.

She turned off the lamp and slid beneath the covers, her thoughts jumbled. Dan, Duncan, her children and Stephen all fought for prominence in her mind. She gave up trying to sort out her feelings, but Daniel Page's green eyes danced before her as she watched the first ravs of daylight fill her room.

Christmas morning was chaotic. Unable to catch even an hour's sleep when she heard the children make their way down the stairs shortly after daybreak, she had joined them, dressed in jeans and a pale blue cable-knit sweater, hoping a strong cup of coffee would help keep her eyelids open.

When Dan Page made an appearance, clean-shaven and wearing a navy wool crew-neck sweater, her heart raced. "Good morning," he said to everyone in the room, but only Eileen paid him any attention. He dropped to the sofa beside her.

"They're busy," he observed, glancing at the children opening their presents.

"Yes," she agreed, smiling.

"Then kiss me," he suggested. "They'll never notice."

His hand cupped her chin as his lips lightly brushed hers. When they broke away and turned, three pairs of curious eyes were watching them. Jordan frowned and the twins were grinning.

"Good morning, children," Dan said, nodding to them. "Is Christmas to your satisfaction?"

He left the sofa and sat on the floor, giving each child his undivided attention as they showed off their gifts. He was even able to draw a few words out of Jordan.

Dan motioned to a gift that had become wedged in the lower branches of the tree. "There's one more. Jolene, can you get it?"

"It's for you, Momma," Jolene exclaimed, crawling out from under the branches of the tree. The tree trembled.

"Don't knock it over, stupid," Jordan scolded.

Jolene handed the present to Eileen.

"It's from Dan," Eileen said, remembering the small box wrapped in gold foil from the night before.

Dan remained on the floor while she opened it.

"Oh, Dan, it's beautiful," she exclaimed, lifting a gold chain from the cotton inside the blue box and displaying a nugget suspended from the chain. "What an unusual shape."

"Is it a real nugget?" Jordan asked.

"Genuine," Dan assured the boy. "It reminded me of an Idaho Russet potato. The jeweler assured me it would grade a number one baker," he said. "It seemed like a perfect gift for a spud lady."

"How much does it weigh?" Jordan asked. "Is it more than an ounce? Did it cost you a lot of money?"

"Jordan!" Eileen scolded. "Thank you, Dan, it's beautiful."

He shrugged. "It's just a trinket that caught my eye." He got to his feet. "Anyone for chow?" he asked. "I need to get back to Boise this afternoon. I have an article to rewrite and I fly to Arizona tomorrow morning."

Eileen's heart sank. "But we have gifts for you. Can't you stay tonight? I thought . . . ?"

"Thank you for the presents," he said, glancing at each one. "I'd like to take them with me. I'll open them on my trip. It will make Christmas last a little longer. I've spent the last several Christmases alone. This one is very special. I'll stay in touch. Count on that." He turned away, unwilling to show the depth of his emotions.

She followed him into the kitchen and together they prepared a light meal, with the children giving conflicting suggestions that inspired laughter and lightened the tense atmosphere in the room. After lunch they lingered in the living room around the barren tree, but the children's presence precluded any serious conversation.

By midafternoon, Dan had packed his suitcase and stowed the gifts in his car. He turned to Eileen, catching her in the middle of a yawn.

"Tired?" he asked.

"I never got to sleep," she confessed.

"Too bad," he said. "I fell asleep immediately."

"Just like a man," she teased, glancing toward the children. "Will you be gone long?" she asked, wishing they could spend more time together.

"I'll be in Arizona for two weeks, then I'm meeting in Los Angeles with a literary agent who thinks he could get me a book contract if I'd expand my series on interesting women." He took her hand in his. "I don't know when I'll be back, but I'll call."

"I'll miss you," she said, her voice unsteady.

He nodded, sliding his hand into the back of her hair and easing her closer to him. "For a woman who insists on no commitments, you're letting your emotions show."

"Don't tease me, or I'll start to cry," she said, blinking away tears.

"I was hoping to take you to some fancy restaurant for New Year's Eve, but we'll have to put that on hold." He wrapped his arms around her and kissed her hard, then climbed into his car.

Rolling down the window, Dan handed her a large manila envelope. "For you and the kids," he said. "I had fun doing them." With that, he drove away.

She clutched the envelope to her breast and watched the vehicle disappear into the distance, then slowly returned to the house, her heart heavy.

"What's that?" Jordan asked, pointing to the envelope.

"It's from Dan," she replied. "Let's see what's inside." She slid the contents of the envelope onto the dining room table and gasped. Prints of the photographs he had taken several weeks earlier scattered across the table, pictures of the children, posed alone and together, family groupings and several of her alone. The prints were in assorted sizes.

The children sorted through them. "You can each choose three to put on your bulletin boards and keep as your very own," Eileen announced. Her only regret was that there were none of Dan.

"Why did he waste so much film?" Jordan asked, rummaging through the pile and retrieving two of himself and one of the family.

"'Cuz he likes us!" Jolene replied, before Eileen could swallow the lump in her throat.

A pall settled over the house that evening and they all retired to their rooms early. The farm routine returned to normal the next day, with livestock to feed, potato cellars to monitor, and business ledgers to post for the upcoming year-end tax work.

Jordan helped her clean out two of the cellars. She chose a few dozen potatoes and bagged them for use in the house, then got the pickup and helped him load the remaining three hundred pounds of potatoes in the back and move them to the full cellar.

Two of the overhead lights had burned out and visibility was limited as they made their way inside.

"Mom, it smells funny in here," Jordan said.

"I'm sure everything is fine," she replied absently, her thoughts on Dan Page.

"Maybe some frosted spuds are spoiling," he said.

"Oh, I don't think so," Eileen replied, leaning against the support beam near the door. She sniffed the air, trying to detect any trace of the ammonia smell that would be a warning that some frozen potatoes had been missed by the sorters. "I think it's just the usual musty odors. We'll keep an eye on it."

She helped him close the big doors to the cellar, hoping all was well. She wasn't sure she could cope with any more problems. The leasing company had called the previous day and she had stooped to asking Jordan to say she wasn't home.

"I'm just a little behind on their payments," she had explained to him. "As soon as I find a new buyer for this last cellar, I'll be able to bring the accounts current.

Dan called on New Year's Eve. "I'm in the White Mountains of Arizona," he said. "I went skiing today."

"Sounds like a rough assignment to me," she said, wishing she were with him.

"I'm checking out the whereabouts of a woman who used to run the place," he explained. "She's in the second installment of the first series of articles," he added.

She fingered the gold nugget resting against her chest.

"Do you have my gift on?" he asked.

"You must be psychic," she said. "I just touched it."

"How is everything there?" he asked.

"Fine."

"That's good. Working hard?"

"So so," she said.

"Did you sell the last of the crop?" he asked.

"I have one cellar left," she replied. "I'm having a little trouble finding a buyer. This year's crop was good, but that can be a mixed blessing." She didn't want to talk about farming. "Are you going to a party tonight?"

"A small one at the ski lodge."

"Have a good time," she said.

"Sure, but I'd have a better time if you were with me. Why don't you hop a plane and come on down?"

She laughed. "No one hops a plane on a moment's notice from this part of the country. You should know that."

"Are the twins behaving themselves?"

"They've always been easy to live with."

"And Jordan?"

"Sullen. What about Stephen? Is he having a good time in Mexico? I think he and Jordan were hoping they could spend the holiday here together."

Dan sighed deeply. "He wrote me a letter from Mexico. He says he hates the military academy and wants to come live with me."

"What are you going to do?" she asked.

"I'll go see Van when I get back to Idaho," he replied. "We'll discuss it again. It won't be the first time he's wanted to leave. That school is so regimented it stifles a child's natural development. Remember when your kids were learning to color and they kept getting outside the lines?"

"Of course," she said, laughing. "It's perfectly normal. Their enthusiasm and motor skills development are much more important than staying inside the lines."

"Well, getting outside the lines would be an unforgivable sin at that place. It's a damned dictatorship with the headmaster in full authority, never to be questioned or challenged. Stephen is a born questioner."

She laughed. "Perhaps he takes after his father."

"Could be."

CHAPTER THIRTEEN

WHEN THE CHILDREN RETURNED to school after their Christmas break, Eileen was alone again at the farm. At noon their first day back her part-time employee arrived.

"Jordan and I ran out of time before we started cleaning cellar three," she said. "Why don't you do it next, Ben? And one of the haystacks has started to slip a little. Can you get it propped up?" She laughed. "I've always had trouble lifting bales of hay, even the smaller ones."

"I'll get right on it," Ben said, walking toward the cellars in the distance, his limp from an old harvester accident throwing his gait to the left.

Eileen returned to the posting of her ledgers. Suddenly she heard a shout, then a scream from the yard. She jumped from her chair and raced to the kitchen door. Ben Yates was breathing hard, gripping his hat in his hand as he leaned against the porch post.

"Oh my God, Mrs. Mills," he gasped. "There's water running under the door of that full cellar...and it stinks like hell!"

Not even stopping to grab her coat, Eileen ran outside and together they hurried to the cellar.

When they arrived, Eileen stepped gingerly over the odorous rivulets coming from beneath the double doors.

"Help me, Ben," she cried, and together they pulled the huge doors open. The stench of ammonia forced them back.

She grabbed the tails of her shirt to cover her nose and took a step inside, but Ben grabbed her arm.

"No, Mrs. Mills, you can't go in there," Ben insisted. "You'll pass out from the fumes. Wait until it airs out a bit. I'll turn the fans up."

She peered into the cellar and her heart stopped when she saw the huge sink holes in the potatoes. What had been a twenty foot wall of potatoes a few days ago was now half that size. She was sure they were caving in before her very eyes. *Will the loss be total?* she wondered, numb with shock. *No, it can't be. I'll be bankrupt!*

"Get the sorters out here, Ben," she shouted. "We've got to save what we can. We'll sort them by hand. Surely some of them haven't rotted. We can work out here. We'll bag the good ones and let the conveyor carry the spoils right into the trucks. Get the trucks. Hurry!"

While Ben set up the equipment, Eileen called her other off-season employees and rehired them on the spot. When the two sorters were in position and the trucks ready to receive the discards, Ben began to empty the cellar, using the front-end loader to scoop the loose potatoes up and deposit them into the hoppers. The employees who had been called arrived within the hour and began the arduous job of examining each potato.

Undamaged potatoes were dropped into burlap bags stationed between the workers and the sorter rail. If the potato was moist or soft or had any mold growing on it or green spots from sunlight, it stayed on the conveyor to fall into the trucks. The trucks filled more rapidly than the burlap bags.

Jodie and Jolene arrived from school and offered to help. Eileen showed them what to look for and they took their places alongside the men, standing on wooden crates to reach their work.

"Don't bring any more spuds from the cellar, Ben," Eileen called as the sun began to descend in the western sky. "If we get too many out, they'll freeze before we get them sorted."

He nodded, and redirected his work to juggling the full trucks. "What'll I do when they're all full, ma'am?"

"We'll dump them on the ground over there," she said, pointing to the open area near the old dairy barn.

Jordan got off the school bus and spotted the activity near the cellars. "What happened?" he shouted, and quickly she explained the catastrophe. "I told you it smelled funny in there, Mom. Why didn't you listen to me? Why didn't you call for me at school? I could have skipped basketball practice. I could have been here helping!"

Before she could reply, he ran to the nearest sorter and began working alongside one of the men.

The encroaching darkness activated the yard light. When the hoppers had all been emptied, the workers stepped down from their stations and two of them lifted the girls to the ground. The number of bags of good potatoes was pitifully small.

In spite of the below-freezing temperature, Eileen wiped perspiration from her brow. "Ben, bring the front-end loader over here," she called, waving him to the bags of potatoes. "Guys, tie the bags and put them in the scoop and Ben will take them to cellar number two."

She wiped her face again, leaving a dirt smudge across her cheek. "That's all we can do tonight. If any of you can stay overnight, we'll start at daybreak tomorrow. I've got to save as many as possible. Use the phone in the kitchen to call your families...and thanks, guys. We would have lost them all without your help."

She surveyed the weary workers. "I have the makings for sandwiches in the kitchen, but you'll have to make your own. I'm going upstairs.'' She turned away and walked stiffly toward the house, unwilling to let the others see the tears trickling down her cheeks.

Upstairs, she showered and changed into clean jeans and a sweatshirt, then phoned three dairy farmers who had been close friends of Duncan's. When she explained the situation, two of them offered to pay a token amount if she could deliver the spoiled potatoes to their farms. The third volunteered to pick up a load, but he couldn't pay.

"I can chop them up," he said. "The cows love them, but they choke on them if the pieces are very big. Sorry I can't pay you, but farming's not good for me right now."

"I understand. Thanks," she said. "Come on over."

She called the manager of the local employment office at home and explained her predicament. "I'll feed workers and house them if necessary," she added. The manager promised to do what he could.

Scoop by scoop, day by day, the cellar was unloaded. As the decomposition completed its cycle, the ammonia smell dissipated until the workers no longer choked when they went near the cellar.

Eileen knew she would never forget the smell of rotting potatoes. One in a ten-pound bag was bad enough, but when the major portion of three million pounds of potatoes decayed at once, the odor was unbearable.

Five days later the workers had disposed of eighty percent of the cellar's contents. The bags were stacked along one wall of the next cellar. The empty cellar was scraped and cleaned, then opened to allow any lingering fumes to dissipate.

Her phone rang on the second Monday in January.

"How is the Mills family today?" a cheerful Harold Quincy asked. "Have a great holiday?"

"Fine," she said, her spirit still numbed.

"Say, about those spuds we should have picked up last week, if you still have them, I'd like to send my trucks out to get them, today if possible. Those girls on the line can really put out the work when they see overtime on their paychecks. They're yelling for more hours. How can I disappoint those pretty little ladies? Okay if we come this morning?" he asked, chuckling.

"Sure," she said. "You're welcome to all I have left, but at the first price you offered me."

"That's fair enough, Mrs. Mills," he replied.

Nothing's fair, she thought, as she returned to her work.

Later that day, a stunned Harold Quincy was still scratching his head as his men loaded the potatoes on two of the five trucks he had brought. "Geez, Mrs. Mills, I'm sorry. I'll get that check in the mail to you first thing tomorrow morning. Geez, I'm sorry." He turned, and motioned his men to start their engines.

"So am I," Eileen murmured, as she watched the last of her crop go to market.

DAN CALLED two days later. "Take a message," she requested of Jolene. "I can't talk to him now."

When he called again two weeks later, she was in one of the fields, staring at the plowed rows. The furrows were white with snow that had fallen the night before. *Is this catastrophe my punishment? A reminder of my guilt for becoming involved with Dan? But if that's true, why did Duncan die?* She had done nothing to deserve widowhood. Or was there something in her past, some deed long forgotten for which she was now paying penance? She stared at the barren furrows and wondered what unforeseen catastrophe lay waiting to snare her in the months ahead.

"Tell him to call back," she said.

"But Momma, he said it's important. He said I had to come get you or else," Jolene insisted.

Eileen sighed deeply, knowing that sooner or later she would have to talk to him. "Tell him . . . I'm coming."

"It's been awhile since we've spoken," Dan said, his voice a distant comfort to her ears. "How are you?"

"Fine," she replied, longing for his arms to hold her.

"You don't sound very cheerful."

"I'm fine, but . . . I miss you."

"I miss you, too," he said. "I've got to do something about all this travelling."

"I thought that was the part of your job you like best," she said. "The freedom to go places, to meet people."

"It used to be, but since meeting you . . . well, can't a man change his mind?" he asked. "Eileen?"

"Yes?"

"About Christmas . . . were you safe?"

"Yes," she murmured. "I've had my period and you needn't worry about complications."

He chuckled. "Honey, just knowing you brings complications and I love every one of them. I wanted you to know I'll be by Saturday. I have the tear sheets from the updated article."

A shield of defensiveness surrounded her. "I don't know if I can live up to your description."

"I only write the truth . . . as I see it, of course. Sometimes I'm biased but I try to let the reader know if that's the case."

"I'm sure you did a fine job," she said. "You're very talented. Lucky too."

"Luck has little to do with it," he replied. "I work hard and when a person plans ahead, everything usually works out. But you know all about that, don't you? I wanted to let you have an advance look. You're my star feature. I concede to a total lack of objectivity. You'll love the photos. You and the children look so happy and the one I used with you and the kids and Waite around the table shows just the mood I wanted to get across to the readers about farming and farm families. I'm quite pleased with the results.''

She closed her eyes, trying to maintain her self-control. ''Dan, it doesn't really matter,'' she replied. ''I have to go. Goodbye.'' Quietly, she replaced the receiver and returned to the barren field, feeling alone and desolate.

DAN SAT at the small table in the restaurant, feeling totally alienated from the woman he loved. When Eileen had hung up on him earlier in the day, his first reaction had been disbelief. Wounded pride had followed, then anger, but some sixth sense had made him realize that some unknown complication had occurred.

That being the case, Eileen was probably letting her mis-guided sense of pride overrule her good judgment. She didn't have to carry the burden alone. But what burden? Did she have problems worse than the bad-checks fiasco? Had she withheld information from him? Lied? And if so, why?

Leaving his meal half eaten, he returned to his motel room. When he dialed Eileen's number, Jordan answered.

''Is your mother there?'' Dan asked.

''She went shopping,'' Jordan replied.

''Shopping?'' Dan glanced at his watch. ''At this hour?''

''I ain't lying!''

''Of course not, Jordan, I never said you were, but wouldn't the stores all be closed in Shelley at this hour?'' Dan asked. ''Did she drive into Idaho Falls?''

''She went to Pocatello.''

''Pocatello? Why not Idaho Falls?'' Dan frowned. ''Who's staying with you children? Who's baby-sitting?''

"We don't need a baby-sitter," Jordan said. "Mom left me in charge. We can take care of ourselves."

"I'm sure you can." He decided to take a different approach with the boy. "How is everything?"

"Fine."

"Jordan, level with me," Dan said. "I want to help if I can. I know something is wrong. Now what has happened to make your mother so... distant, so withdrawn?"

"We can take care of ourselves," Jordan said. "My dad taught me how to do most of the work, and my dad and my mom always worked together and now my mom and I can handle everything just fine. When Mr. Waite comes back, he'll help us. We'll be able to get the crops planted and I can help with irrigation and..."

"Jordan, stop it! I want to help. Now tell me what's wrong with your mother."

"She's... she's just... she cries, but I know it's because she misses my dad... they always did everything together... and he didn't go off on trips... and... and she says our problems are our business, our private business... and she said to not gossip about it... and what do you care, anyway?"

"I care a hell of a lot, Jordan," Dan replied. "Tell her I'll be there Saturday... and she had better be there, or I'm going to hunt her down, so she might as well give up trying to avoid me. I want to get to the bottom of this whole business and help if I can, so we can get on with our lives. Tell her that."

Jordan didn't reply.

"Did you hear me?" Dan asked, beginning to lose his patience with the sullen boy.

"Yes, sir," Jordan said.

"Just tell her, please," Dan added.

When he arrived on Saturday morning, the house was empty. He glanced at the calendar on the wall in the kitchen. "Jordan to soccer practice, nine to noon," was written in Eileen's neat handwriting just below another note that read, "Twins to library."

Perhaps Eileen hadn't returned, he thought, but he'd seen her car through the open garage door when he had parked his own vehicle. He knew he'd probably find her on the property somewhere.

"Eileen, are you in there?" Dan called, approaching one of the huge potato cellars. He pulled the handle and felt it give. He eased the door partially open and slipped inside. "Eileen? Are you in here?" he called, waiting for his eyes to adjust to the darkness. "Pugh, it smells in here. What happened?"

She brushed past him out into the sunlight. He turned and grabbed her arm before she could get away.

"Eileen, what the devil is going on around here?" he asked, his temper rising by the minute.

"Nothing," she exclaimed. "Nothing at all…other than we lost a whole cellar full of spuds because of my carelessness. Three and a half million pounds of spuds, that's all. Enough to pay off the balance of my line of credit, enough to bring the loans up to date, enough to keep the place from foreclosure. Instead I sold them for cattle feed. The bill collectors are calling every day and I'm running out of excuses."

Her fists clenched and unclenched. "The bank is warning me it might want to reconsider my line of credit for next spring, and the leasing company where Duncan got the new spud harvester is threatening to repossess it but I've padlocked the door of the equipment shed and I won't let them have it. Other than *those little problems*, everything is fine, just fine."

"Eileen, I don't understand." Dan took her hand and pulled her across the yard into the house then into the kitchen. "Sit down and tell me about all this. What really happened?" Eileen tried to pull away but he tightened his grip on her hand. "I don't want to hear any bull about everything being fine because I know better. Damn it, Eileen, tell me."

She dropped into a chair but refused to look at him. Briefly, she detailed the events that had taken place since the first of the year. "Still want to help?" she asked.

He ran his hand through his hair. "I don't understand. I know you had some loans. Most farmers do, but how you could go from a financially sound position to this in so short a time? It's impossible."

"Not for me," she replied cynically.

"You had a good season."

She shrugged, but didn't reply.

"Duncan told me he had a few loans but I thought you had been keeping them current."

"With what?" she cried. "A flake of a potato broker skipped the country after writing me a check for one hundred fifty thousand dollars . . . and it bounced!"

He frowned. "Is that why you had the notices from the bank?"

She nodded.

"Why didn't you level with me then?" he asked. "Maybe I could have helped you work it out."

"I managed to sell the spuds to another company but the price was much lower."

"Have you seen an attorney?" he asked. "Pressed charges?"

"Sure. Thomas Cameron is my attorney and he's filing a suit, but I'm just one of nine growers left with bad checks. Two have already filed for bankruptcy. I covered the checks

I wrote but that left nothing in reserve for the loans that were due in November. I've been shifting funds ever since and stalling off the creditors."

He sighed. "Maybe you can refinance."

"They all say they'd be glad to if Duncan were still alive, but they have no faith in my ability."

"Isn't that sexual discrimination?" he asked.

"They say it's just good business judgment."

Dan remembered a remark Duncan Mills had made to him many months earlier. "Have you always been in debt?"

She shrugged. "Most crop farmers operate on a line of credit. I explained all that to you. Even the homesteaders a hundred years ago did the same thing. They would borrow for seed and pay off after harvest time." Her shoulders sank. "It's a treadmill, isn't it? Farmers have been losing their land for decades because they never get caught up. The banks make out because there's always some green would-be farmer who wants to prove to the local yokels that he knows more about farming than they do." She grimaced. "They don't know what stress is until they have a foreclosure around the corner and a financial officer breathing down their necks." She seemed to shrink before his eyes.

He studied her defeated posture. "But you've always managed before, haven't you? I assumed...damn it, that was my mistake. You and Duncan were partners and I thought, when he got sick, that you took up the reins and... Was I wrong, Eileen? Has this all been a farce?"

She met his gaze and he saw the defiance return to her eyes. "When Duncan grew weaker, he bought new equipment that was more automated and he refinanced some of the loans," she explained. "Interest rates were high when he did it. I thought I could handle it. I promised him." She backed away from Dan. "The yields were good and the weather was perfect, except for that frost in October. I just never planned for these two problems.''

"Why didn't you tell me about this sooner?" he asked, "Why the deception?"

She stiffened. "It was none of your business."

"But Eileen, we've..."

"What we did doesn't matter now," she replied.

"Doesn't matter? We made love and you say it doesn't matter?" His face flushed. "Are you that casual about your intimate relationships?"

She met his angry gaze. "When it's necessary. Why not? It was enjoyable, but that's in the past. This is today. The future of the farm is what's important now. The Mills family has lived in the area since the turn of the century—before any of this was under cultivation. They broke ground here after World War II. Duncan was born here. I promised I'd keep this farm for my children. What you and I had was—" Her gaze darted around the room. "It was a brief moment... it doesn't matter now."

Dan wanted to grab her and shake her, force her to show some emotion. "You're a fraud, Eileen Mills, a fraud and a fool."

"You saw me the way you wanted to see me," she replied, trying to ignore the expression of disbelief in his eyes. "Now I have work to do, so why don't you just leave and take your silly pictures with you? I don't want to see them anymore. I don't want to see the article, and I don't want you hanging around here. I have work to do. Jordan and I have talked about it and between us, we can manage."

He squinted at her profile. "You'd burden a boy with a man's responsibilities? Is that fair to your son?"

"We can hardly expect some city reporter to save the farm for us," she said, taking another step away from him.

"Save the farm?" Dan asked. "Is it that bad?"

Eileen walked to the door, her body rigid. She held the door open. "When Hogan returns in March, we'll be fine. It's no concern of yours. Now please leave, before you force me to call the authorities."

"Eileen..."

"Leave!"

EILEEN SANK against the door. Driving him out of her life had been one of the most deplorable things she had ever done, as painful as losing Duncan. The emptiness in the pit of her stomach turned to sharp stabs of pain and she doubled over, seeking relief. Clutching her midsection, she went to the refrigerator and poured a glass of milk, then heated it in the microwave.

When the discomfort began to subside, she forced herself to think of the work scheduled for the day. She tried not to think about how losing Duncan had been out of her control and how driving Daniel Page away had been by choice.

As the days passed she began to see how getting Dan off her property had been easy compared to keeping him out of her mind. The daylight hours were filled with activity, but at night his imaginary arms would slide around her and hold her, and his lips would caress hers, and he would love her, and they would talk in the darkness.

Perhaps he was thinking of her, too, she imagined, for his spirit helped her get through the busy days and empty nights.

She wondered if she might still be adjusting to losing Duncan. Yet in the still of the night, it was Dan Page she missed. Had their friendship, begun when they had talked on the phone almost two years earlier, evolved into much more? Passion could be driven from her body and soul, cleansed with forgiveness and forgetting, but love? Her heart ached. Yes, she loved him, she loved him and she'd driven him away without ever telling him so.

DAN PAGE was deep in thought when Vanessa sat down.

"I invited you here to discuss our son, Dan," she said.

"What's wrong now?" he asked tensely.

She waved a manicured hand in the air. "Physically, he's fine, but in Mexico he refused to join in most of the activities I had planned with the other families. He wasn't pouting, but...oh, I don't know. The older he gets, the worse it is for both of us. What are we going to do with this son of ours?"

He smiled. "If men and women knew what lay ahead of them, would they think twice before having children?"

"I doubt it," she replied.

"He wants to leave the academy," Dan said.

"And he wants to live with you," Vanessa added, stroking the fabric on the sofa on which she sat. "Frankly, I wouldn't be opposed to a change in residence, but you're home less than I am."

"Did he tell you about the two boys who ran away?" Dan asked.

She nodded. "We must do something before he becomes desperate. He's growing less patient each time he comes home."

"He needs a live-in mother and father," Dan said. "I might know a place where he can spend the summer," he said. As he uttered the suggestion, he knew he was crazy. Eileen had thrown him off her farm and out of her life. Why would she accept the care and feeding of his son? Maybe if he offered her a generous amount for room and board and insisted Stephen be put to work on the farm, she would accept. She could use the money. Would he stoop to using his son and his son's friendship with Jordan to get to Eileen? *Maybe,* he realized.

Vanessa took a sip of tea from a delicate china cup. The fine lines around her mouth softened. "He's my son no matter where he lives." She straightened and set her cup back on the coffee table. "Let me know if you can make arrangements. It will buy us time before the fall term starts at the academy. He could stay with me in Boise, but there's a restriction against children here in this building. Maybe I'll have to move. He'll be in high school soon. Oh, why does parenthood have to be so difficult?"

"We'll work something out," Dan agreed. "Let's just hope Stephen will hang in at the academy until school lets out." He watched her hand stroke the muted pattern of the sofa.

"How do you like my latest addition to the collection?" Vanessa asked. "It's in remarkable condition. It's an early Sheraton, probably made between 1800 and 1810."

Dan shrugged. Glad to change the subject he said, "Nice, but too formal." A vision of Eileen Mills's comfortable, nondescript overstuffed sofa came to him, quickly followed by a memory of the brief but erotic encounter they had had there.

"Dan, whatever is the matter with you?" Vanessa asked. "You hardly said a word during dinner. Are you ill?"

"It's a personal matter."

Vanessa leaned forward and touched his trousered knee. "We never had secrets, Dan. Careers may have gotten in the way of our marriage but we were never hesitant to discuss our problems. We were always very perceptive to each other's needs." She brushed a thick strand of silvery blond hair away from her temple and tucked it behind her ear, pulled her feet up beneath her, and studied him.

Her svelte posture, as she sat in the designer hostess skirt and blouse, harmonized with the clean lines of the sofa on which she sat. Vanessa's beauty had caught his attention that first morning they had met. They'd both been newly hired administrative assistants fresh from college and they had each been filled with dreams of success. Together, they had set their goals and objectives, knowing that success could be theirs for the taking. Within months they had shared much more than just their career goals.

Now, sixteen years later, his ex-wife was no less stunning, possibly more so, with the added maturity. Her floral hostess skirt reminded him of the elegant red velvet skirt Eileen had worn the evening they had made love. His stomach tightened into a discomforting cramp. Before he realized what he was doing, he shared the story, withholding only the more intimate details.

As the tale unfolded, she gave him her undivided attention. When he finished, she smiled. "Dan Page, the gadabout journalist falling in love with a little farm girl? I think it's delightful!" She reached for his hand and squeezed it. Elegantly, she rose from the sofa and left the living room, returning a few minutes later with the three issues of *Western Living* in her hand.

She tossed them in his lap. "Which one is she? I'm sure you can find her faster than I can."

He straightened. "I didn't say I had interviewed her."

"How else would you have found a woman living near the lava beds of eastern Idaho? Come now, I know you better than that."

He grinned and tossed the last issue back to her. "Page thirty-four." He went to the bathroom, stalling to give her time to read the section on Eileen. When he returned, she sat staring at Eileen's photograph.

"Well?" he asked.

"She's very pretty, clean and country, unsophisticated and honest. Your writing makes her appear to be very warm and loving." She handed the magazine back to him. "She looks petite. How tall is she?" she asked.

He shrugged and drew an imaginary line across his chin. "Just right." Vanessa laughed.

"I paid more attention to the part about myself than to the others in the articles." She smiled, her blue eyes sparkling. "I wanted to make sure your writing was accurate and fair."

"And?"

"As always, you did a magnificent job," she said. "You've had a few casual involvements since our divorce. So have I."

He nodded.

"There was a time after our divorce, when I would have been receptive to a reconciliation," she said. "Did you know that?"

"Are you talking about when I returned from Texas?"

"Yes," she admitted. "Stephen was asking me why we had divorced and I couldn't really give him an answer he could understand. How does one explain to a five-year-old why he no longer has a mother and father who live under the same roof?"

"What made you reconsider?" he asked.

"Do you remember that night we...needed each other...?"

Dan grimaced. "A mistake I never made again. That was the last time we made love. I stopped free-lancing, accepted Gil's offer to become a staff reporter, and moved into a new apartment."

"Yes, and I spent the next week trying to explain to Stephen why you had gone away again," she said. "When you moved to Texas, he cried a lot and then you came back and he thought...well, he assumed we had reconciled when you started hanging around again."

"Hanging around?" He rubbed the tight muscles in his neck. "I never stopped to think about the effect it was having on Stephen," he admitted. "I was at loose ends."

"Perhaps I was lonely, too," she conceded. "One reason I insisted on enrolling Stephen in military school was to spare him the emotional upset of seeing his mother and father becoming involved again, but it never happened."

"We make better friends than lovers."

"I agree," she said. "Now, what can I do to help?"

"Nothing," he said, reaching for his jacket. "She needs time, but I don't want to wait too long."

Vanessa rose and followed him to the door. "Are there other men in her life?"

"Damn it, Van, I don't know. I do know we have nothing in common."

"Do you love her, Dan?" Vanessa asked, touching his forearm.

"What?"

"Do you love her...love her unconditionally?"

He closed his eyes for several seconds, then looked directly at her. "Yes."

"Then you have something in common...if she loves you, too."

CHAPTER FOURTEEN

DAN DROVE AWAY from Vanessa's apartment, vowing to drive to the academy as soon as possible and tell Stephen that they were working on a solution to his unhappiness.

Each of Stephen's letters had become more insistent about leaving the private school. In his most recent letter, he had described in lurid detail how two other students had solved their unhappiness with the restrictions of the school. One boy had run away while the other had attempted suicide. Both stories had sent a chill down Dan's spine. His problems with his son seemed as unsolvable as his difficulties with Eileen Mills.

Suddenly a possibility materialized. He let himself into his quiet apartment and went directly to his Rolodex, searching for the phone number of the couple who might be able to help him. A glance at his watch confirmed the lateness of the hour, but he punched the numbers anyway.

"Grasten Livestock," a woman's voice said.

"Abbie...Abbie, is that you?" Dan asked. "I'm sorry it's so late, but I had to call."

"Who is this?" she asked, her voice growing more cautious.

"This is Daniel Page. We've met a few times and—"

"Of course," Abbie said. "I didn't recognize your voice. Dane is already asleep and I was...reading...in bed. How are you? I'm sorry we didn't get to visit at the wedding, but you know how weddings can be."

"Especially for the bride and groom," he agreed. "Eileen said you had taken a trip."

"We took a cruise to Australia and spent three weeks there, then visited a sheep farmer in New Zealand. The farmer's son interned with Dane several years ago. That was work, but we took a side trip into the back country. Can you imagine, this Kentucky gal spending six weeks traveling around the world?"

"Sounds like you had a great time," Dan said. "How did you get Dane to leave the ranch for that long?"

She laughed again. "I convinced him he would profit by seeing the sheep business in Australia and New Zealand first-hand, then I slipped some fun in when he wasn't looking. November and December are quiet around here. Moses and Wilma Parish are the most dependable assistants we could ever want. They took care of the last lambs we had for sale. So, we up and went! Say, why don't you come up and see our photos? We took tons of them."

"I'd love to see them," Dan said, mentally checking his agenda for the coming week. "What if I stopped by? I need a sounding board, Abbie, and you being her cousin you might be able to help."

"Cousin? Is something wrong with Eileen?" Abbie exclaimed. "Dan, what's wrong? I haven't called or written Eileen since we returned except for a Christmas card."

"Why don't I tell you in person?" he said. "I'll be there for coffee break tomorrow morning."

"We start shearing tomorrow afternoon," she said. "We'll put you to work. Working with sheep is therapeutic and great exercise."

"Isn't it a little early for shearing?" he asked.

"Dane has always sheared in May but I read an article in *Sheep Magazine* and convinced Dane we should try it. We're doing the Finns and if they do well, we'll consider changing completely. Plan to stay a day or two. We have lots of room. You can write an article about the pros and cons of shearing in February.''

''Sounds great,'' Dan replied, and as he hung up the receiver, he hoped he would be able to find answers to the problems plaguing his relationship with Eileen. After tossing and turning for hours, Dan left Boise shortly after three in the morning. When Dane and Abbie Grasten greeted him at their door, he hoped the drive was going to be worth the effort.

They sat around the table in the cheery yellow-and-white kitchen. ''Now tell us why you really drove all this way?'' Abbie said. ''I'm sure it isn't to see our photos.''

Dane Grasten leaned back in his chair, tilting it a few inches. ''Let me guess. It hasn't been that long since Abbie was driving me crazy. She set foot on the place in March and my life has never been the same since.'' He laughed when she punched him in the ribs. ''No regrets, mind you, but she put me through hell before she came to her senses and agreed to marry me. Knowing one Hardesty like I do, I'll bet a day's wages, your problem is her cousin.''

Dan frowned and nodded. ''Eileen is so damned determined to do everything alone,'' he explained. ''She made these promises to Duncan and now she can't keep them and it's tearing her apart . . . tearing us apart, too.''

Abbie rested her head against her fist and leaned forward. ''How involved are you with her? Or is that too personal to ask?''

''Too much to be objective,'' Dan admitted. ''Damn it, I've never had to ask for help before, especially about how to get along with a woman, but I can't just drop it. She means too much to me. Why does she have to be so proud and stubborn?''

Grasten glanced at Abbie. "The Hardesty women have to prove to the world they can do it, whatever *it* may be. Asking a man for help isn't in their repertoire." He winked at Abbie. "Except for certain biological acts. They carry their interests to the extreme. When they decide they're in love, there's no changing their minds. They're loyal to a fault, but they have this irritating quality of separating their love for a man from what they see as their other duties. Abbie and I still have our differences, but I've never doubted her love for me. Especially now."

Abbie blushed and her hand dropped out of sight below the table. "I wasn't going to tell anyone, but time is taking care of our secret," she admitted. "We're doing together the one thing I could never do alone." She smiled. "We're going to have a baby."

"That's great," Dan said. "When?"

"It either happened in the outback of Australia or when we went backpacking in the mountains of New Zealand," Abbie replied, glancing at her husband.

Dane kissed her cheek. "I think he meant when is it due."

"Oh," Abbie gasped, covering her mouth. "August."

"That's wonderful," Dan agreed. "I'm happy for you and I'm sure Eileen is, also."

"She doesn't know yet," Abbie said. "I've been waiting until I was sure nothing would happen. It's almost four months now. Maybe next month I'll tell people, starting with my favorite cousin."

Dan shook his head. "I understand the drive to succeed, but why does Eileen think she has to do it all by herself?"

"Growing up in Kentucky the way we did wasn't easy," Abbie said. "All the Hardesty families were dirt poor until the last few years. It's much better now, but when we went to school, education didn't have a high priority in the state. Consistently, Kentucky students placed at the bottom of the test scores nationally. When Eileen and I decided we wanted to go on to college, we had to fight our way out from under the prejudice of the state's students in the eyes of the out-of-state colleges . . . and we did.

"Our parents were pretty much self-educated. My Uncle Harry graduated from the eighth grade but Aunt Minnie was pulled from school in the second grade. She knows the alphabet and can sign her name but her reading level is still borderline illiterate at best. They and my other uncles drummed into all of us Hardesty cousins the importance of doing well in school."

"Isn't that the normal attitude of parents?" Dan asked.

"Not in Kentucky," Abbie explained. "They didn't want us to be like some of our cousins who live in eastern Kentucky."

"I don't understand," Dan said. "What happened to the so-called War on Poverty movement of the sixties?"

"Many of the people fell through the cracks," she explained. "Their incentive and pride had been destroyed by what had happened in that area during the time of heavy coal exploitation." She frowned. "It's complicated, but now they need job opportunities and training, not just more giveaways. Ask Callie the next time you meet her. She spent three summers there. It's horrible to think people still live in that kind of poverty, but they do."

She stared out the window at the snowcapped Montana peaks in the distance. Her husband and Dan Page waited quietly for her to continue. She smiled. "Sorry, guys, but I still get nostalgic when I think about those days. Eileen, Callie and I made a vow when we were still in grade school to break free. Eileen and I succeeded by getting away. Callie is still fighting her own battle. She'll make it in time."

"A child shouldn't have to run away from home in order to survive," Dan said.

"We each found our own way out," Abbie said. "Eileen and I left the state. Our neighbors in the Rainbow Hills are still talking about those Hardesty girls. Whatever we did, we did it with gusto, even Callie."

Abbie left her seat and began to pace the room. "Each of us was the only girl in a family of boys. We were more like sisters than cousins. We were very different in personalities but we never tried to dominate each other. Yes, we squabbled, especially Callie and me, but most of the time we meshed and harmonized. Callie was the most romantic and the prettiest of the three."

"You're all beautiful women," Dan said.

Abbie stopped behind Dane's chair and put her hands on his broad shoulders. "Thank you, but that doesn't make life any easier," she said. "Callie's beauty got her lots of boyfriends but her heart belonged to a boy who was worthless and no one could talk sense to her." She smiled. "I was the dreamer. I wanted to be free and control every facet of my life, and my weaving career gave me that opportunity. That quest for knowledge is what brought me here." She kissed her husband's cheek.

"How did Eileen fit into your sisterhood?" Dan asked.

"Eileen was the leader," Abbie said. "If we had a problem, she would solve it. Duncan depended on her the same way. She's always accepted the responsibilities thrust upon her."

Dan shook his head. "A person can carry only so much, then they begin to stumble. Eileen is stumbling and won't admit it."

"Eileen tends to play mother hen," Abbie said. "She'll fight off the forces threatening to harm her and her brood until her back is to the wall and all seems hopeless, and still she'll find strength to fight some more. It's in her genes."

Dane Grasten peeked out the window at three vehicles pulling into the yard. "The shearers just arrived. We had better get out to the sheep shed. Want to do some hands-on research, Page?"

"Sure," Dan said. "Maybe we can find a way to help Eileen in spite of her pigheaded nature. What a stubborn bunch of cousins."

"That's for sure," Dane said, ignoring the disdainful glare Abbie shot his way.

Dan spent part of the afternoon sweeping wool tags from the wooden floor so the fleeces would be relatively clean when tamped into the wool bags. "Challenging," he said when Grasten asked him how he liked his work. Grasten grinned and reassigned him to wrangling the sheep through the chutes for the rest of the day.

Two days later, Dan packed his suitcase. Abbie followed him to his car. "She needs your support, Abbie, before she breaks. I've never dealt with such an obstinate woman in my life."

"Sounds like you're smitten," Abbie teased.

"I wish she was," Dan replied.

"Maybe she is," Abbie said. "Have you considered the possibility that she's in love with you and feels guilty?"

"But she's been a widow for a year," he said.

"She told me once she felt attracted to you from the first," Abbie said. "Did you know that?"

"She was a married woman," he replied. "I liked Duncan when I met him. I felt at ease with her. That's as far as it went."

"You and I know that, she knows that too," Abbie said, "but did that stop the two of you from giving each other comfort? The mind can play tricks on a person. She told me once that she and Duncan stopped having sexual relations long before his death. A woman continues to have sexual needs even when there's no way she will allow herself to express or satisfy them. Do you understand what I'm trying to say?''

"She feels she's been unfaithful to Duncan because of me?" Dan asked. "Good Lord, how can she? I knew Duncan was probably too sick to be a normal husband to her, but that didn't mean I was ready to take his place. I respected their marriage too much to be a negative force in their remaining time together. I cared, about her, about them.''

"Then you, too, felt the attraction from the start?''

"Sure, but . . .''

"Then perhaps you both need to face your guilt over the past and put your cards on the table, if you want to have a future together. You make a special couple, Dan. I could tell that each time I saw you together. There's a harmony between you.''

"Right now, it's discord," Dan said.

DAN PAGE AND GIL HADLEY waited for the waitress to return with their charge cards and receipts.

"Didn't you grow up on a farm?" Gil Hadley asked, counting out coins for a tip.

"In New Jersey," Dan said.

Gil chuckled. "You're the only person I've ever met who was actually born in New Jersey.''

Dan frowned at the tired joke. "Do I have two heads or six fingers or some other abnormality because of my birth place?''

"Sorry," Gil said.

The waitress slid the tray and credit cards onto the table. "Thanks, honey," Gil said, admiring her swinging hips as she left.

"Remember your age and your wife," Dan mumbled, retrieving his card and putting it back into his billfold.

Gil laughed. "Who's the boss here? Don't answer. You never were one to show respect for your superiors."

"I hate that word," Dan said. "We're all equal. Some of us use our talents, some of us get lucky, but we're all equal under the skin. Now what's behind this joint lunch, Gil? The least you could have done was pick up the tab."

"I have a story idea for you," Gil said.

"I'm assuming I have no choice in this next assignment?" Dan said, smiling.

"Have I ever shoved a story idea down your throat?" Gil asked, looking hurt.

"No, but you've held my mouth closed a few times until I swallowed."

"You'll like this one," Gil said, reaching into his pocket and withdrawing a roll of pink paper. "Here's a flyer I spotted over the weekend. It was one of several. How would you like to do an article on farm foreclosure?"

"Not particularly," Dan replied. *Why have my own nose rubbed in the very problems that are tearing Eileen apart?* he thought.

"Go to some farm auctions," Gil said, ignoring Dan's disagreeable expression. "Concentrate on the human interest angle. Get the feel of the people. They're neighbors and I'll bet you a steak dinner they feel like scavengers when they bid on their neighbor's belongings, even if they get them at a good price." He unrolled the flyer and waved it at Dan. "This auction is Saturday near Burley. Cover it."

Reluctantly, Dan took the curling pink flyer. He'd been putting off his visit to Eileen's farm for weeks now, not wanting to face one more rejection. Three on the phone had been enough.

The magazine with the follow-up article had been released, but he still had extra copies set aside for her. Reaching for the issue Gil had brought, he turned to the article. As he reread his words and stared at her photo, he was torn between his love for her and resentment over the promises she had made to the ghost of a husband, promises that continued to keep them apart. His cynicism fought with his desire to find happiness with her. Loving her had become his own cross to bear and he wanted to lay it down.

EVEN A NEW VEHICLE hadn't boosted Dan's spirits, but as he shifted into four-wheel drive to cope with the deep ruts, he was thankful he had bought the blue Blazer. Since he had rammed the sedan into the ditch near Eileen's place, the steering had never handled quite right and he had traded it in on the more practical Blazer.

The spring thaw had turned the farm road into a quagmire and the steady stream of trucks going to the auction didn't help. Mud splashed against his windshield from the truck in front of him. He turned on his wipers and applied several squirts of cleaner.

He found a parking space alongside an older truck and flatbed trailer several hundred yards from the farmer's yard. A public address speaker from the auctioneer's platform announced the beginning of the sale with household furniture, to be followed immediately by the farm equipment.

"If anyone is interested in the land, please speak to..." The public address system crackled and Dan stopped listening. His rubber boots sank a few inches into the mud when he climbed from the Blazer. He wore faded jeans and a camel-colored chamois shirt, wanting to blend with the locals as he observed them. The early spring weather was warm but breezy. He left his lightweight jacket in the cab but reached for a brown baseball cap, left from a brief stint when he and Stephen had tried to play league ball together one summer. An out-of-state trip had cut his coaching career short and he had never tried the sport again.

He worked his way to the edge of the crowd. The ground was higher and packed hard by the foot traffic. A table had been set up near an equipment shed and two women were selling coffee.

"Morning, ladies," he said. "Coffee black and two donuts." He dug some coins from his jeans pocket. "Too bad, isn't it, about things like this happening?"

The gray-headed woman nodded. "A real shame. The Wallenbergs have been around here since 1910. Oscar must be rolling over in his grave at what his grandson has come to."

"What did he do?" Dan asked.

"He expanded, just when he got the place all paid off," the younger woman said. "He bought out his neighbor and used the two places as collateral to buy a third place. Maybe he got greedy. Land prices were going up, but so were interest rates and when he refinanced, he got caught in the squeeze. He took a big loss two years ago when half his crop froze in the field. Last year, he panicked and signed contracts in the spring for all his spuds. Harvest time spud prices were great but he was tied to his contracts. He thought he could make it up with his barley but it was a bumper year for grain and he held his too long."

The younger woman stuck out her lower lip. "He can't even start up his planter. He ain't got no seed taters 'cuz the grower in Montana claims he forgot to pay last year's bill. No one will give him credit. He finally just threw up his hands and told the two banks they could draw straws for the place. His wife says they're moving back to Tennessee." She shook her head sadly.

"How do you know so much about their problems?" Dan asked. "I would think they would keep quiet."

The younger woman shrugged. "She's my cousin and her folks have a sorghum farm near Cowen. They usta grow cotton but the mill closed. Now they make home-grown sorghum and put it in fancy jars and sell it to the city folks in the South. Besides, my John knows Rudy Fellows who runs the elevators west of town. Rudy's brother is a banker in town and when the men gather in the cafe for coffee, tongues wag. Why men are worse gossipers than their women. It's no different than any other town...big city too, only we know our neighbors 'cuz people don't move in and out so often."

"It's not all bad," the other woman added. "This is the first time I've seen most of these folks since the fair last fall. It's a shame for the Wallenbergs but I sure do enjoy visiting with everyone again. Winter tends to keep us home, you know."

Dan laid his coins on the table. "Thanks, ladies," He milled around, listening to the conversations. Some were derogatory, but most were sympathetic to the family's plight. Occasionally, names of other farm families were mentioned, with comments that they, too, might be forced into a similar situation.

A woman in the crowd to his left caught his attention. Her sky-blue bulky knit sweater looked familiar. Slight of build, the woman's movements recalled vivid images of Eileen Mills. *No, it can't be.* Her profile was similar but her hair was much shorter. Golden highlights glistened in the bright morning sun as the woman turned her head and wrote something down on a small note pad she was clutching in her hand.

Dan's pulse quickened as he studied the woman, the soft waves of her warm brown hair brushing against her cheek as she wrote. Why would Eileen be here in Burley? Where were the children? When she straightened and her attention returned to the auctioneer, she brushed wispy curls from her temple. *Of course, she has to be Eileen. No other woman has mannerisms quite like hers. Haven't I memorized each and every one of them? Hadn't she threatened to cut her hair?*

Dan worked his way through the crowd. Several middle-aged farmers wearing bib overalls separated them. When her profile was in plain view, he saw the grim expression that had narrowed the usual full curves of her lips. As he continued to study her, her motivation for being at the auction became clear to him. Was she experiencing her own future through this family's loss? Sensing the bitter strength in her eyes to survive made his heart ache for her. *Why, Eileen? Why suffer alone? Let me help you.*

The crowd shifted to the first piece of harvesting equipment, a sorter similar to one Dan had seen at the Mills farm. Eileen's pen was poised to record the price of the highest bidder.

Dan worked his way around the visiting men in overalls and stopped by Eileen's side. She completed her notation.

"Good morning," he murmured, shoving his fists into his pockets to keep from touching her.

She glanced up. "Dan?" The color drained from her cheeks.

"I didn't recognize you at first." He admired the sprightly hair cut. "I like it."

Her attention darted between the opening bid on a potato planter and Dan. She blinked away the tears collecting in the corners of her eyes. "What are you doing here?" she asked.

"Learning how a farm auction works," he replied. "And you?"

"Nothing." She bit off the word and ducked her face. The auctioneer's voice sang the escalating bids as the crowd got caught up in the sale. Dan touched Eileen's arm. Suddenly she buried her face against his shirt. "Oh, Dan, everything is so wrong and I'm so miserable."

"Good," he murmured as he pulled his other hand from his pocket and wrapped his arms around her, patting her shoulder as she tried to suppress the tears. He fished a handkerchief from his hip pocket and handed it to her. "This one is clean, too. I carry it for crying women I meet at farm auctions."

She accepted the handkerchief and wiped her eyes and nose. "What's so good about all this?" she asked.

"What's so good? You've admitted things aren't going smoothly and you need help. For you, that's a turning point."

"You're insensitive," she muttered into the handkerchief.

"No, I'm not," he challenged. "I'm honest enough to know you're suffering alone when you don't need to. Good grief, Eileen, don't you think I care? How do you think I felt each time you hung up on me or refused to come to the phone?"

"You should have walked away," she said.

"God knows I tried."

"Why didn't you forget me?" she asked.

He shook his head. "The moment I spotted you, all those old feelings came back. So here I am, holding you, and it feels wonderful."

"Sold," the auctioneer shouted.

"Five thousand, six hundred," Dan said.

"What?"

"The planter went for fifty-six hundred," he said, motioning to her pad and pen. "Here, let me." He jotted the figures down and handed the pad and pen back to her, guiding her to the next piece of equipment going on the auction block. Piece by piece the assets of the farm were sold.

Eileen's note pad filled with notations. She missed a few key amounts when her thoughts shifted abruptly to Dan. Fortunately the auctioneer took a short break and she didn't have to fight the hopeless challenge of ignoring him.

"Let's get something to eat," Dan suggested. After a quick break of hotdogs and coffee, they returned to the crowd following the auctioneer's flatbed truck as it crept down one aisle and returned on the next.

"May I?" Dan asked, relieving her of the note pad.

"Be sure to add a descriptive note when it's appropriate," she said. "Age of the piece, condition, that kind of comment."

"Yes, boss," he said, glad to see a subtle smile soften her mouth. He followed behind her, occasionally missing a final bid when he made the mistake of allowing his gaze to follow her hips, which swung delightfully as she hurried ahead to the next item for sale. Had she gained weight? Her hips seemed to fill the jeans yet her waist was smaller than ever if that was possible. He missed a third final bid and cursed softly beneath his breath.

"What's the matter?" she asked, glancing over her shoulder.

"I was distracted," he admitted.

"It went for nine hundred," she said, motioning to the pad. "Terrible price. It should have sold for twice that amount."

The sun was hanging low in the western sky when the auctioneer accepted the top bid on the final piece of equipment. "That's all, folks. Thanks for coming. There will be another auction on the Smith place near..." The public address system cut in and out and the announcement was garbled.

"Let's go," Dan said, putting his arm around Eileen's shoulders and turning her away. "I suppose there will be a whole string of these affairs this spring."

They walked toward the field where the vehicles were parked.

"I'm surprised Jordan and the twins aren't with you," he said.

"I needed to get away," she explained.

"Are you going home now?" he asked as they reached her car.

"I have a motel in town. I'll go home tomorrow."

His heart jumped. "Who's staying with the children?"

"Mrs. Sherman, a friend from our church," she said. "Jordan thinks he's old enough to be in charge, but not overnight. Of course Hogan Waite is back—and the other men, so they're not really alone. We've planted five hundred acres of spuds already. I'm cutting back this year, even on the barley. Two sections of land will lay fallow. I just didn't want to worry about..." She ducked her head. "I'm rambling, aren't I?"

When she met his gaze, the expression in his green eyes was unreadable. "Are you going back to Boise now?" she asked.

"My plans are flexible," he said. People around them were driving away. "Would you have dinner with me?"

"I'd like that," she said solemnly. "Why don't you follow me back to the motel? I have a reservation at the American Inn. I'll register and we can visit awhile. You're welcome to shower and get some of this mud off if you wish. Maybe I'll do the same. I ... I'm prattling again, aren't I?"

"Yes." He took her keys and unlocked her door, returned the keys to her palm, and opened the door. "We're wasting time."

CHAPTER FIFTEEN

"BRING YOUR THINGS inside," Eileen said. "I won't be but a few minutes. You can use my shower and then we can talk until it's time to eat." Her eyes were unfathomable as she watched him lingering by the motel room door. "I'm repeating myself. Well, anyway, I'll hurry." She disappeared into the bathroom.

Maybe he should just say goodbye through the locked bathroom door and head for home, Dan deliberated. A vision of her in the shower, sudsy shampoo trickling down her slender neck and her hands gliding over her wet body was his undoing. How could he leave her now? His rejection of her invitation might even the score between them but why keep tally when she had extended this offering of peace?

Before he could come up with more reasons to leave, he grabbed a hanger with clean slacks and a sports shirt and his overnight kit and returned to the room. He closed the door softly behind him, set the dead bolt, and tossed the hanger and case onto a nearby chair.

The bathroom door opened. Steam swirled around her. She was wearing the white fleece robe. "You can have the bathroom," she said. "I can dry my hair out here." She turned away, searching the walls for an electrical outlet for her blow dryer.

"Thanks," he said, closing the bathroom door behind him.

"You can use my shampoo," she called to him.

"Okay."

She dried her hair and ran a pick through it. As she touched the shoulder-length tips and swished them around her face, she smiled. Putting the blow dryer back in her suitcase, she studied her reflection in the mirror and knew the symbolic gesture had been a necessary step in leaving the past behind. Standing in the center of the spacious motel room, away from the farm and her children, was part of the journey of liberation. Did the man in her bathroom complete the trek? Listening as he turned the shower off, she knew what she wanted and needed.

The door opened and he reappeared, his shoulders tan and muscular above the motel's white towel he had wrapped around his hips. A drop of moisture trickled down his chest and was quickly absorbed by the towel.

"Sorry, I forgot my clothes." He motioned to his slacks and shirt. She took a few hesitant steps toward him.

He met her at the foot of the bed. "To hell with clothes," he said. "It's you I want, not a meal or an evening of talking."

"Yes," she whispered. "Oh, Dan, I want you to love me."

"Be sure," he murmured, and not until she nodded her assent did he untie the belt of her robe. He brushed the robe from her shoulders and it fell to the floor. Her hand rested on his naked hips for an instant before she tugged the tip of the towel from where he had tucked it.

He touched her cheek before burying his hand in her curling hair. "I've missed you so much," he whispered. "I didn't know how much longer I could survive without you."

"You were always with me," she replied, stepping closer and kissing his chest.

He tipped her face up to his. "I don't understand."

"I have no photos of you except for those tiny little ones that appear in your magazine, but each time I saw one of the prints you left, you were there looking over my shoulder. I would go into the guest room and I could see you there waiting for me. When I put on my robe, you were there to remove it. When I baked bread, you were there to enjoy it. You are a very difficult man to forget." Her fingers trailed down his body. "You gave me wonderful memories. I may have ordered you from the farm, but you haunted me constantly, day and night."

"Memories aren't enough, not when we can have so much more." He pulled her hard against him. Her head fell back as his mouth explored her throat. The pressure of her palms on his shoulders guided him downward and he buried his face between her breasts.

Still she wasn't satisfied. "Touch me," she moaned. "Kiss me everywhere. I can't bear to be without you anymore." A tremor shook her as his mouth found her nipple, playing across it with his tongue before suckling gently. She pressed against him, shaking her head as he moved to her other breast. Her body was on fire and nothing but his loving touch would assuage her now.

"No," she cried as his mouth left her body, but their separation was brief. He swept her into his arms and carried her to the bed. Gently he laid her down and joined her, his hand caressing her body.

He hesitated. "Safety first."

"I have nothing," she whispered.

He smiled. "It's my turn." Tiny sparks seemed to follow his hands when he resumed his exploration. He counted each vertebra with his mouth, leaving a trail of kisses down her spine. While he concentrated on the small of her back, his hand slid between her thighs and found the warm moist center of her passion. When he buried his fingers in her, she gasped and closed around him, surging to ecstasy in seconds.

Her heart thundered in her chest as he rolled her over and settled between her thighs. Wrapping her legs around him, she met his thrusts. She pulled his head down and claimed his mouth, encouraging him to take her again to that special place in the universe where they could share the passion of their union and find peace together again.

His mouth massaged hers and she wanted his kisses to go on forever. Suddenly he pulled away and buried his face in her hair, holding her tightly against him as he carried her along with him to fulfillment.

"I'VE NEVER FELT so at peace before," she said, rising on her elbow to gaze at him. "Are you asleep?" she whispered, admiring the brush of cinnamon-brown lashes resting against his tan cheeks. The subtle rising and falling of his chest told her he was drifting away. As she lay back beside him, she felt his hand caressing her back.

"I don't want to fall asleep," he said, his voice little more than a whisper. "We should get dressed and go to dinner. That's why we came here."

"No," she confessed, tracing the outline of his mouth with her finger tip.

He opened one eye, then rolled onto his side and gazed down at her. "I was sincere."

She laid down beside him again. "Thank goodness you were prepared. I never considered this happening...until I looked up and saw you beside me at the auction. Then I knew."

He chuckled. "Don't get the wrong idea. I'm not johnny-on-the-spot in these matters, but for your sake, I'm glad it worked out."   "And so am I," she replied. "I pretended at first that we would have dinner and go our separate ways, but I wanted you to stay long enough to kiss me, to hold me. I wanted to say how sorry I was, to tell you how miserable I've been . . . and to ask you to forgive me.''

His hand stroked her rounded hip. ''How is everything back at the farm?''

''Better,'' she said. ''The bank is giving me one more year to get back on my feet. We finished planting the spuds last week. Some of them are already peeking up out of the ground. The barley is in. We put another section into alfalfa. Spuds are heavy feeders, you know, and the alfalfa will replenish the nitrogen in a few years. We're looking forward to summer. Can you imagine it's April already?''

''Sounds like you're back on top of everything,'' Dan said. ''Is this Hogan fellow a big help?''

''Oh, yes, we'd have a hard time getting along without Hogan. He's like one of the family.''

''Where does he stay?''

''Stay?'' she asked. ''Why, on the farm, of course.''

''Does he live in the house?''

She pulled away. ''Of course not. None of my hired hands live in our house, not even the foreman. They never have. What difference does it make to you? Why do you care?''

''Because I don't want some other man being in your house, whatever the reason.'' He tightened his arm around her. ''Damn it all, Eileen, I love you!''

''What?''

''I love you. Is that so strange? I have nothing to offer you. I certainly know next to nothing about this business of yours, and I gallivant all over the country, but that didn't stop me from falling in love with you. I just wanted you to know . . . in case that good-looking hulk of a foreman has designs on you.''

She curled into his side. ''There has never been anything between Hogan and me. He's family . . . a brother . . . an uncle to the children." She nestled down in his arms, not expecting a reply.

"Does he know that?" he asked.

She pulled free and sat up, staring wide-eyed at him. "I certainly hope so."

He laughed and pulled her back down. "If you were half as miserable as I've been, you'll agree we can't live without each other, so why not live with each other? There would be problems to work out . . . I'd probably keep my apartment in Boise for a while, and I have to resolve some problems with Stephen and Vanessa, and I need to talk to Gil Hadley. He's my publisher. He expects me to go wherever he points, and we'll have to work that out."

"It sounds pretty impulsive to me," she said.

"I know, but wouldn't it be better to spend what time we have together than apart? I can't expect you to come to my place, and I couldn't spend the nights at your place, with the children there, unless we were . . . husband and wife."

"You did once," she said, kissing his cheek.

He grinned. "Yes, and that was the most memorable Christmas I've ever had." His expression sobered. "But on a regular basis . . . well I don't know. You haven't said no. Does that mean yes? Will you marry me, Eileen?"

She kissed him lightly. "Oh, Dan, I love you very much. I wanted to come to you but I couldn't. What if we have misunderstandings again?"

"Just say yes or no," he suggested. "We'll deal with the problems one at a time, together."

Her eyes glistened. "No, I can't marry you. Not until I work out my business problems and . . . and more time has passed." Her hand began to explore his body and beneath her touch he reacted.

"You love me but you won't marry me?"

"I have my reasons," she replied. "Come spend the weekends at the farm. We'll try a little modern togetherness first. Maybe you'll find you don't want the responsibility that goes with taking on a young widow and three ready-made children."

"Are you sure?" He rolled her over onto her back.

"Yes, and bring Stephen," she added. "He and Jordan get along so well, it will make our trial run go smoother."

"And if problems arise?"

"Then we can count our lucky stars that we didn't complicate them by marrying. This way you can walk away if you choose. Now would you love me again before we go to dinner?"

He tried to see beneath the liberated facade she presented. "We'll try it," he whispered, pulling her hands away, teasing her body into readiness. As she accepted him and her hands slid around his neck, the need for words subsided and rapture took its place.

THEIR FIRST TRIAL WEEKEND together included a drive to Pocatello, where they had lunch with Gil Hadley and his wife, who had been briefed earlier in the week by Dan.

"And now what?" Gil asked, as he picked up the check for lunch and looked from Dan to Eileen, then the children.

Dan frowned. "Eileen can't get away and I have another trip to John Day, Oregon."

"And I have to be back at school for tests," Stephen said.

"I have a track meet on Wednesday," Jordan said.

"We're in a play at school and we practice all this week," Jolene said, with Jodie nodding her support.

Eileen sighed. "We'll just all go about our separate lives as usual. For now, we're all going to the farm and try to get to know each other. We have a day and a half."

Dan squeezed her hand. "We'll manage."

"Love is on your side," Elizabeth Hadley said. "Give it time to grow and you'll become a family sooner than you realize."

The trip to the farm was noisy. Stephen and Jordan sat in the rear of the Blazer, plotting the coming summer. The twins recited the lines of the play over and over again until Dan began to prompt them when they forgot their parts.

Dan and his son drove away midafternoon on Sunday and the routine returned to normal. During the lonely evenings, after the children had gone to bed, Eileen wrote brief letters to her relatives, detailing enough about Dan to satisfy their curiosity.

The phone rang late that Friday as Eileen waited for Dan to arrive for the weekend.

"Hi, it's Abbie," an excited voice said.

"Abbie? Good grief, it's been months," Eileen exclaimed.

"You could have called if you were worried," Abbie said.

"Touché. How are you?"

"Fine," Abbie said. "Could you meet us for dinner on Sunday at the school house cafe in Dell? I know it's more miles for you but I really need to visit with you."

"Sure, but why?"

"I just need to see you, to talk over old times."

"Are you and Dane having problems?" Eileen asked.

"Let's talk about it then," Abbie hedged.

"Will you be alone? If so, come on down to Shelley."

"No, Dane will be with me."

Eileen exhaled. "That's a relief. I know how you two are. Have you learned how to get along?"

Abbie laughed. "We're still practicing, but our lives have taken a new twist. Lambing is almost finished. We can leave the Parishes in charge.

"We're cultivating the spuds." Eileen began to describe the work necessary in the early part of the season.

She heard the door downstairs open and close. Within minutes Dan appeared and set his suitcase on the floor. He sat down on the bed and she tried to concentrate on the phone conversation. He kissed her neck and she started to giggle.

"What's going on there?" Abbie asked. "Are you alone?"

Eileen pushed Dan away. "We'll see you at noon on Sunday," she promised. "I have to go now."

Dan removed the phone from her hand and laid it to rest. "Aren't you going to welcome the weary traveler home?" he asked.

"Welcome home, darling," she murmured, pulling him close again. "I missed you so much."

His mouth claimed hers and they rolled across the bed, enjoying the intimacy of her body against his. He left the bed and locked the door. In minutes they were undressed and together.

They lay in each other's arms and talked about the week that had passed. He told her of the new article he was working on and she filled him in on the happenings on the farm.

"Sounds pretty normal," he said, nuzzling her hair.

"Except for calls from Stephen and Vanessa," she said.

"Van? Van called you? Why?"

"Stephen wants to quit school," she said. "Isn't that silly for a twelve-year-old boy? How did Vanessa know about me? I wasn't sure if you had told her about us."

He kissed her forehead and pulled her closer. "I gave her your number in case of an emergency. Good Lord, I don't understand my son sometimes."

She traced the muscle flexing in his forearm. "He could spend the summer here," she said. "I wouldn't want to cause trouble between you and Van, but he would be welcome."

"I'll have to talk to her, but no matter what is decided, he has to finish the term." Dan nuzzled her ear, nibbling on the lobe. "Let's worry about my son tomorrow. I have other things on my mind tonight."

"Me too," she whispered, surrendering to his lovemaking.

ON THE STROKE of noon, Dan, Eileen and the four children arrived at a quaint restaurant 120 miles north of the farm.

They climbed from Dan's Blazer as the Grasten's Eagle rolled to a stop next to them. Dane went to the passenger side of the vehicle, opened the door, and gave Abbie a hand.

Eileen stepped closer and held out her arms. "Well, what have you two been up to?" Her eyes widened as she took in the green and yellow knit maternity top Abbie was wearing. "Oh, Abbie, I can't believe it. You? Pregnant?"

Abbie laughed and gazed up at her blond husband. "See, I told you she wouldn't believe it unless she saw me."

Eileen shook her head slowly from side to side. "All these years you've always said kids weren't necessary, a nuisance."

Abbie's hand touched her protruding abdomen. "The way this one kicks, they're still a nuisance, but this one is absolutely necessary."

"When?" Eileen asked.

Dane and Dan broke into laughter. Eileen looked puzzled.

Abbie blushed. "The expected delivery date is early August. I'm almost six months pregnant! I have other subjects to discuss with you, too, but that's enough until after dinner. So how is everyone?'' One by one, she hugged the children. She smiled at the second boy. ''And this must be Stephen. Can I give you a hug as well?'' she asked.

Stephen kicked at the stone near his toe. ''Guess so,'' he said, grinning.

Abbie turned her attention to Eileen and Dan. ''How are you?'' Her gaze shifted from Eileen to Dan and back to Eileen. ''At least you must be speaking.''

''It's a complicated story,'' Dan said. ''Courting between Boise and the farm isn't easy.''

''We manage,'' Eileen added.

''Oh, Eileen, I'm so happy for you both. Try. Try and you'll make it work.'' Abbie's eyes filled with tears and she hugged her cousin as tightly as her pregnancy would allow.

The brick building had once been a rural school. They went inside and found several empty chairs around a large table in the rear of the room. Two other couples occupied seats at the same table. In spite of the conversion to a family-style restaurant, the flavor of the one-room schoolhouse had been preserved, with reading sentence strips, a chalkboard and textbooks, and numerous antiques from the area decorating the walls.

After they ordered, Abbie and Eileen began to catch up on each other's lives. Dan listened while Dane described the current lambing season.

Jordan gave a report on the market outlook for the potato crop. ''Mom decided to cut way back this year,'' he said. ''She had a real estate salesman out on Thursday. I hope she can't find anyone to buy the place.''

''Buy the place?'' Dan asked, frowning as he looked from Eileen to Jordan. ''Are you thinking of selling? You never...said anything.''

Eileen shrugged. ''I'm not closing any doors. I wanted to know what the place might go for...in case I needed the money. I still have obligations . . . I try to not worry." She smiled. "Let's not discuss farm finances." She took a sip from her bowl of soup. "Delicious. Shall we eat?"

After trips to a salad bar, the main course of roast beef was served family style, with bowls of mashed potatoes and gravy following a platter overflowing with thick slices of beef.

Abbie reached into her purse and withdrew a yellow envelope. She waited until everyone was eating, then turned to Eileen. "I received a letter from Callie."

"You did?" Eileen said. "She called me a month ago, but she would only talk for ten minutes. She said that was all her budget could stand. She was using her mom's phone and . . . well you know how Callie is, too proud to impose on others."

Dan cleared his throat. "Pride can cause unnecessary problems for anyone."

"And you Hardesty cousins have perfected pride to a new art form," Dane Grasten added.

"Now, cut it out, you two," Eileen said. "Go on, Abbie, what did Callie have to say?"

Abbie looked at Eileen pensively. "I wrote her last month. I asked her to see if she could find my mother. I know she's ignored me most of my life, but I'd like to know more about her. Maybe, now that I'm about to be a mother myself, I can understand what made her act the way she did. Anyway, Callie and Aunt Minnie are trying to locate her."

"Callie sounded much more optimistic than usual," Eileen said. "Maybe she's met someone."

"I doubt that," Abbie said. "After that horrible Bobby Joe, well, you know what Aunt Minnie says: 'Once burned, twice shy.'"

Dane Grasten inclined his head thoughtfully. "I don't know about that."

Abbie laughed. "There are exceptions to every saying. Now eat, and leave these matters of the heart to the women." He winked at her and returned his attention to his plate.

"If she calls again, I'll simply ask," Eileen said.

Abbie beamed. "Leave it to Eileen, the problem solver, to cut through the mystery."

"It's usually easier to solve other people's problems than one's own," Eileen conceded, "but I do hope she finds happiness. She deserves it."

Abbie nodded. "Keep me posted. Now, while we enjoy this delicious dinner, tell us what you remember about my mother and father. Perhaps your memories are better than mine."

"I do remember one time," Eileen said. "You were about four and you came with this tall dark-haired man and red-headed woman. She was tall, about your height." Soon Eileen was able to share more and more memories of Abbie's early childhood. With a promise to stay in closer touch, they parted a few hours later.

"She and Dane appear to be very happy," Eileen said as Dan drove them home.

"Yeah, and now they're gonna have a baby," Jolene said, sighing deeply.

"Babies, yuck," Jordan groaned.

"Momma, are you ever gonna have another baby?" Jodie asked.

"I hope not," Jordan said, before Eileen could reply. "A baby would really spoil everything."

Eileen was quiet as they drove over Monida Pass and into Idaho. "What's wrong?" Dan asked.

"Abbie and Dane are lucky to work together," Eileen said. "I miss you during the week."

Dan nodded. "I'm working on a change, but I have commitments. Be patient."

In the rear of the Blazer, Jordan and Stephen whispered. Curious, Eileen tried to catch a few words but couldn't. She caught Dan's gaze. "What are they talking about?" she asked.

He glanced into the rearview mirror. The boys looked up and saw him watching them. The whispering stopped.

SCHOOL WOULD BE OUT in two weeks and the children were tense with anticipation. As they sat around the supper table, teasing each other about their upcoming report cards, the doorbell rang.

Eileen hurried to the front door, hoping Dan had made an unexpected midweek stop, perhaps to make up for the two weekends he had missed. She reached for the knob, feeling a mixture of resentment and love for this man who had begun to display the irritating habit of showing up at her doorstep only when it proved convenient. His career was important, yet at times she needed him, for moral support, if nothing else.

A sweaty and disheveled Stephen Page leaned against the porch post, much as his father had done numerous times in the past.

"Stephen? What are you doing here?" she asked. Uncertainty about the stability of the nontraditional family she and Dan had formed had held her back on bringing Stephen into her home. "Come inside. Are you hungry? Do you want to freshen up? Go upstairs and then join us at the table. We always have room for one more."

Without a word, he climbed the stairs.

She returned to the kitchen.

"Who was it?" Jordan asked.

"Stephen," Eileen said, still perplexed about finding him on her doorstep.

"Stephen? Great!" Jordan exclaimed. "He actually did it." He shot from his chair and bounded up the stairs.

When Jordan returned to the kitchen, he had Stephen in tow. "I bet him he wouldn't do it. This is one bet I'm glad I lost."

Eileen motioned the boys to sit down. "What was the bet?" she asked.

Jordan eyed his mother, the wisdom of his actions now doubtful. "Stephen's school runs until the middle of June," he explained. "His mom and dad wouldn't say yes or no. They have to always *talk* about him, and we got tired of waiting."

Eileen frowned. "Waiting for what?"

"I bet him five bucks he wouldn't hitchhike here. I bet him another five bucks that when he got off the interstate he couldn't find our farm and that he'd have to call for directions." He grinned. "For a city kid, he's smarter than I thought."

Stephen raised his head, brushing his brown hair from his eyes. "My dad is gonna kill me, and when he's finished my mom will kill me all over again. She says if my grades drop, she's gonna stick me back into that academy for the summer. But I won't stay. I told her that."

"Does your mother know you're here?" Eileen asked, wishing Dan were present. Why did he always seem to be gone when problems arose? What kind of relationship had they fallen into? Bedroom privileges on the weekend, and then only when the weekend was convenient? She shifted her attention from one boy to the other, trying to ignore the nausea churning in the pit of her stomach. "You can't stay here, Stephen!"

"Why not?" Jordan demanded. "His dad stays here whenever he feels like it. Why not Stephen?"

"The school will report him missing. He can't hide here until his father decides to show up," she said, resenting being stuck in the middle of Dan's and Van's problems.

"But we planned..." Jordan said.

"I don't care what you planned, young man, he can't stay here!" Her voice was almost a shout.

"Stephen and I have made plans," Jordan insisted. "I don't see why you're so mean when you let his dad..."

"Shut up, Jordan, just shut up!" Eileen squeezed her eyes shut and counted silently. "Jordan," she said, more softly, "if you ran away, I'd be frantic. Stephen can stay here tonight, but he must call his mother. Now!"

Stephen flinched at her sharp words. Eileen stood by while he called his mother and told her what he had done, then Eileen took the phone. "Stephen and my son cooked this up," she said.

"The headmaster called just a few minutes ago," Vanessa replied. "Sometimes I don't know what to do with him. His school has a summer program but he's already expressed himself quite clearly about that." She cleared her throat. "Could you call Dan?"

"I'll try to find him," Eileen said. "Stephen is welcome to stay here tonight," Eileen said, determined to stand firm until she could talk to Dan. "I'll drive him to Boise tomorrow morning. Should we go to your place or to the school?"

Van hesitated. "If you don't mind, take him to the academy and I'll go there in the afternoon and talk to the administration. Thank you, Mrs. Mills, for helping."

"That's fine," Eileen said.

When she hung up, she glared at the boys. "How did you get me into the middle of all this?"

Stephen smiled, his eyes reminding her of Dan's. "I figured if my dad stays here now, there was no reason why I can't stay here too." He shook his head slowly from side to side. "I'd sure like to live here all the time. I hate that school. The headmaster is a tyrant and our football team stinks. They never win a game because the other guys just goof off and we don't have cheerleaders because there are no girls."

"Yeah, his school is for boys only." Jordan chimed in. "I told him about some of the girls who will be in the eighth grade next year. I told him about the swimming pool in town and how we could go swimming as often as we wanted to and—"

"Did you tell him that you had to bicycle in and back, and that you weren't allowed to go unless you'd finished your work? That work comes before play on this farm?"

"Sure." He grinned. "Can you imagine going to a school with no girls?"

Eileen frowned at the glint in Jordan's eyes. "I thought you hated girls."

He stiffened. "Well, maybe I did at the first of the year, but some of them are . . . you know . . . changing."

Eileen remembered Dan's theory of pubescent boys and girls. "Yes, I know, but I'm still very upset with both of you. Jordan, take Stephen outside and feed the livestock while I try to locate his father."

She dialed all the motels in John Day and surrounding area, but no Daniel Page was registered. Eileen felt trapped and resentful. When the boys returned from doing the chores, they raced passed her and up the stairs and she followed them.

"I'm never going back to that school," Stephen insisted.

"Right on, man," Jordan agreed and they slapped palms. "We can make plans."

Eileen followed them into their room. "The only plans you two had better make is how to explain all this to Stephen's mother and father and to the school principal."

"Headmaster," Jordan said, sneering.

"Watch your tone, young man," Eileen said.

"Why? You don't care what I want," he said, his voice growing loud and harsh. "You don't care about anything or anybody, just about having Stephen's dad come here. You don't wanna know what I think. You don't care! Well, you're gonna be sorry because I don't care either. Stephen and I have plans and we're gonna keep 'em."

CHAPTER SIXTEEN

EILEEN'S HEAD was throbbing the next morning when the alarm sounded. First she would see that her own children were safely on the school bus, talk to Hogan about the day's activities, then she'd take Stephen back to his school. The trip would take most of the day. Resentment of this unexpected intrusion on her tight schedule put her in a foul mood by the time she headed for the stairs. Her patience had become thin as tissue paper the last few weeks.

In the kitchen, the twins were standing beside the coffee maker, watching the pot fill with brewed coffee.

"Why thank you, girls, how thoughtful," she said. "But don't try to pour it. You might burn yourselves." She filled a cup and sat down at the table. "What would you like for breakfast?" When neither of them replied, she looked up. Their usually bright faces were somber. "What's wrong, Jolene? Jodie?"

"They're gone," Jolene said.

"We went to their room to play a trick on them this morning and...they're gone," Jodie said.

Eileen smiled. "No, they must be outside doing the morning chores, or shooting baskets...or something." Her smile faded when the twins continued to shake their heads.

"We looked," Jolene said. "Jordan's knapsack is gone and so is the one in the hall closet that Daddy used to use. I think they've run away. Both of Jordan's bikes are gone too. His new one and his old blue one."

"Run away?" Eileen ran her hand across her forehead. "Why would they do that? Surely they knew we could work this out."

Jodie shook her head. "Jordan was real mad last night."

"Jordan has always had a sullen streak, but it's time he learned that he can't have his way all the time." Eileen ran up the stairs to her son's room. Inside, the contents of the room looked as though a tornado had struck. Clothes were strewn across the beds. Jordan's room was seldom neat, but it had never looked as bad as this. In his closet, she searched for his favorite spring windbreaker with all the NASA patches he had collected.

"His space jacket is gone, eh?" Jolene asked.

Eileen nodded. Slowly the full impact of what her son had done began to sink in. "Why would he do this?" she asked.

"They have been planning all kinds of things to do together," Jodie said. "Maybe running away to a new home was one of them."

"But this is their home!" Eileen exclaimed.

Jodie shook her head. "Just Jordan's."

"Stephen doesn't have a home," Jolene added. "He says his dad is gone all the time and his mom doesn't want him around."

Jodie's head bobbed in agreement. "Sometimes he signs his name Stephen Street."

"Street? Why Street?" Eileen asked.

"He said people who live in the streets in Boise don't have homes and neither does he." Jodie shrugged. "So he's Stephen Street but his mom and dad don't pay any attention."

The girls' comments stayed with her as she returned to the kitchen, trying to remain calm and act rationally.

"They must be hungry," she murmured.

"They made sandwiches," Jodie said.

"No, they didn't," Jolene replied. "Jordan only eats peanut butter and jam sandwiches and he always leaves the jar out and the lid off. The peanut butter is in the cupboard. I checked.''

"Jordan's a slob," Jodie replied. "Stephen is neat. Look in the sink. There's a knife and it had peanut butter on it. I smelled it. Stephen cleaned up after messy old Jordan.''

They all peered at the knife lying in the bottom of the kitchen sink. *If the situation wasn't so serious,* Eileen thought, *we could laugh at this,* but she found nothing amusing about her son running away. She reached for the phone and quickly punched out four numbers, paused, and hung up the receiver. The police wouldn't be interested. No use filing a report yet. They would laugh at her for being an overprotective mother.

Where was Dan? Why wasn't he here? Why had he dumped all this on her? She didn't even know what state he was in. Oregon still? He hadn't called for several days. "Girls, you get ready for school. I'll fix breakfast. Surely the boys will come back when they get hungry.'' She smiled gamely. "Hurry now, the bus will be here in thirty minutes. I'll make cinnamon toast and hot chocolate. Everything will be fine, just fine. Don't worry.''

As she watched her daughters leave for school, Eileen's confidence began to crumble. If she called the police, she would have to explain the argument, and then they would ask questions about why Dan and his son considered the farm their second home, and the authorities would hold her accountable for the boys' home environments. How could she convince them that she had always been a good mother? She rubbed her temples. No, she would just keep calm for an hour or two and wait for the boys to return.

A few minutes after ten o'clock, the phone rang.

"This is the Idaho Falls Police Department," a husky voice said. "One of our officers found two bicycles abandoned near the falls. Our records show the license on the newer bike registered to a Mrs. Eileen Mills of Shelley. Would that be you, ma'am?''

"Yes," she said, her voice unsteady. "The falls?"

"Ma'am, do you have sons?"

"One, and he had a friend here... last night. We had an argument. They must have ridden them away during the night or early this morning but why the falls? Oh, my God, could they have fallen in the river? Oh, no! My God!''

"Keep calm now, ma'am," the officer said. "Give me their descriptions and we'll start looking for them."

"I've got to come," she said.

"No, you stay by the phone, in case they're all right and decide to check in," he said. "You know how young fellows can be. They'll probably show up when their stomaches tell them it's time to eat again. You let us know."

Sick with fear, Eileen sat by the phone for an hour. Hogan found her there, rigid and pale. "Any word yet, ma'am?" She shook her head and he patted her shoulder. "I'm sure they're fine," he said, "but if you want, I can go into the city and see what's going on. Would you feel better if I did that?"

"Yes," she whispered, "and thank you."

Images of their lifeless bodies washed onto the rocky banks of the Snake River formed. *Another funeral. More loved ones whisked away. Call my parents. No. Call Duncan's parents. Not yet. Why alarm everyone? Call Abbie. But what could she do so far away? Wait by the phone. Find Dan. Yes, find Dan.*

The phone rang again. "Yes!" she cried.

"Hi, honey, how's everything?" Dan asked, his voice jovial.

"Oh, my God, Dan. The boys, oh the boys... they ran away and now they're missing but their bikes were found near the river in Idaho Falls and no one can find them."

"What are you talking about?" he asked. "Stephen's in school and I'm sure Jordan is too."

"No." As calmly as she could she summarized the events from the previous night. "This morning they were gone! You've got to come."

"Let me check my schedule and ..."

"Your schedule? You'd let your damned appointments take precedence over the very lives of our children?"

"No, you don't understand," he said. "Honey, you're hysterical."

"Of course I'm hysterical," she cried. "Our children may be dead. Dead! Doesn't that mean anything to you?"

"Of course it does," he replied. "I need to think."

"Well, think all you want," she shouted. "Take all the time you need, but if you won't come now ... don't come at all ... ever!"

"I'm in American Falls," he said, his voice sounding more distant with each word. "It will take me about an hour to get there. It's interstate highway all the way to Shelley, so God help me if the cops and their radar are out. Hang tight, sweetheart, I'm coming."

An hour later, Dan drove into the yard, a cloud of dust swirling around the vehicle as he slammed on the brakes. In seconds he was in the house and with Eileen, whispering soothing words to her as she clung to him.

"I was afraid you wouldn't come," she sobbed. "I thought you didn't care enough to come."

He tightened his arms around her. "Shush now," he crooned.

"What if they never find them?" she cried. "What if we spend the rest of our lives wondering what happened to them?" She looked up into his face. "Have we lost our sons before we've had a chance to make them a real family?"

"No, no," he murmured, kissing her lightly, "We'll find them." He led her to the sofa, holding her in his arms until some of the tension drained from her. "I'll call the police again and see if they've learned anything new." He untangled himself and went to the kitchen. *God, protect them* he prayed, as he dialed. Relief clashed with fear when the officer reported that other than the bicycles, nothing had been found.

The phone rang again and he grabbed it as Eileen joined him.

"Hello?" he said.

"Grasten here. Is that you, Page?"

"Yes," Dan said, "but I can't talk or tie up the phone. We have a problem here. It's pretty serious."

"Could it be about two missing boys...oh, about twelve years old and both sandy-haired?" Dane Grasten asked.

"My God," Dan sighed. "Are they there?"

Eileen grabbed the receiver from his hand. "They're with you?" she asked. "How did they get all the way up there?"

Dan leaned close to the receiver to hear Grasten's response to Eileen's question. "The dispatcher from the sheriff's office called me about four this morning," Grasten explained. "Two kids got off the northbound bus in the middle of the night. At first they wouldn't say who they were and they didn't have any identification. When the officer pulled a bluff on them and threatened to throw them in jail, Jordan insisted he was Abbie's son. The dispatcher called to see if I'd like to claim them."

Eileen began to sob against Dan's chest. The phone slid from her hand and Dan grabbed it before it could hit the floor.

"Grasten, we owe you one for this," Dan said. "Eileen was afraid that . . . well, never mind now. Are they in town or out at the ranch? We'll come get them right away."

Grasten chuckled. "They're here at the ranch. Take your time, Page. Let them stew in their own juices for a few hours. Jordan is still angry, but Stephen is pretty upset about what they did. I bought them breakfast when I came in to get them. Seems Jordan dropped a knapsack full of sandwiches into the Snake while they were waiting for the bus to come.''

"Where did they get enough money for bus tickets?" Dan asked.

"They said they have been saving their allowances for some summer fun, but when Eileen said Stephen couldn't stay, they pooled their funds and managed to come up with ninety-one dollars and thirty-five cents. The fares were forty-five dollars each. It was Jordan's idea to come here, but Stephen could have said no. The driver must have been dozing a little. He should have questioned them before ever letting them on the bus. Anyway, they're safe. Abbie and I didn't want you to worry.''

"Worry is a gross understatement," Dan replied. "I didn't know a thing about it until an hour ago, but they've put Eileen through hell. You hold them. We'll arrange for a sitter and leave right away. Thanks, Grasten. Those boys have some big explaining to do. Bye for now.''

"I'll call Mrs. Sherman and leave a note for Hogan," Eileen said, her mind reeling. "And call the police in Idaho Falls." She smiled weakly. "Tell them our sons are safe.''

Later, they traveled in silence to Dane's and Abbie's, holding hands. A few miles into Montana, he took the exit into the small rural town of Lima.

"Let's have lunch," he said. "When did you eat last?''

"Yesterday, I think," she admitted.

He parked in front of a cafe and took her hand before she could open the door. "Eileen, I've been thinking . . . about us, the children. I've asked before and you've turned me down. Now I'm asking again. Will you marry me? This would never have happened if you'd said yes the first time.''

"Are you saying this is all my fault?" She pulled her hand from his.

"No, of course not." He grabbed her hand again. "You keep calling the boys 'our sons.' They are our sons. The twins are my girls, too. I think about the children we could have some day. I think of you as my wife. We're a family in every way but the legal one. I want more than weekend privileges with you in bed. I want the title and responsibility that goes along with marriage. Is that so unreasonable?"

"Half the time you can't even manage to claim weekend privileges," she retorted. "I couldn't find you this morning. I thought you were still in Oregon, or Salt Lake. How could I have known you were in American Falls? You never told me!"

He dropped his gaze. "I should have given you my itinerary. I'm sorry. I was coming home from Elko, Nevada. I heard about a cowboy poet gathering there and...it sounded interesting."

"You see," she murmured. "As long as you travel around the country, free as a bird who can flit from place to place, you need to be unencumbered by a wife and family. You might meet someone."

"I did meet someone," he insisted. "She's right here with me now."

"You must have other women scattered around the country."

He withdrew his arm. "Do you think I've been fooling around with other women since becoming involved with you?"

"I would assume..."

"You assume wrong." He jammed the key back in the ignition and shoved the gear shift into reverse, then roared out of the parking lot and back onto the interstate highway.

They didn't speak again until they arrived at the Grasten Livestock home ranch.

Dane Grasten opened the door for them. "The wayward ones are in the kitchen filling their hollow legs. I've raked them both over the coals about the consequences of their actions. You might as well add to it. Frankly, they deserve it, even if they did present a pretty good case of parental neglect."

Eileen stopped just inside the door. "Parental neglect? Dane, how could you? I love my son!"

Dan laid his hand on Eileen's shoulder. "Benign neglect is what he means and I agree, at least on my part. Stephen has been sending me messages for the past two years. Van and I ignored them because we thought he would get over his rebellion. Meeting Jordan only made his dissatisfaction grow."

She turned to him. "Are you saying if you hadn't gotten involved with the Mills family, none of this would have happened? How dare you! I'm not responsible for you refusing to listen to your son and I would never stick my child in a cold impersonal military academy just because he was a bother to me."

"Stop," Dane insisted, laying a firm hand on each of their shoulders. "If I didn't know better, I'd think you two hated each other. Do you?"

Eileen's features turned pale when she turned to Dan. The worry lines around Dan's mouth had deepened since she had first met him. His eyes, the color of a field of barley about to turn, were deeply troubled. His hair seemed lighter, and she realized it was due to the white at his temples that matched his sideburns. Had she taken him so much for granted that she had failed to see the changes in him since they had first met? Had knowing her taken this toll on him?

"I don't hate Dan," she murmured. "I love him."

"Nor do I hate her," Dan replied, taking her hands in his. His gaze roamed her features, seeing only the beauty he had always found there, not the physical attractiveness of her feminine features but the total person inside, the strength and loving concern, the determination to protect her loved ones, the practicality of her approach to living. He didn't even notice her haggard expression. He smiled as he admired her now shoulder-length hair. Would he ever see that braid hanging down her back again? Did it matter? He cared about her just as she was, because in spite of their difficulties he loved her to distraction.

Grasten smiled and pushed them closer. "This domestic counseling is intriguing," he said. "Hope I never need it myself. Now why don't you two go down the hall to Abbie's and my bedroom?"

"Why?" Eileen asked, dragging her gaze from Dan's face. "I want to see the boys."

"Kiss and make up a little," Grasten suggested. "You need to present a united front to those two insecure kids in the kitchen. They're both scared stiff that you two are never going to get married. If you don't get married, they'll never be brothers. They want that more than anything else in the world right now, other than having a mother and father who love them. No one should be forced into matrimony, but you've involved four children in this situation. What are you going to do about them?" He pointed down the hallway. "It's at the end, just beyond the blue nursery. Excuse the mess. We're doing some remodeling."

They found the room and walked inside. Dan closed the door. "Need the bathroom?" he asked, glancing at the door on the other side of the room.

She shook her head stubbornly.

"Well, I do," he said, and disappeared, closing the door a little harder than necessary. She looked about the room, her attention drawn to the unusual carved headboard. She approached it cautiously. This was where Abbie and Dane Grasten slept . . . made love . . . where they had built a marriage sound and strong, one that made Eileen uncomfortable in its implications. What had Dan and she established? Nothing but a big mess.

Dan's hand touched her shoulder. "It's impressive, isn't it?" he asked, his breath stirring the curls near her ear.

"Yes," she replied softly. "They seem so happy. Abbie says they never argue but that they discuss a lot, and sometimes their voices get a little loud." Her gaze lingered on the ornate headboard and the scenes it depicted. "They've found love."

Dan turned her around to face him. "Look at me, Eileen, please." Her mouth was tight, her jaw stiff when she looked into his eyes. "We've found love, too." His hands slid into her hair. "We've let it wander, abused it, neglected it, like we did our sons. Let's bring it back and let it grow. I love you more than life itself." His lips brushed hers. *Ask once more, Page, or you're a fool,* he thought. He claimed her mouth again, feeling her lips soften beneath his as their bodies touched.

Her hands began to work their way up his chest, to his throat, and as her arms slid around his neck, she succumbed to his overtures, meeting him with her own ardor, pressing against him and stretching on her toes to reach his face. "Yes, and I love you, maybe too much. I'm afraid."

"Never, sweetheart, never be afraid again," he whispered. "If you love me and I love you, then why won't you marry me?" Dan asked softly.

When she didn't reply, he shook her. "Communicate with me, Eileen. Isn't that what this is all about? Talk to me. Tell me how you feel. A man can only take so many rejections and he begins to wonder if he's wasting his time. Don't you think it hurts me when you keep saying no?"

"I never meant to hurt you," she exclaimed, her face screwing up as she tried to stop the tears. "But you're always gone. You're never home when I need you. It's as if I'm still a widow."

"What about you?" he challenged. "I asked you to come with me several times and you always had an excuse to say no."

"A farmer can't just walk away," she retorted.

"Well, she can certainly get a sitter. If you can get a sitter for all those kids, why not a sitter for the farm? Do you have to be tied to the land so tightly it becomes an albatross?"

"I seldom get a sitter for my children," she said.

"And that's another problem," he said. "All those kids. How do you think I feel, making love to you and wondering when some kid is going to knock on the door?"

"It's not all my fault. One of them is yours!"

Gradually he began chuckling.

"What's so funny?" she asked, smiling in spite of herself.

"Here we are, arguing about the very things that can make us a family. I love those kids...but I do get a little tense when I hear them walking the halls outside our locked door at night."

"Maybe we could get away occasionally...to a motel..." She smiled at him. "We could go into Idaho Falls. That's all of ten miles away. Can you stay long enough to travel that far?"

He looked pained. "Am I that bad about staying away?"

She touched his shirt. "Sometimes. I worry that you won't come back, that you'll have an accident and I'll loose you...permanently."

"Oh, honey," he murmured against her hair. "I understand. Losing Duncan was unavoidable. Neither of you could have done a thing about it, but us? We can work at being together. Now, for the third and last time: Will you marry me?"

Time hung suspended as he waited for her response.

"It won't be easy," she cautioned. "Are you sure you want to take on a young widow and three ready-made children?"

"Stephen makes it four," he said. "Then there are the ones to come. Don't forget them."

"Ones to come! Don't rush me, Mr. Page."

He grinned. "Does this mean you accept?"

"What if we have misunderstandings? What if..."

"Just say yes or no," he coaxed. "We'll deal with the problems one at a time, together."

Her eyes glistened. "Yes, I'll marry you. We'll probably have lots of problems and lots of confusion, Daniel Page, but I promise you lots of love, too."

"That sounds great to me, sweetheart," he replied, kissing her soundly. "A little confusion keeps a man on his toes and a lot of loving is just what I have in mind, beginning tonight when we get those two wayward boys of ours home to do evening chores. In fact we'll call Mrs. Sherman from here and see if she can stay the night. We'll drop Jordan and Stephen off and head for the big city." He kissed her cheeks, then the tip of her nose. "Want to spend the night in Idaho Falls with your future husband?"

"I'd love to," she replied, resting her forehead against his chest. "This is a start, isn't it?"

"Yes," he said. "Now let's tackle our first two problems."

THEY WERE MARRIED a week later at the county courthouse in Blackfoot, with Dane and Abbie as their witnesses and the four children in attendance.

For a month, Dan stayed at the farm, working on revisions. Once he convinced Eileen to accompany him to Boise to deliver several assignments to Gil Hadley. A side trip to Weiser enabled her to meet his parents. On the way home, they stopped at George and Geraldine Mills's home and told them of the wedding. George was jubilant but Eileen's former mother-in-law was quiet.

"You'll always be their grandparents," Dan said. "I hope you'll have room in your hearts for my son Stephen as well. Not all children have four sets of grandparents. Let's make the most of his good fortune.

Arrangements were made for Stephen to finish the year at the academy. Van would bring him to the farm for the summer.

WHEN THE PHONE RANG midmorning on a late June day and Eileen answered it, some sixth sense warned her the honeymoon was about to come to an abrupt halt. "Dan, it's Gil Hadley. He says it's urgent."

The one-sided conversation continued for a half hour, with Dan taking notes furiously. Eileen tried to get her husband's attention but he waved her to silence. She couldn't make out the total picture, but knew he had accepted another assignment.

Forty-five minutes later he turned to her. "A really major story has broken and Gil thinks it would make a great human interest cover. He wants Susan Gallagher, himself and me to take a late flight out of Boise. I can get a commuter flight from Idaho Falls to Boise. Gil will meet me."

The excitement in his voice was matched by the gleam in his eyes. How could she remind him of the promises he had made when this was what he was trained for, his profession? And hers? Spuds and earthen cellars, manure, barley; not at all romantic and exciting; unlike this spectacular assignment he had just been given.

She suppressed her disappointment. "What kind of story?"

"Turn on the television. Gil says all the networks are carrying it. There's been an earthquake. Its epicenter is right on the international border between Arizona and Mexico.

It's devastated the two towns. They're poor towns, but the town on the U.S. side is more fortunate and those residents are trying to do what they can for their Mexican neighbors." He glanced at his notes. "I'd better make my reservations. I think a flight leaves at 2:00 p.m." He tossed his pen in the air and caught it. "Damn, it will be good to be back in the thick of things again. Let's have lunch early so I have time to pack and we can talk."

He called the airlines, only to learn that the flight was full. "I could take a chance on a no-show but that would be risky. I'd better drive to Boise." He turned to her. "I'll call as soon as I have a place to stay, but don't worry if it's several days. They've been having trouble with the phone lines."

"Dan, you're a plain old-fashioned news reporter more than a fancy journalist."

He laughed. "Once the excitement of covering breaking news gets in your blood, it's hopeless."

She walked with him to his Blazer. "I've got to go or I'll miss the flight out of Boise. I love you," he said and then he was gone.

SATURDAY MORNING Vanessa Harcourt called to say she wanted to come for a visit.

"Okay, but Dan's not here," Eileen said, reluctant to be with Dan's ex-wife alone. "He's on assignment."

"Frankly, it's you I'm curious about," Van said.

Stephen and Jordan had mixed emotions about Van coming. "What if she wants him to go back to Boise?" Jordan asked.

"Then we'll discuss it, won't we?" Eileen said.

When Vanessa arrived, Jordan got right to the point. "Can he stay with us?"

"Of course, for the summer," Vanessa said.

"He wants to go to my school this fall," Jordan added. "It's cheaper than that stupid military school."

Vanessa arched a brow at the outspoken boy. "Money isn't a factor. What does Stephen want? Can't he speak for himself?"

Stephen met his mother's gaze directly. "I want to live here all the time."

Vanessa tensed. "Permanently? You don't want to visit me in Boise? Ever?"

"Sure, sometimes," Stephen replied, grinning. "Maybe when the fair is on or BSU is playing a football game."

"Doesn't Eileen have enough children already?" Van asked. "Have you talked this over with her and your father?"

"There's always room for one more here," Eileen assured her, "and Dan has wanted to have his son with him for some time."

"Yes, but still..." Van's gaze shifted from the boys to Eileen and back.

"So? Can he live here with us?" Jordan asked, and Eileen gave him a warning look.

Vanessa sighed. "If living here is your decision," she said, glancing curiously at Jordan, "so be it. But I'll miss you, Stephen. You're still my child and I love you. I just don't always understand what's brewing in that mind of yours." She wrote out a generous check and handed it to Eileen. "His appetite is insatiable at times. I don't want him to be a financial drain on you. Groceries cost money even when you live on a farm."

"That's not necessary," Eileen replied. "Dan has already..."

Vanessa slid the check into Eileen's palm. "Take it anyway. Save it for something special for him." She glanced around the comfortable informal living room. "I'm glad Dan has found happiness here." She extended her hand.

Eileen accepted the check. "Thank you."

Vanessa kissed Stephen on his cheek and he gave her a quick hug before leaving the room. She turned to Eileen again. "I'm glad the boys have left. May I talk quite frankly?"

"Of course," Eileen said.

"Seeing where Stephen was living was only one reason for my coming," Van said. "Dan and I never tried to work at our marriage. We went about our separate careers. Stephen's arrival hardly caused a ripple for either of us. We made good salaries and I had a live-in nanny. She stayed with me until I found the private school. I never had to get up at night to tend Stephen. Neither did Dan."

She looked forlorn. "Don't let that happen here. Stay involved with each other's lives. Don't drift apart. Confront Dan if necessary. If a marriage isn't a partnership it isn't a true marriage. Dan and I never formed that partnership."

She smiled ruefully, pulling herself to her full height. "I have many talents but motherhood isn't one of them. I recognize that limitation. Fate must have had a hand in all our lives, or you and Dan would never have met. Stephen has never had this kind of family life. Dan has never been a full-time father. Perhaps they've both been deprived."

CHAPTER SEVENTEEN

DAN STARED at the calendar. Although he had managed to call at least once a week, he had to accept the harsh fact of being gone for eight weeks.

His father had called earlier in the day and left a message that his mother had had a heart attack and had been taken to a Boise hospital and that he would call again as soon as possible.

The earthquake story had mushroomed into a complex project when an offer from a national television network had proven irresistible, and Dan had agreed to cover the story for them as well as *Western Living*. He had done some television reporting in both Texas and Idaho and had always enjoyed the media and the excitement of on-site reporting. A trip to Los Angeles for an appearance on a late-night talk show had been followed by an all-expense-paid flight to a daytime talk show from the east coast during which he had escorted three of the survivors to and from the local area. The weeks had rolled by.

Eileen had said during their most recent late-night call that she had seen more of him on television than in person. "Perhaps we've rushed the marriage after all," she'd suggested.

He mulled over her words as his fingers drummed the desk, waiting for the phone to ring.

Thank goodness Eileen and the children are all healthy, he thought. Another catastrophe would be more than he could handle at the present. He had wrapped up the work near the border and made reservations for a flight from Phoenix to Idaho Falls in the midafternoon, after a four-hour drive from the small motel where he'd lived for two months. He had tried to get Eileen to join him, but she had begged off, saying they were into heavy irrigating and spraying for peach aphids and making preliminary plans for digging the spuds.

He planned to call Eileen as soon as he knew more about his mother's condition and have her meet him at the Idaho Falls airport. He would pick up the Blazer from the Boise airport's long-term parking later.

The phone rang and Dan had it to his ear instantly. "Yes, Dad, how is she?"

"Not so good, son," his father said. "How soon could you get here? She has been asking for you. Your sister is on her way from New Jersey. The doc just doesn't know which way she might go. Oh, damn it, son, just get here pronto."

"Sure," Dan said. "I'll change my flight and call Eileen. I'll see you tomorrow afternoon."

When he called the farm, no one answered. He frowned, wondering where they might be. He called early the next morning and a sleepy Eileen answered. He explained the situation.

"Of course, she needs you," Eileen said. "Call me after you've talked to the heart specialists."

"I called last night," he said. "Where was everyone?"

"Hogan Waite took us to dinner and then to a movie."

"Why would Waite take you all out?" he asked.

"He said we had been working too hard," she explained. "Since you weren't here and I didn't know when you might call, I accepted his offer. The children all love Hogan. Even Stephen finds him fascinating, especially when he tells his stories about Alaska. We've been sitting outside on the porch lately and it's peaceful. I wish you could be with us." She cleared her throat before he could respond. "Anyway, it was good to get away. Sorry we missed you. The children send their love . . . and I do too.''

"Could you get away and meet me in Boise?" he asked.

"I have a meeting on Monday morning in Idaho Falls with the banker who monitors our line of credit," she said. "I have to bring the books up to date and prepare some budgets for the next two years. It will take me all weekend to get everything ready. The meeting is very important, and I really can't change it again unless . . . oh Dan, I hope and pray your mother will be all right.''

"Sure," he murmured. But as he drove the long lonely miles on State Route 85 through the desert past Ajo and Gila Bend to Phoenix, the image of tall, handsome, charismatic Hogan Waite escorting Eileen about town gnawed at his gut.

As EILEEN LAY in bed that night, wishing desperately Dan was beside her, her hand settled on her lower abdomen. How could she tell him over the phone that their lives were going to become even more complicated the following spring?

She hadn't had a period since the runaway escapade. Afterward, they had implemented Dan's suggestion and spent the night away from the family. They hadn't made love again until after the wedding and by the time they thought back to what they had done, the consequences of their night of ecstasy were irrevocable.

At first Eileen had credited the delay to the excitement of the wedding and having Dan around full-time. They had made love during the day, while the children had been in school, but had always been careful. But now it looked as if their caution had been after the fact.

More recently, she had been troubled with nausea each evening. She reached for a salt cracker, wondering why she couldn't have normal morning sickness like other pregnant women.

FRIDAY EVENINGS had become the most difficult for Eileen during Dan's absence. Hogan had accepted her invitation to join them for dinner, taking his place at the table at least once a week.

Hogan had become distant when Dan had begun to spend the weekends at the farm, but after she had told him of their marriage and the weeks had passed, he had regained his former good-natured disposition. In Dan's continued absence, she had passed on more of the responsibilities to Hogan and he had assumed his new duties with gusto.

Surprisingly, she had grown closer to Hogan since her involvement with Dan. Her affection for him had developed into the kind of affection she'd felt for her four brothers, and in recent weeks, whenever a problem arose, she found herself turning more and more to Hogan for the solution.

When Dan's absence had been extended by his mother's illness, she began to feel as if she was being slowly cut into fragments. Dan's mother's condition had improved. An angioplasty was scheduled in a few days and her condition would improve quickly if the procedure went well.

Although Dan had called several times from Boise, each successive call had left a bitter taste in Eileen's mouth, reminding her once again that they had become two strangers who shared the marriage bed and found passion and fulfillment there whenever their paths happened to cross, which hadn't been very often. But often enough, she acknowledged. She had put off making an appointment with her gynecologist for birth control. Now she had had a prenatal checkup instead.

Within a few weeks the physician would be able to determine if she was carrying a single fetus or twins. The way her clothing had begun to tighten, she feared it might be the latter. Two more children with an absentee father was a possibility that brought her little joy.

THE MEETING with the bank officer took an unexpected twist when he asked Eileen to bring additional papers to a second meeting scheduled for the following week, papers that would confirm the collateral to the notes which would be due in a few months.

She felt like a cornered animal during the meeting and when it ended, the wounds were deep. Two other officers had attended and they had explained the bank's change in policy.

The bank's capital stock had been purchased by a large midwestern bank holding company and the out-of-state management had decided to shift the direction of their lending portfolios.

"We're calling all our agricultural loans as they mature, Mrs. Page, so please make plans to pay everything off. Any note unpaid by December first will be considered in default, which is quite within the bank's right. We've been quite lenient with many of you farmers. Now it's time you took control of your affairs. Perhaps a thinning of the ranks is in order."

Hogan, whom she'd asked to accompany her, took her arm and led her from the office. The summer day was hot, but a chill made her skin feel clammy. When Hogan put his arms around her in the bank parking lot, she sank into his embrace and succumbed to the tears that had been burning her eyes during most of the meeting.

"Oh, Hogan, what am I going to do now?" she asked, sobbing against his broad chest.

He patted her shoulders and guided her to the truck. "We'll work it out somehow. You, Duncan and me, we saved the place more than once. We can do it again. It's too bad that damned hus—" He looked at her. "Sorry, ma'am, but why isn't your husband here with you? I don't mind helping one bit, but it's his place to hold you when you cry, not your foreman's."

Eileen could think of no appropriate reply. "Let's stop at the restaurant down the street," she suggested, brushing at the damp spots on his shirt front. "We might as well enjoy a meal while we're in town. Those vultures won't be able to find us if we stay away from the phones for an hour or two."

Hogan grinned, his blue eyes twinkling, his teeth gleaming beneath his dark mustache. "Sounds great to me. We'll play hooky a little while. Can't see what difference it would make now."

When they arrived back at the farm, Stephen waved to her.

"Dad called while you were gone," he said. "I told him where you were. He said he would call when he could and that Grandmother is getting better, but she's had a complication."

Eileen loved Dan to distraction when he was with her, but he had been gone so much, she had begun to wonder if they had a solid love at all. He had offered her little hope for finding solutions to her problems, just a declaration of his affection.

What she needed now was someone she could count on. Perhaps an expert spud foreman would be more beneficial than a willing lover who knew nothing about the potato business.

"DAMN IT," Dan Page grumbled as he waited for Jordan to find Eileen. *Doesn't she ever stay home anymore? Why isn't she in the house where she belongs?* He groaned at his own chauvinism. Vanessa had never stayed home. Eileen had a career as important as Van's, her own business to run, even if it did originate from her home. *Home is not the same as a kitchen. Home is more than a place where you eat and sleep.* He had been no help in establishing a home. The weeks away had slipped into months. His priorities had slipped as well, distracted by the excitement of his profession, often thousands of miles from his new bride.

Forsaking all others...wasn't that what the justice of the peace had said? He had forsaken his own wife. He rubbed his temples as he counted the time since that special day. It was hard to believe that they had said their vows more than three months earlier, pushing four. If he didn't hustle, the summer would be over and he would have missed it all, missed his son's company, getting to know her children, but most of all spending the days and nights with Eileen. Soon, he vowed, soon he would be with her to stay. Only one more side trip to make and he would be home. It was high time he settled down.

The last two evenings he had called, she had been asleep. "So early?" he had asked Jolene.

"She's got the summer flu or something," the girl had replied. "She pukes."

"She what?"

"You know, upchucks, throws up. She can't eat supper anymore."

The slamming of a door caught his ear and he straightened, excited at the prospect of hearing Eileen's voice again.

"Waite, here." Hogan Waite's booming baritone filled his ear.

"I wanted Eileen."

"She's not here, Page."

"Where is she?"

"At the doctor's."

"Is she still sick?" Dan asked, his heart thudding.

"Nothing that time won't cure, but if I were you, Page, I'd get the hell back here and face up to what you've done before she runs out of time and patience."

"What are you talking about?" Dan asked.

"I held her in my arms the other day when she was crying, and damn it, it should have been you. What kind of liberated marriage is this you've trapped her in? If she decides to dump you for desertion, I'd seriously consider making a play for her myself just to know she was being taken care of the way she deserves. Do you hear me, Page?'' Hogan's voice grew louder, his anger obvious.

"I don't know what you're talking about, Waite, but you'd better keep your hands off Eileen or you'll have me to answer to."

"Hah," Hogan snorted. "You're no husband to her. She's a woman who needs loving, even in her condition."

"Condition? What condition?" Dan asked.

"Why, you don't even know, do you?" Hogan said. "Your wife is going to have a baby. I suspect at times she thinks you've skipped out on her, just like poor Duncan did. But Duncan couldn't do a thing about it. What's your excuse, Page?"

He slammed down the receiver in Dan's ear.

"WHAT DID THEY FIND?" Eileen asked, watching the U.S. Immigration Service patrol car drive away. She leaned against the sink, welcoming the hard ledge pressing into her hips because it made her feel alert.

Hogan shook his head. "I'm sorry to tell you this, Mrs. Page. I suspected all along that Hector and Julio might be illegals, but they had papers and we needed them. How were we to know their papers were false? They looked authentic to me. You know how hard I tried to get someone from town. No one wants to move pipe anymore...except illegal aliens. I'll bet a day's wages that most of the pipe movers in the west are just like Julio and his cousin."

"Oh, no," Eileen groaned.

"Anyway, to make a long story short, they're in the back seat of the patrol car and now we're short-handed again. I hate to tell you this, knowing how you've been feeling lately, but that old story about the bounced paychecks has been circulating again. Frank Asbury came to me just yesterday. Said he had heard it at Elsie's Cafe last week.''

"Would it help if I talked to him?" she asked, fighting the recurring nausea that now occurred at midday, instead of evening.

Hogan shook his head. "Wait until payday. Meanwhile I'll keep my ears open and let you know if I hear any more rumors. You should be spared this kind of thing, ma'am.''

"Don't, Hogan," she said, turning away. "Please, not today.''

The next day, Frank Asbury collected his paycheck. "I'd better get it to the bank before it's too late," he mumbled, then gave his notice and left.

They were unable to replace the two seasonal pipe movers. Stephen and Jordan volunteered to help, and Hogan showed them a few techniques that would make the work a little easier, but the irrigation cycle fell seriously behind schedule.

"It's a good thing we have the two pivot systems," she said, as they gathered around the table that evening.

Hogan shrugged. "It could be worse.''

"Yes, I know," she replied. "Only another week of irrigating and we can start drying out for digging. We have a month to find new laborers.''

Hogan patted her hand. "We'll manage. Don't we always?''

Before retiring late that night, Eileen placed a call to Dan's father's home in Weiser.

"He's not here," her father-in-law replied. "He packed his suitcase and drove away about an hour ago. His mother is much better now. The pleurisy has cleared up and the hemorrhaging in her leg has stopped. It was from the blood thinner, you know. She looked like raw liver for a while. She gets to come home next Tuesday. Dan tried to call you but no one answered the phone.''

"We were all out in the fields," she said. She choked on using the word home. "Is he coming here?"

"I think he was going back to Boise," the elder Page said. "He said he had some matters to take care of. Say, why don't you and Dan come here again real soon? We'd sure love to meet those new grandkids of ours. Dan has told us about your farm. We used to be farmers ourselves. You just have to get away once in awhile."

She had stopped listening after hearing of Dan's destination. Had he chosen his apartment in Boise over her place? Why? He had promised to cancel the lease and move his belongings to the farm, but never seemed to be free long enough to follow through.

Eileen lay awake far into the night, numbed by the cold reality that they had gone their separate ways before their marriage had been given a chance to get off the ground.

WHEN HOGAN WAITE'S harsh words sank in, Dan accepted the blame for what their marriage had become—only a legality. He tried to call her again, but no one answered. Perhaps Hogan had taken Eileen and the four children to town again. She had no time to come to him, her husband, yet she found time to spend evenings with Hogan.

"You're a fool," he said aloud, as he drove away from his parents' place. *Eileen would never cotton up to another man.* Such an idea would be as alien to her as any he could think of but if she had changed and did just that, he had no one to blame but himself. *Page, you're a number-one fool, and I just hope you can get there in time to tell her so.*

He drove to Boise and his apartment, gathered most of the clothing in his closets and dresser and shoved them into boxes. Gil Hadley's home was his next stop. He got the sleepy man out of bed just after midnight. Dan handed Gil the final drafts of several articles he had been working on, as well as his own written resignation.

Over coffee, he spilled his problems to Gil and Elizabeth Hadley, shared the discovery of Eileen's pregnancy, and divulged the fear that he was failing at his marriage. From a distance, he had created a fantasy home life, when in reality, he had made Eileen a grass widow by being an absent husband.

"Stay awhile," Elizabeth insisted. "You don't want to leave her alone again because you fell asleep at the wheel. At least nap for a few hours."

Together Gil and his wife convinced Dan they were right. He settled onto the Hadley's living room sofa, intending to rest for an hour or so. He fell into a sound sleep, waking with a start as day broke anew. Unwilling to admit defeat yet, he vowed to tell her in person what he had been unable to say over the phone.

Several hours later, Dan turned into the Mills Farm driveway and braked to a stop on top of the culvert. The name Mills on the sign leaped out at him. *Ironic,* he thought, knowing that in reality, she was still Eileen Mills. In name, she had become Eileen Hardesty Page, but in his absence she had been forced to reclaim the world of her deceased husband and carry the burdens alone because he himself had been one hell of a negligent husband.

As he drove toward the house, an avalanche of love filled him and with it, confidence that she still loved him. He parked near the kitchen door and took the porch steps in one leap.

"Eileen!"

No sound greeted him. The aroma of beef stew simmering in a slow cooker on the counter filled the room, reminding him that he hadn't eaten since the previous day. He returned to the yard and shielded his eyes from the early-morning sun. In the distance, he saw the giant wheels of the pivot systems methodically circling in two of the potato fields. One of the trucks was parked on the edge of the dirt road, to the left of the potato fields. He saw Hogan's giant form leave the grain field and climb into the vehicle. The barley was already turning golden.

Dan scanned the next potato field. Only when the fields were in full growth, with the foliage coming to a man's knees or above and the pale blossoms spiking a few inches above that, did one realize the full size of Eileen's operation. He spotted Jordan and Stephen struggling with long pieces of irrigation pipe.

Stephen staggered under the weight, stumbled, then regained his footing and moved ahead, keeping in line with Jordan. When they reached their destination—sixty feet down the field—they reconnected the pieces and raced to the center of the pipe to give each other a high five slap of success. They met at the next piece of pipe and, together, lifted it to drain the water. Then one would run forty feet to the other end and together they would start trudging again through the rows of potato vines. Stephen spotted him first and waved, immediately throwing Jordan off balance and he disappeared into the lush greenery.

Dan shifted his gaze to the next field and saw someone moving pipe alone. The figure was slight, not much taller than the boys and dressed in an oversized shirt and a floppy brimmed straw hat. *Surely Eileen wasn't doing manual labor in the fields. Where are the men hired to move pipe?* He watched as she heaved one end up enough to drain it, then stepped over the plants and worked her way to the middle of the pipe.

"No, Eileen," he hissed, "it's too heavy." He took several steps and stopped, amazed at the sight of her actually lifting the piece of heavy pipe. "No!" he shouted and began to run toward her. "Eileen!"

She stumbled and lost her grip on the pipe. Her straw hat fell from her head and disappeared into the vines. She turned as he reached the edge of the field. The tops of his shoes sank into the muddy furrow where the irrigation had already been completed.

"Eileen, don't lift that," he called.

She brushed the perspiration from her brow with her gloved hand, but the glove was dripping with water and her face was wetter than before.

The mud claimed his shoes and he stepped out of them. She started to bend over the pipe and he shouted again. "No! I'll do it for you. Wait until I get there and I'll help you." The expression on her flushed face stopped him twenty feet away.

"It's not necessary for you to stoop to doing the work of a migrant farm laborer," she said haughtily. She glanced down at his feet. "Where are your shoes?"

"The mud got them."

"You've ruined them, your trousers, too." She glared at him. "Your father said you went to Boise." She returned her attention to the pipe at her feet. "If you want to help, take that end and lift."

The instant he reached the opposite end, she began to lift hers. Without a word, they moved several sections.

"Eileen, I want to talk to you," he said, wiping his hands on his pant legs and wincing at the blood seeping from the abrasions on his bare palms.

She frowned. "You won't be able to type if you do this kind of work without gloves. Go back to the house. I'll be there in an hour or so." She turned away and bent over the foliage.

He couldn't see what she was doing. "Eileen, please talk to me. I'm sorry... about everything, being gone so long, being..."

She came to his end. "Do it like this," she said briskly, showing him how to connect the sections. She turned without looking directly at him and walked away, the mud sucking at her irrigation boots. "Hurry up. We're behind schedule and the potatoes will show the lack of water. This is our last time to irrigate, then we dry the fields for three weeks or so. Get a move on,'' she said over her shoulder.

He wiped his forehead. "Why the hell don't you have a power-driven system here?" he called to her rigid back.

"We have two of them." She pointed across the fields to the giant water systems. "Each one had a fifty thousand dollar mortgage hanging from its motor when we bought it and they aren't paid for yet. Maybe Santa Claus will bring us one for Christmas."

She could tell by the subtle change in his expression that her cynicism had found its mark. He looked ridiculous splattered with mud. His necktie was soiled. *No doubt, it's a designer tie. Serves him right,* she thought. *If he isn't careful, he'll get it caught in the equipment and strangle himself and then I'll have to rescue him.*

"Go back to your precious reporting," she shouted. "We've gotten along without you all summer. Why show up now? You're only a disruption around here. We don't need you."

She turned away. When she reached the end of the pipe, she stooped over and tried to lift it. Her wet gloves slipped and she stopped the falling pipe with her knees, tugging the heavy pipe until she had balanced it on her thighs.

Why is he here now? she thought, angry at herself for letting his presence get to her. She had forgotten to empty the pipe and the weight of the water inside was staggering. A surge of tears obscured her vision and she could do nothing to stop them.

Embarrassed by her clumsiness, she turned her fury toward Dan. *Why had he surprised her, catching her with her guard down?* She hadn't heard a car drive up and yet, when she had turned there he had stood, dressed in a fancy white dress shirt and a maroon tie, beige slacks and expensive leather shoes, looking debonair and perfectly ridiculous as if he had returned from a day at the office. Even with a scruffy day's growth of reddish beard, he looked handsome, and she hated him for the effect he was having on her.

It served him right for attempting to do farm work in dress clothes. He was stupid and very much out of his element, looking silly standing ankle-deep in the mud. She was stupid for caring how he looked, but the set of his tanned features was as readable as an open book. She didn't want his concern or pity now. She just wanted him to evaporate into thin air.

"Eileen, put that pipe down and come to the house," he pleaded. "I know you're upset but—"

"Upset! What on earth are you talking about? What reasons do I have for being upset? I married you because I loved you, but all you wanted was a place to hang your pants...and I let you...and I'm paying the price. Damn you, Daniel Page, for ever coming into my life!" Her grip on the pipe slackened and it began to roll down her thighs.

As she grabbed at the pipe, her boot tangled in a potato vine. She tried to free her foot and pulled up several small Russet potatoes, their moist beige skins glistening in the sun. A wave of dizziness struck her and she staggered again. Wrapping her arms around the silver pipe, she clung to it, determined to keep it in her grasp. Her boot broke from the suction of the mud and she staggered.

The pipe seemed to be turning, rolling her beneath it. Her wrist was being pulled apart, but the pain in her arm was nothing compared to the snapping sound she felt in her leg.

The back of her head settled into the mud. The sun beating down on her face blinded her. As she felt the cool mud against her cheek, she yearned to sink beneath its chilling numbness and let it take away the excruciating agony in her leg and wrist. Merciful blackness swept over her for a moment, but someone was calling to her, lifting her head from the mud. She opened her eyes. Dan knelt over her, blocking the powerful rays of the sun from her face.

"Oh God, Eileen, you're not Superwoman. Why did you do such a foolish stunt? Are you trying to kill yourself?"

His eyes were brimming with tears. The sight of Dan Page, mud splattered and breathing hard, reduced to tears on her account was one straw more than even she could handle. His image blurred and swam, and she blinked several times. His face came closer as he kissed her on her muddy cheek and smiled.

"You're just here between trips," she said, groaning as she tried to shift her position.

"No, love, I'm here to stay," he replied, touching her chin with his fingers.

She tried to shake her head. The tremor in his warm touch fragmented her emotions. "Why?"

"Because I love you and I want to be your husband. I'll tell you more later. Now what can I do to help you?"

The sun's rays changed to icicles and she fought to stay awake. She wanted to hear what he had to say, but his voice changed to a distant ringing coming from a deep tunnel. Positive she was sliding down the inside of a piece of irrigation pipe, she tried to smile but couldn't feel her facial muscles respond. "You might move . . . the pipe."

CHAPTER EIGHTEEN

"SHE'S FAINTED!" Dan murmured, peering down at her pale features, beautiful in spite of the mud caked on her cheek and in her hair. He scanned the horizon. "Help," he shouted. "I need help."

Jordan and Stephen raced across the field, whooping as they hurdled the rows of greenery. The twins, who had been gathering eggs from the nesting geese and chickens, heard the boys' screams and dropped their baskets, running to see what was wrong.

In his peripheral vision, Dan saw the truck that Hogan had been driving stop on the dirt lane between the fields. Hogan leaped from the vehicle and ran toward them.

"What happened?" Hogan asked, squatting beside Dan. "I saw her fall. She had no business trying to move pipe in her condition." He smiled affectionately at Eileen and touched her hair. "Stubbornest woman I ever knew."

She stirred, her eyes fluttering open for a moment.

"She's trapped," Dan said. "Her arm and leg are under the pipe. Help me get it off."

"You stay put, Page," Hogan said, touching his shoulder. The foreman motioned to Jordan and Stephen. "Grab that end and let's get this off your mom." They picked it up and moved it to the ground several feet away from Eileen.

Dan ran his hand down her arm. Eileen cried out when he touched her wrist. He bent her arm at the elbow and gently laid her hand on her stomach. The rounded curve of her abdomen beneath the plaid cotton shirt distracted him for a moment.

"Her jeans are so muddy I can't see where she's injured," he said. "Let's get her to the hospital in town."

"Momma's dead," Jodie sobbed, clinging to Dan's arm. Her grip slipped as he lifted Eileen in his arms and stood up. "Momma's dead and you're taking her away just like they did Daddy. I know it. I know it and we'll never see her again!" She screamed, tugging on Eileen's muddy pant leg.

Eileen stiffened in Dan's arms and her complexion turned ashen. Her eyes flew open. "Don't touch my leg," she gasped. "I heard it snap. Just . . . don't touch it!"

Hogan swept Jodie up and set her in the crook of his left arm, then reached for Jolene and held her in his other arm. He straightened. "See, little ladies, your momma is going to be fine. Your new daddy is going to take good care of her." Hogan met Dan's troubled gaze. "You look as bad as the missus does, Page, almost as muddy, too."

"Is she gonna be all right, Dad?" Stephen asked.

"We'll take her to the hospital and find out," Dan said. "Waite, can you drive us?"

"Of course," Hogan replied. He carried the girls down the rows to the truck and put them on the ground. Dan followed with Eileen in his arms and waited while Hogan dropped the tailgate.

"Can we go, too?" Jordan asked, the tremor in his young voice revealing his anxiety.

Dan's gaze flickered to Hogan before resting on Jordan's anxious face. "Sure, son, climb in."

"If he goes, I go," Stephen said, vaulting over the side and into the flatbed.

"And me," Jolene insisted.

"Me, too?" Jodie asked, clutching tightly to Dan's pocket.

Dan chuckled. "Why not? The more the merrier. Waite, would you do the honors again, please?"

"My pleasure." One by one he lifted the girls into the back of the truck, then gave Dan a boost up, and slammed the tailgate closed again.

Dan eased down onto a wooden box near the cab and adjusted Eileen on his lap. She stirred in his arms and opened her eyes.

"Where are we?" she asked, smiling weakly at all the faces hovering around her.

"I thought you were…" Jodie dropped her head for a few seconds before looking sheepishly into Eileen's face. "Are you gonna be okay?"

"I've hurt my arm and leg," Eileen said, settling against Dan's chest.

"Please sit down, children," Dan said. "Your mom is going to be fine. I promise." He glanced down at Eileen. "I keep my promises."

The children returned to their seats as Hogan turned onto the paved road and accelerated toward town.

Dan brushed the muddy curls from her temple. She looked up at him. "And… the child?" he asked.

"You know?" she asked. "Who told you?"

"Hogan," he admitted. "I'm ashamed, really ashamed to have to hear from another man that my wife is going to have a baby."

"*Babies*," she said softly.

"What?" He tensed, tightening his hold on her.

"Babies… plural," she murmured against his shirt. "I have this hereditary tendency to have my children in sets."

"Sets?" He frowned. "How many is in a set?"

"I hope just two. I have twin brothers. My grandmother had three sets of twins, and I have an aunt who has triplets."

"Good Lord!"

At the hospital Dan carried Eileen into the emergency area, followed closely by Jodie, Jolene, Jordan and Stephen. Hogan brought up the rear.

As Dan shifted Eileen slightly, clumps of dried mud fell to the floor.

"Good gracious, what's this?" a plump nurse exclaimed, bustling from an examination room. "Have you two been mud wrestling?" She tossed her head back and laughed. "Frankly, I can't tell who won and who lost." Immediately, she was all business. "Bring her in here." She turned and disappeared behind a white curtain. When Dan didn't follow, the nurse peeked out and cocked her head. "Pronto," she directed and Dan hustled.

He laid Eileen on a gurney and stayed close by, holding her uninjured hand.

The nurse peered over a pair of half glasses at Dan. "Name?"

"Eileen . . . Page."

"Are you sure?"

He frowned. "I'm sure."

"And you?"

"I'm her husband. Daniel Page." Eileen groaned. "Listen, can't we take care of the paperwork later," he asked. "My wife is injured."

"Address?"

He grimaced and gave the address, then explained what had happened. "It's her right hand and her right leg, but she may have sustained other injuries. The mud . . . I couldn't tell."

"Yes, Doctor Page," the nurse said, smiling sweetly, "but to be sure, why don't you step outside? We'll get her cleaned up a bit and Doctor Lewis will be here in a few minutes."

"But, I—"

"...should do as the nurse says." She tried to find a clean spot on his arm and gave up, then took his hand and led him outside. "Listen, Mr. Page, we'll do our work—"

"But how do you know if—"

"This is what we're trained for, Mr. Page. Trust us. We'll let you know how she is just as soon as we've examined her. Now," she said, pausing as she glanced up and down his body. "Why don't you go down the hall? There's a bathroom where you can at least get the dirt off your arms and face." She nudged him in the direction of the public restroom and disappeared back into the room.

He washed as best he could and returned to the waiting room where the four children and Hogan waited.

Hogan glanced up as Dan approached. "Sit down, Page, you don't look so good."

Dan shook his head. "I'd make a mess of the furniture." He motioned to the magazine lying open on Hogan's knees. "Alaska?"

Hogan nodded. "Alaska, northern Idaho and western Montana are my three favorite states. God, I love those mountains."

Dan stared down at the other man. "Then what keeps you coming back to this flat country? If it weren't for the Snake River irrigation project, this land would still be the Great American Desert."

Hogan shrugged. "This family, more than anything, I reckon." He eyed Dan for several seconds. "Duncan and I met in a bar in Idaho Falls several years ago. No, he wasn't a drinker, but he usually managed to find some seasonal workers there each year, and we hit it off right away. Maybe it was our size . . . he was a big guy, too, you know."

Dan nodded. "We can't do much about our heights. I'm five ten. Duncan was six three. Jordan made sure I knew that several months ago." He glanced at Jordan who shrugged and returned his attention to a magazine. "My height has nothing to do with why I fell in love with Eileen.''

''Conceded,'' Hogan said, holding up his hand. ''But Duncan was also a great husband and father, and I liked that. I found it downright pleasant to be around the Mills family. I've never married. Only met a few women who interested me enough to even speculate on the possibility. But if ever I knew a strong, close family, it was Duncan and Eileen and their children.''

''Sounds like a hard act to follow,'' Dan said.

Hogan frowned deeply. ''When Duncan got sick, I thought it was one of the cruelest dirty tricks of fate I'd ever witnessed.''

''I met Duncan twice,'' Dan said. ''I spent several hours with him. I agree, he was a unique man.''

Hogan left his chair and began to pace the floor. ''I had my doubts about you, Page, when you started hanging around. She just didn't seem like your kind of woman.''

Dan began to pace in the opposite direction from Hogan. ''I love her,'' he said, gesturing wildly. ''Given a chance, we'll make the best of our differences and draw on our likenesses. If she still loves me, and will swallow some of that damned pride of hers, I'll help her resolve these problems she's having with finances. And if we can't save the farm, we'll try something else, together.''

''I made Duncan promises,'' Hogan said, ''that I would make sure she was doing okay before I pulled out, that I'd take care of her myself if need be.''

''Damn those promises,'' Dan exclaimed. ''Are promises made to Duncan going to haunt me to my dying day? Is that what he wanted to happen? I can't believe it. The promises Eileen made have been the major cause of her problems right now.''

''She's loyal by nature,'' Hogan said. ''So am I.''

They met in the center of the room and Dan squinted up at Hogan. "Sometimes I wonder just how you feel about her yourself."

"How I feel about the missus is my own business," Hogan said, "but let me tell you this, Page, if I ever hear that you've neglected her or abused her or been mean to one of these kids, I'll come back here and settle the score. And if you did skip out on her, I'll hunt you down and . . ." He grinned. "Well, never mind what I might do. Just don't make it necessary to find out. Do you get my drift, Page?"

Dan extended his hand. "Sounds fair enough, but I'd much rather have you as a friend."

Jodie came and stood between the two men. She took Dan's hand. "Please don't have a fight. Mr. Waite, Mr. Page is our daddy now and you mustn't hurt him. He's not as big as you or our first daddy, but we sure love him a lot and we want him to stay with us. If you beat him up, he might leave again and Momma would be sad and she would cry again like she used to do and . . . and, well just be nice to him." Her blue eyes glistened and tears trickled down her cheek.

Dan knelt on one knee and put his arm around her. "Don't cry, honey, I love you too. All of you, even stubborn old Jordan over there who gives me such a hard time." He nodded to Jordan who grinned. "Stephen may be my first son, but the rest of you are my children too, and I have no plans to leave you. And you know what?" He winked at Jolene who had come over to join them.

"What?" Jolene asked.

He lifted the loose brown hair from one of the twin's neck. "No mark," he said boastfully. "This pretty girl must be Jodie. Am I right?"

"Yes," Jolene exclaimed. "You're the only one since my momma and daddy who could remember. Even Mr. Waite still gets mixed up sometimes." She giggled and threw her arms around Dan's neck and squeezed him tight, then gave him a smacking kiss on his cheek. "You need to shave... Daddy." She pulled away a few inches. "Momma said we didn't have to call you Daddy unless we wanted to, but I want to. Is that okay?"

"I think that would be wonderful," Dan said, closing his eyes to keep the tears in his eyes from falling.

Someone cleared his throat behind Dan and Dan untangled himself from the twins' arms and rose to his feet.

A tall gray-haired man in a white knee-length coat stood nearby holding a clipboard in his hand. "Mr. Page?"

"Yes," Dan said, extending his hand. "How is she?"

"She has a dislocated wrist, which is almost as bad as a break and just as painful," the physician said. "By the way, I'm Doctor Lewis. I've taken care of the Mills family for years. Welcome to the fold. Now, about Eileen. She has a simple fracture of the fibula in her right leg. That's the smaller bone and the break was undoubtedly caused by direct violence."

"Violence?" Dan exclaimed.

"Eileen says the pipe fell on it. Unfortunately, today's media has distorted the meaning of the word. The nurses are cleaning her up. She's been X-rayed and now we'll be moving her to another room where we'll be setting the leg with a cast to her knee. The wrist will be braced and wrapped and put in a sling. She's to keep it immobile for a month. Same for the leg. I told her she would have to give up moving pipe for this season," he said with a smile.

"What about... the pregnancy?" Dan asked.

"If the pipe had fallen directly on her abdomen, she would very likely have injured the babies." The physician raised one brow. "She told me you had been away on a business trip. Did you know she was carrying twins?"

"Not until today," Dan said.

"Then when she's comfortable in her room, I would like to talk to both of you. The prenatal care for a woman carrying twins is a little more complicated than usual." He studied the children. "Why don't you all go home? You can see your mother tomorrow. We're going to keep her here for a day or two. She's been working too hard. She needs a rest, away from cooking and cleaning and pipe moving...and noisy children."

"I want to see her," Dan said.

"You go home and clean yourself up while we do our work and get her settled in," Doctor Lewis insisted. "Then come back and stay as long as you wish." He laughed. "I delivered the girls when I still had a family practice. They were healthy babies for twins and almost full term. We want the next pair to be the same."

Jolene giggled and Jordan elbowed her in the ribs. "Cut it out, Jordan, or I'll..."

"See what I mean?" the physician said. "Spare your mother for a few days. She's earned a vacation."

"I WAS SO DIRTY," Eileen said aloud. She was settled in her hospital room, her foot propped on several pillows and her arm immobilized against her stomach, appreciating her pristine condition after her muddy accident.

The door swung open and Dan entered. He lingered at the foot of the bed, his hands pushed deep into the pockets of his white chino pants. The cherry-red knit shirt accented his tan, but it was the troubled expression in his eyes, not his good looks that made her heart begin to thud.

Her hand began to shake as he walked along the side of the bed.

"How are you feeling?" he asked, sitting on the edge of her bed, but hesitant to touch her.

"Terrible," she admitted.

He reached for her left hand and held it between his. "Eileen, there's so much I want to say to you." He stared down at their hands before meeting her gaze again. "I came so close to losing you," he said, his eyes glistening. "And it was all my own making." He blinked, trying to suppress his tears, without success. She freed her hand and wiped his cheek.

"The accident wasn't your fault," she said.

He shook his head. "I mean everything. My staying away too long, leaving you to carry the responsibilities at home. You were right when you said I wanted a place to hang my pants, but God, I want more than that . . . for you and me, for the children." His hand splayed across her abdomen. "For these children . . . Good Lord, Eileen, do you realize I'm going from being a father of one son to a parent of six children in a year's time?"

She wiped his cheek again. "It takes time to adjust, darling . . . and I wasn't very cooperative. I was angry. I married you and yet I was still living like a widow, and I didn't think it was fair. I should have told you more about what was going on here, including the babies, but you were so excited about all your gallivanting around the country and I reacted in my usual stubborn way. I was proud of you, especially when I saw you reporting on the television screen. You were very professional. I had no idea you were so talented."

He grinned. "Television has always been a strong side interest for me, but it can control your life if you let it."

"I felt so cut off from everything you were doing," she continued. "Once I saw that Susan Gallagher standing next to you and I felt very jealous."

"Susan?" He laughed. "Susan has a husband and two teenage boys in Eagle and she was the first one to return home. I should have taken a lesson from her."

"I convinced myself you didn't want to come home, and I was going to prove to you and the world that I could go it alone," she said. "I loved and hated you at the same time!"

His hand slid beneath her hair and settled on her neck. "I skipped out and left you carrying the same load I promised to help you carry. I'm sorry."

She leaned against his palm, savoring its warmth. "I'm sorry, too. We made love and then went our separate ways. That wasn't the way it should have been."

"No, my love, but we had something very special, didn't we?" He wiped the tears from her cheeks as she had done to his.

"Yes," she said. "Those memories carried me through the day, but the nights were so lonely without you."

"Never again," he vowed. "Never again."

Her hand covered his. "I love you so much," she whispered. "I tried to stop but I couldn't."

"And I love you," he replied, cupping her face in his hands. His lips hovered inches from hers. "May I kiss you?"

"Please," she whispered.

His mouth covered hers, exploring her soft lips beneath his. When he pulled away, her eyes glistened.

"Are you really home to stay?" she asked.

"While I was in Weiser at my folks' home, I had this vision of my future alone again, and it wasn't the way I wanted to spend the rest of my life. I remembered an earlier vision, of the two of us loving each other and growing old together, seeing our children bring grandchildren into our lives. I got so damned sentimental. I made my decision right then and there. I tried to call you but no one answered. I drove to Boise and got poor Gil Hadley out of bed in the middle of the night and turned in my resignation."

"Are you sure you did the right thing?" she asked.

He nodded. "Meet Daniel Page, free-lance writer once again and soon-to-be father of six."

"How does an unemployed father of six provide for his wife and houseful of children? Maybe you were hasty."

"I'll be able to work at home from now on," he explained. "The agent I visited in Los Angeles has found a publisher who is excited about our proposal to expand my series on successful women into a book. The publisher wants it out in the book stores in time for a year from this Christmas. They're working out the contract now. That, my darling wife, means an advance up front. Can we find a room for me to write in at that noisy farmhouse?"

"We'll manage." She stroked his forearm with her finger tips. "I still have all those loans and a crop to bring in. We start digging spuds in a few weeks. How can I work like this?"

"We'll discuss it when you're home and feeling better." He stood up. "Now you get some rest. I'm going to the farm to check on that brood of ours. I'll talk to Hogan a minute, and hit the sack. I'm bushed, sweetheart. A man at my age needs his rest. Enjoy your vacation," he murmured, brushing her lips with his. "And when you get back home, you won't be alone, ever again."

CHAPTER NINETEEN

EILEEN EASED HERSELF from the bed, trying not to disturb Dan. Today was the day they should begin to dig spuds, but when she mentally counted the crew, she wondered if the potatoes were destined to rot in the fields. Eileen had an arm in a sling and a leg in a walking cast. Dan was still a journalist who had never ridden a harvester. The children were out of school for two weeks during Spud Vacation, and Stephen and Jordan were old enough to do part of the harvesting if the work wasn't too difficult, but the twins were much too young. Hogan Waite, her foreman, would try to cover for everyone else's inadequacies.

"Where do you think you're going?" Dan asked, grabbing her nightgown and slowly drawing her back to the bed.

"I'm looking for a miracle," she confessed. "I thought I might find it in a fresh-brewed cup of coffee."

"I'll go with you," he said. "Hogan is due at seven. I promised him breakfast in exchange for his ideas on this little problem of ours."

She rolled into his arms. "Little problem? That is the understatement of the century, Farmer Page."

"We'll think of something," he replied. "Three heads should be better than one." He propped himself up on an elbow and studied her face. "You get prettier every day. Is this the pregnant woman syndrome?"

She smiled. "I'd rather think of it as the opinion of a husband in love, because I could lie here in bed day and night and look at you." She touched his lips and he kissed her finger.

"Kiss me?" he asked.

Her left arm slid around his neck and slowly drew his head down. "How can I refuse?" His lips touched hers and her lips parted, encouraging his exploration of her warm moist mouth.

Breathing heavily, he pulled away. "We can either get dressed and meet the day before it gets a head start on us...or we can say to heck with it all and just stay here. What do you say?"

"You were the one who invited the hired help to breakfast," Eileen replied, kissing him at the base of his throat.

"I'll know to keep my mouth shut next time," Dan growled. His hand slid over her hip and down her thigh as she rolled away.

"Get dressed, darling," she suggested primly. "I was the one willing to get up and spend some time trying to solve our problems and all you want to do is lie around and wrestle and make love and do all that old stuff."

"Old stuff? Old stuff, is it?" He grabbed at her gown again, but she escaped and hobbled to the bathroom.

"Better luck next time," she teased.

While he dressed, Dan's thoughts gradually shifted from his passionate wife to the very real problem of finding the workers they needed for the harvest. The longer the potatoes stayed in the ground, the closer the first frost of the season came. He and Hogan had already baled the third cutting of alfalfa but a cooler August than normal had left him with the feeling that they had wasted their time. He had contracted the combining of the malt barley out to a man from Blackfoot in order for Hogan and him to concentrate on the potatoes. *Surely we can find workers somewhere,* he thought, pulling on a clean pair of jeans and heading for the hall, shoving his shirttails inside and buckling his belt as he went. *This farming takes more of a man's time than I thought. No wonder Eileen couldn't get away to join me.*

Downstairs, the children went out for morning chores as Hogan knocked on the screen door. "I got an idea," Hogan said, as he slid into a chair and accepted a cup of coffee. "Dallas Odell always has more men than he needs. Let's call him and ask to borrow a few."

Eileen shot from her chair, nearly losing her balance. "No. We'll think of something else. Those men who passed around the rumors about our checks being no good are probably working for him right now. We aren't that desperate yet."

Dan scratched his head and reached for the telephone.

"Who are you calling?" Eileen asked.

"Someone who might be willing to come out of retirement," Dan replied. He chatted a few minutes with his mother. "Put Dad on the line." He covered the receiver. "I promised Hogan breakfast but could you get it started?"

"If Hogan can manage the toaster and you can pour the juice, I think I can fry some bacon and scramble eggs, only one of you will have to separate the slices of bacon. I'm not a very good one-handed chef." She smiled at both men. "The next time you promise breakfast, Mr. Page, you cook."

Dan grinned and gave her a mock salute, then spoke into the receiver. "Dad! How would you like to go back to work for a few weeks?" He explained their predicament. "Eileen is supposed to stay off her leg as much as possible. Could you and Mom both help?"

He was silent again, nodding. "Thanks. We'll see you early tomorrow morning." He turned to his two curious listeners. "Mom has an appointment with the heart specialist in Boise this morning, but they'll pack their things before they leave Weiser. They'll be here this evening. Dad knows farm equipment, Hogan. You'll find him a fast learner on the harvester. My mother has volunteered to take over kitchen duties. You—" and he gave Eileen a quick kiss on her startled mouth "—are on a medical leave of absence." He frowned. "We have a seventy-year-old retired tomato farmer from New Jersey and his wife who has a heart condition. Maybe we need some more solutions."

Eileen grew quiet.

"Now what's wrong?" Dan asked. "Are you angry with me?"

"No, no," she said with a wave of her hand. "Why don't we call George and Gerry Mills? Who knows more about spud harvesting than two old spud farmers?" She chuckled. "Gerry would be very displeased if she heard me call her an old anything."

"I'll call them," Dan volunteered. "It's time Gerry Mills and I made peace."

He dialed the number and let it ring. "They're not home."

"They must be," Eileen said, reaching for the phone herself and letting it ring more than a dozen times. "Now what do we do?"

"We start digging with the help we have," Dan said, trying not to read too much into Hogan Waite's furrowed brow. "We'll start with one crew. I'll drive the spud truck. Hogan can drive the harvester and if you can ride it with Jordan and Stephen, you can tell them what to look for. But let them do the work! We'll take it slow and if your leg or arm begins to ache too much, we'll just stop." He shrugged. "Whatever potatoes we manage to dig will be that many more than if we did nothing."

"Sure," she mumbled.

"Right," Hogan replied, slapping Dan's shoulder. "Nothing ventured, nothing gained. Up in Alaska the fishermen have a saying about no one ever catching fish when his boat is in port. We'll manage, at least for today."

Hogan sat a platter of buttered toast down as the children returned. The boys were excited over their jobs.

"What do you do when you ride a harvester?" Stephen asked.

"You stand on a platform on the back. The harvester digs the spuds and a conveyor belt carries the spuds into the trucks," Hogan explained. "You have to watch them and when you find a dirt clod or a cut potato, you throw it out so it doesn't get into the cellars. You look for spuds with green spots." He described the job in more detail. "Think you could handle that?"

"Sure," Stephen boasted. He turned to Jordan.

"I did it last year," Jordan said. "I'll help you learn what to look for. But I know a guy who lost his arm and . . ."

Hogan held up his hand. "You have to stay out of the way of the belts and pulleys and other moving parts. Keep your shirts tucked in your jeans, your hair under your caps, and your fingers inside your gloves. Don't get caught in the moving parts! It's that simple, but your mom knows all about it. Listen to her! I don't want to end the season with any three-fingered boys around this place. Do you hear me?"

"Yes, sir!" Jordan and Stephen replied.

"What about us?" Jolene asked. "Don't we get to work?"

"Yes," Eileen said. "You girls are in charge of the house and dinner. There are three packages of cold cuts in the fridge. Count heads and make two or three sandwiches a piece."

"Math? When we're not even in school?" Jolene asked.

"It's easy," Jodie said, "I'll do the math and you can put on the mayonnaise and lettuce."

Eileen smiled. In spite of her shyness, Jodie could always come up with a solution to the twins' problems. "Have them ready by noon. I'll warm soup in the microwave. Make some with meat and some with peanut butter. That should please everyone.'' She glanced toward her son, and he grinned and ducked his head.

Having Jordan share a room with Stephen had brought about a significant change in her son's habits. More than once she had overheard Stephen sounding like a drill instructor giving Jordan orders on keeping their room neat. Perhaps the military academy had its positive side, after all.

During their lunch break, Dan placed another call to the George Mills residence. When he hung up, he beamed with delight. ''Gerry Mills called me 'son' and promised they would be here tomorrow in time to help with breakfast. I'll be damned. Add two more names to your list, Hogan.''

Hogan jotted down the names and frowned. ''We need several more people just to make a decent start.''

As they finished the meal, the phone rang. ''I'll get it,'' Eileen said, hoping it wasn't bad news.

''It's me,'' Esther Cameron said. ''My mother called and told me about your problems. Well, I called Thomas at the office and asked if he could arrange an emergency vacation. His partner in the firm just got back from a trip to Hawaii. They have no cases going to trial for the rest of the month. Isn't that great? We'll be there tomorrow morning early. It's been a few years, but I'd love to ride the harvester again or drive a truck. The weather is perfect. Let's hope it doesn't turn cold and frost. The boys are out of school and they want to work, too, so we'll see you tomorrow, honey.''

''Thanks, Esther,'' Eileen said.

Two adults and two teenage boys were added to Hogan's list.

''I know someone,'' Eileen said. ''Remember that pretty blond nurse I introduced you to at the hospital?''

Dan smiled. ''Unforgettable.''

Eileen leered at him. "Her husband teaches at the high school so he's off for two weeks. I'm going to call her. She said once she'd help me in any way she could. Now I'm going to hold her to her promise."

Her friend promised to check with the hospital about adjusting her schedule and to call back. She did an hour later, shortly after Eileen had given up riding with the boys and returned to the house for a rest.

"Paul and I can work. We both know how to drive spud trucks. We did it for Paul's dad before they sold their property to Dallas Odell. We'll be there by seven tomorrow morning."

Around the table that evening, Dan and Eileen studied the growing list of volunteer workers. "We still need some truck drivers, four at least, and some laborers in the fields and in the cellars," Hogan said. He shook his head. "It's a start, but that's all. We should have twice this many spuds in the cellars by this time."

"We've drained the pool of relatives dry," Dan said. "I think we're overlooking the obvious here. Dallas Odell is the biggest spud grower in Idaho. Maybe he can help us. Why do you dislike him?" Dan asked. "I interviewed him once. He seemed like a pretty decent guy to me."

"He's land hungry," Eileen said. "Duncan always said…" She stopped, aware of the silence that had fallen on the room. "I just don't want anything to do with him."

"Even if he can help?"

"He won't," she replied.

Dan glanced at Hogan, who sat stone-faced. "I'm staying out of this discussion," Hogan said.

"Then I'm going to call him," Dan said. "I'll use the phone in the office." He looked at Eileen's bent head. "It's quieter."

The next morning, Eileen sat brooding over the harvest, alone in the living room, her foot propped on a pillow.

Mentally, she weighed her problems against the blessings in her life.

Dan had pitched in and taken charge of the farm, no doubt of that, impressing her with his keenness and knowledge. An outsider would easily think he had grown up on the land. She laughed aloud. He had!

The doorbell rang and she eased her cast off the pillow. "I'll get it," she called to Dan's mother, who was baking pies in the kitchen. To her surprise, Vanessa Harcourt stood on the porch. She was dressed in jeans and a plaid shirt, jogging shoes and a straw hat. A small suitcase sat on the porch beside her.

"Stephen called me last night," Van said. "When he told me about your labor problem, I asked if I could help. He said I was the only 'member of the family' who was not here."

"Come in, Van," Eileen said, motioning the stunning woman inside. "Just what did he say to you?" she asked, offering the woman a cup of coffee.

"He said all the relatives but me were already here working." She smiled. "He can be so funny at times. He scolded me for not knowing more about how potatoes were grown. Perhaps he's right. I've been isolated in the executive office for too long. It's high time I got some dirt under my nails. Can you use me?"

Eileen laughed. "Of course, but you don't really have to do this. Stephen exaggerated a little."

Vanessa nodded. "I know, but once I began to think about what my son had said, I couldn't drop it. I want you all to forget that I'm a vice president. I stopped in Blackfoot and bought a pair of bib overalls in case I needed them. Now, put me to work!"

At the noon meal, Eileen introduced Vanessa to Hogan Waite.

"Treat me like a regular hired hand," Vanessa said, taking Hogan's hand in hers.

Hogan gulped twice before he smiled. "You can ride up front with me and I'll teach you how to drive a harvester. It's not hard at all if you pay attention." Over pot roast prepared by Dan's mother, Hogan had eyes only for Vanessa. At suppertime he announced, "She takes to this farm work like a duck to water, by damn. She may never want to go back to that office of hers."

Vanessa moved into one of the trailers and invited Jordan and Stephen to join her, freeing the boys' room for Dan's parents. On Friday at noon, Hogan announced, "Vanessa and I are going into Idaho Falls for supper tonight, so don't plan on having us at the table. We're going to take in a movie afterward."

To Dan's amusement, Van blushed but didn't say a word and refused to meet his curious gaze.

Saturday was just another work day, but Sunday the equipment remained idle. "The Lord's Day is still for worship and relaxation," Eileen declared, as she and Dan, the six children, both sets of grandparents, and the Camerons climbed into the Cameron's van and drove into Shelley.

After dinner, the children scattered, the older adults went upstairs for a nap and Eileen fell asleep on the sofa while watching an old black-and-white suspense movie. When the doorbell rang, Dan answered it.

"Come in," he said. "Your timing is perfect." As he motioned the tall, black-haired man into the living room, Eileen awoke.

Disoriented, she smoothed her hair and adjusted her clothing. "Did I hear the doorbell? Oh," she gasped, spotting the stranger standing beside Dan. She reached for the cane she used to help her keep her balance.

The man raised his hand. "Don't get up on my account, ma'am. I'll come to you. I should have done just that when

I heard about Duncan's passing. When Dan called me several days ago, I could hardly believe it when he told me you two had married. I think that's just great, ma'am, just great." He dropped into the overstuffed chair across from the sofa.

"Who are you?" Eileen asked. "Do I know you? Have we met?"

Dan cleared his throat. "Eileen, this is Dallas Odell." He sat down beside Eileen and squeezed her hand before she could react. "He's come to talk spuds, honey."

Eileen's mouth narrowed as Dan patted her hand and rose again. "I'll get us some iced tea." He smiled at Eileen. "You two can chat awhile and get to know each other."

In the kitchen, Dan tried to listen to the murmurings coming from the living room, hoping that Eileen would be reasonable and not consider his interference a dirty trick. When he had talked to Dallas earlier in the week, the man had expressed his regrets that at the time he couldn't spare anyone, but that he would like to come and see them on Sunday.

Eileen was beginning to bristle at the restrictions of being a semi-invalid, sitting idle day after day while others bustled around her. As they sipped their tea, Odell described his complex operations in considerable detail, and Eileen perked up.

"So you see, ma'am, I'm running to stay ahead of the creditors just like everyone else. But this has been a good year for me and I need some more land in order to rotate the crops. I've been looking for another pivot system and if I found a used spud truck or two, I'd sure be willing to pay cash."

Eileen sat quietly for several minutes. Dan and the other man exchanged glances but neither spoke. Finally, she reached for the cane and stood. "This is my land and my equipment," she said, her voice clear and confident. "So it must be my decision. Perhaps the time has come to take some steps backward in order to move ahead. Dan?" She held out her hand and he took it. "Mr. Odell, come with us." She led the two men outside and toward Dan's Blazer. "Dan, would you drive us around the property?"

As Dan helped her into the cab, she whispered, "This was a devious and dirty trick, Dan Page, and we'll talk about it later."

An hour later, they followed Eileen into the office.

"I'd sure like to have one of those pivots," Odell said.

"It's expensive but it sure beats moving pipe manually." She chuckled.

Dallas Odell grinned, his handsome brown eyes gleaming. "Page told me about how you broke your leg, ma'am."

"I'll talk it over with the boys, sweetheart," Dan volunteered. "If we can work it out, you can have the pivot system."

"And the extra trucks. I could give you..." Odell scratched his thick dark hair and named a price.

"Too low," Eileen said levelly. But within minutes, they had settled on an amount a few hundred dollars less than Eileen's first counteroffer. "You can have the two blue vehicles as soon as we've finished digging." She straightened in her chair. "I've already had a call from Jeremy Dixon. His land is just north of ours and I'm going to accept his offer for an outright purchase of a section. I don't want to sell anymore but I'd be willing to lease you up to a thousand acres for the next two years."

She glanced at Dan, who eyed her with newfound respect. "I might want to expand again...when we get our house in order. I always thought I'd be giving this land to my children but now I don't know if I'd be doing them any favors." She smiled lovingly at Dan. "As you can tell, our family will be expanding next spring. Twins. I want to hold on to my future options."

The men laughed.

"And I want a cash lease only," Eileen continued. "I don't want to fool around with any sharecropping arrangements."

Odell nodded. He started to rise.

"One more thing, Mr. Odell," she said.

He dropped back into his chair. "Call me Dallas, please ma'am. I don't need anything more."

"But we do." She glanced toward Dan. "We need four men for three weeks to help us finish digging spuds. Laborers are in short supply this fall. Do you know where we might find some reliable laborers who know how to work spuds?"

He grinned. "I have more than a hundred men working for me, ma'am. I think I could spare some. I'll have five here tomorrow morning at 7:00 a.m. sharp. Here it is mid-September already. Yesterday I thought I smelled frost in the air. You wouldn't want to get caught with spuds in the fields. You know what frozen spuds can do to a cellar."

Her eyes widened. "Yes, . . . Dallas, I know what frozen spuds can do to a cellar, and to a farm, and to a relationship, and I don't want to ever lose a cellar that way again!"

Dan looked at her with love in his eyes, nodding his heartfelt agreement.

EPILOGUE

"HAPPY BIRTHDAY," Dan murmured, as he slid his arms around Eileen. They stood on the porch, watching the last three potato trucks leave the farm on their way to the processor in Firth.

She leaned against him and sighed. "It's been a good season after all, hasn't it?" she asked.

"Yes," he agreed. "Now let's sit down. Doctor Lewis said you should stay off your feet as much as possible." He took her hand and led her to the porch swing nearby. "Are you cold? Perhaps we should go inside."

"No, I want to say goodbye again to Hogan before he leaves," she said, reaching for Dan's hand. "I know we've said goodbye already, but I'm afraid he might not come back next year." He squeezed her hand. "This is the earliest we've ever emptied the cellars. We probably should have held part of the crop until after Christmas. The prices would be higher and—"

He touched her lips with his fingers. "No, love, we have other priorities in the coming months. I can imagine you out checking on your spuds while you're in labor. I don't intend to bring these children into the world in a spud cellar."

"I suppose you're right, but it's hard not to worry." Her hand went to her throat and she adjusted the clasp on the gold chain resting against her blue smock.

He smiled. "You have your old locket on."

"I always wear it on my birthday," she said. "It brings back all those good memories when I had the world by the tail on a downhill pull. I knew it all, that summer. I was ready to conquer the world and find my destiny." The metal warmed beneath her fingers.

"I haven't seen you wear it since that night in Montana when Abbie got married," he said.

She smiled, not saying a word.

"Perhaps you have found your destiny," he suggested. "It just took a little longer than you expected. Does it open?"

"Yes," she said, pushing on the clasp.

He turned the locket toward the light coming from the kitchen window. "When did you get it?"

"One summer when I was twelve," she replied. "And here I am a woman of thirty-four. How time flies."

" . . . when you're having fun?" he teased.

"It hasn't all been fun."

"No, but the future will be brighter," he assured her. He studied the image of a brown-haired girl inside the locket, her eyes too large for the rest of her features, but her smile confident and shining. "You were a pretty girl," he said. "Jodie and Jolene look a lot like you did. They've changed so much since I first met them."

"Yes, they're nine going on fifteen," she said. "Jolene thinks we should get cable television or a satellite dish so she can watch the music videos of the rock stars. I told her no."

"Insensitive mother," he replied. "Next she'll think she needs a training bra."

"She's already asked for that," Eileen said. "I told her to wait until after Christmas. She said I didn't understand." She chuckled. "Remember when you told me about your theories on teenage girls and boys? We're in for some rough times ahead."

"We'll manage," he replied. "We'll practice with the boys and by the time the girls get to be teenagers, we'll know what to do."

"By then, the rules will have changed," she murmured. "Jordan has grown three inches this year. He's taller than Stephen now. I hope that doesn't interfere with their friendship. I worried so much about him. He resented his father dying and..." She was silent for a while, then turned to him and smiled. "Jordan thought you were a creep who was hanging around his mother and he was very vocal until he met Stephen. I'm so glad Van agreed to let Stephen live with us permanently."

"Van has her practical side," he said, fingering the counted cross-stitched scene on the front of the locket. "Are the trees symbolic of you and your cousins?"

She nodded. "Aunt Minnie did the stitching that summer. She is a warm, wonderful and very down-to-earth woman. She saw a rainbow in every dark storm. What Aunt Minnie lacks in formal education, she has made up for in other talents. She's a brilliant quilter, a weaver, and the best darned baker of stone-ground wheat bread ever. She taught me how to bake."

"Then I'm indebted to her," Dan said, nuzzling her hair. "I'll take you there someday," he promised. "Children need to meet all their relatives. Ours are fortunate to have so many."

They held one another for a few minutes in silence.

"I could never have made it through harvest without you, Dan," she said, taking his hand in hers. "You took charge as if you had always worked on a farm. You haven't been able to jog a single morning since you moved here. Do you miss it?"

He lifted her hand to his mouth. "Farm work, and especially moving that damned pipe, has more than taken the place of how I used to exercise. And mud is much better on a man's joints than concrete.'' He began to chuckle. ''Did you ever expect help to come from so many directions?''

She grinned. ''No and it was wonderful. It was difficult for me at first,'' she said, resting her head against his arm. ''My bossy nature and all.''

''You're not bossy, just a born leader. Yet even leaders need to give their followers a chance to stretch their abilities. We made it, didn't we?''

Eileen turned to Dan. ''Our blessings overflowed.''

He nodded. ''They will continue to overflow, sweetheart.''

''I'm glad I sold the acreage to your parents,'' Eileen said. ''I don't understand why they wanted half a section, though, when they're supposed to be retired.''

''Dad wants to build a greenhouse,'' he said. ''He's been reading about growing hydroponic tomatoes. As soon as the house is finished, we'll have new neighbors. You used Dallas's money wisely.''

She had applied the funds to the land mortgage, as well as the proceeds from the sale of acreage to her neighbor.

''I'm down to less than a thousand acres now, if I don't count what I leased to Dallas Odell. You tricked me on that.''

Dan laughed. ''True, he's a little land greedy, but he's paid you a good price and now you don't have to worry for two years. He bought that pivot system, and you were able to pay off the lien against the other unit.''

Dan had talked over the irrigation situation with the two boys and they had jumped at the chance to earn steady money the next summer. ''I'll handle the pivot system we have left and the boys can do the pipe moving. I'm going to start pricing another wheel line this winter. Maybe in a few years, we can afford to pick up a used pivot from someone going out of business.''

She frowned and he arched a brow. "I know," he said, "it came too close to home, but we're better off than last year. The judgment against the broker didn't hurt."

"I never expected to get a dime and instead we got fifty cents on the dollar, when Thomas's investigator located that secret bank account in New York City. It pays to have a lawyer in the extended family."

They had closed out the credit line in full, and paid off two out of the three loans against the land and equipment. After several discussions with another bank in town, they had been able to borrow enough to pay off the third loan and replace it with one at a lower interest rate on the newer bank. Eileen had swallowed her pride and not asked if having Dan in the picture had made the loan committee more receptive. It probably had. The bank had also extended them a promise of operating credit for next spring.

"I'm sorry we had to sell the trucks," she said, "but Dallas gave us a good price on them. He's not as bad as I'd thought. It's just that he's so successful and the rest of us seem to scrape by, and some don't even manage to do that. It's not fair!"

"Don't fret," Dan said, pulling her into his arms. "Odell's affairs are his business, but I've heard by the grapevine that he's mortgaged to the hilt, operating on other people's money. We're one of the few farms to get cash out of him."

She slapped playfully at his hand as it caressed her breast. "You? Listening to gossip?"

"Who cares what the gossips say? We have one mortgage left and if my book sells as well as the publisher thinks, we'll work on that mortgage as well." He stroked her arm. "With less crops to worry about, we can get away from here once in a while. When my folks finish building their new house, they'll be close enough to cover for us. You, my love," and he kissed her cheek, "can go with me on some of my research trips."

She smiled. "But not for more than a few days," she warned.

"I promise."

They settled against the back of the porch swing.

"Abbie and Dane will be here next Sunday," she reminded him. "They say they want to make sure we're all doing fine, but I think they really want to show off their daughter. Can you imagine, little Anna is almost three months old? Imagine my cousin a mother! She was never the type until she met Dane."

"That's what love does to a person," he said. "Here comes Waite." He helped her from the swing.

She groaned aloud and touched her stomach. "Sometimes I get tired of incubating these babies of ours," she said. Her eyes widened and she gasped. "They must be boys. One of them just kicked a punt and the other tried to catch it."

Dan led her across the yard to where Hogan Waite was putting a suitcase and a steamer truck into the back of his truck.

Hogan turned, his large handsome features somber, his eyes hooded in the dusk of late October.

"You don't have to leave," Dan said.

"You're one of the family," Eileen said. "Won't you stay?"

Hogan shook his head. "You're in good hands here, ma'am," he said, motioning toward Dan. "We've both fulfilled our promises. A man knows when it's time to move on."

"Where are you going?" Dan asked.

"I thought I'd check out Arizona," Hogan replied. "A friend of mine has a place down by Patagonia."

Dan smiled. "No snow-capped peaks there."

"Then I can always come back to Alaska or Idaho." He hunched his broad shoulders.

"If you change your mind, you have a standing job here as foreman, Waite," Dan said. "I still have a lot to learn about this spud business."

Hogan laughed and slapped Dan's shoulder, knocking him slightly off balance. "You're going to make it, Page. You've got the smarts to learn the business and the guts to survive, and I know you and the missus have something special. I wish I could be here to see the next set of twins growing up around this place." He glanced away toward the fields then back to Dan and Eileen. "Well, I'll say goodbye now. You take good care of her, Page, or you'll have to answer to me."

Eileen blinked the tears away, then threw her arms around the big man's neck and kissed his cheek.

Hogan extended his hand and Dan accepted it. "Well, Page, I might see you around sometime."

"Come back next March," Dan said. "See the kids and help plant some seed potatoes."

"Might do that." Hogan turned away and climbed into the cab. He waved but didn't look back.

They watched the red glow of his taillights fade into the darkness. Dan turned to Eileen and took her hands in his. "So, birthday lady, how about going inside and changing into that new outfit of yours? Mrs. Sherman will be here in a few minutes. I've been trying to take you to dinner in a fancy restaurant all alone for a year and this is the night."

"Are you sure you want to be seen with a woman in my condition?" she asked, her eyes glistening as she gazed up at him.

"More than anything in this world," he replied, pulling her as close as he could. "You're the woman I've loved since the first day we met. The time was wrong then, but it's perfect now.''

"Oh, Dan," she sighed, melting in his arms. She claimed his kiss, then accepted his hand as he led her inside.

Harlequin Superromance

COMING NEXT MONTH

#278 NIGHT INTO DAY • Sandra Canfield
When their eyes meet across a crowded New Orleans
dance floor, travel agent Alex Farrell and sports
celebrity Patrick O'Casey learn the meaning of
Kismet. Alex, a semi-invalid stricken with
rheumatoid arthritis, refuses to burden Patrick with
her illness, but he decides she'll be his wife—
no matter what the obstacles!

#279 ROOM FOR ONE MORE • Virginia Nielson
Brock Morley loves Charlotte Emlyn and is
determined to marry her—until her teenage son
reveals he's fathered a child. Brock is ready to
be a husband and stepfather, but a grandfather...?

#280 THE WHOLE TRUTH • Jenny Loring
Besides integrity, Susannah Ross brings a certain
poise to her judgeship—and nothing threatens that
more than seeing lawyer Dan Sullivan in her
courtroom. Difficult as the situation seems, this time
they are both determined to make their love work.
Ten years has been too long.

#281 THE ARRANGEMENT • Sally Bradford
Juliet Cavanagh is a no-nonsense lawyer with a
practical approach to motherhood—she wants a
child but not the complications of a marriage. She
advertises for a prospective father and attracts a
candidate with his own conditions. Brady Talcott is
handsome, wealthy, intelligent and healthy, and he
insists on living with Juliet—especially when he
learns he can't live without her!

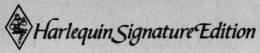

Harlequin Signature Edition

Penny Jordan

Stronger Than Yearning

He was the man of her dreams!

The same dark hair, the same mocking eyes; it was as if the
Regency rake of the portrait, the seducer of Jenna's dream, had
come to life. Jenna, believing the last of the Deverils dead, was
determined to buy the great old Yorkshire Hall—to claim it for
her daughter, Lucy, and put to rest some of the painful memories of Lucy's birth. She had no way of knowing that a direct des-
cendant of the black sheep Deveril even existed—or that James
Allingham and his own powerful yearnings would disrupt her
plan entirely.

Penny Jordan's first Harlequin Signature Edition *Love's Choices* was an
outstanding success. Penny Jordan has written more than 40 best-sell-
ing titles—more than 4 million copies sold.

Now, be sure to buy her latest bestseller, *Stronger Than Yearning*. Avail-
able wherever paperbacks are sold—in October.

Harlequin Intrigue

In October
Watch for the new look of

Harlequin Intrigue

...because romance can be quite an adventure!

Each time, Harlequin Intrigue brings you great stories, mixing a contemporary, sophisticated romance with the surprising twists and turns of a puzzler...romance with "something more."

Plus...
in next month's publications of Harlequin Intrigue we offer you the chance to win one of four mysterious and exciting weekends. Don't miss the opportunity! Read the October Harlequin Intrigues!